HELL'S JUDGEMENT
Birth of the Dark Princess

by Michael D. Benson

HELL'S JUDGEMENT
Birth of the Dark Princess

This is a work of fiction. Any references to historical events, real locales, real people, or real organizations are used fictitiously. Other characters, names, incidents and places, are a product of the author's imagination and any relationship to other persons living or dead is purely coincidental.

ISBN-13: 978-1-7320330-1-6

Visit Michael D. Benson's website at
www.mikebensonbooks.com

Published by
Huntsmen Books
June 2018

To Sean, Shane, and Shad

Prologue

The weather forecast was set to air in thirty seconds, at 6:00 a.m. sharp. On this, the first day of winter, millions across England sat before their televisions with mounting apprehension. Rumor had it that England would experience a harsh winter weather season like no other. According to the predictions, it would be more severe than any recorded in human history.

When the program aired, Englanders sat stunned as, instead of the usual weather report, the ghost of Albert Finney appeared on their television screens—Albert Finney, the Academy Award-winning filmmaker who had dropped dead of a heart attack just weeks after he had completed his last movie, *The Rebellious Winter*. The film was a horror story about an attack of Mother Nature, in the form of terrifying natural disasters that took the lives of an entire country and left no survivors to tell the tale. Unfortunately, Finney didn't live to see the great success of his film, or even its premier.

Viewers watched in shocked disbelief as Finney's ghost, wearing the black tuxedo he had been buried in, composed himself at the news desk. He took a few seconds to digest the words on the teleprompter before greeting his audience.

"Good morning, citizens of England," he said sternly. "Although my live appearance on national television may seem, well, mysterious—indeed, inconceivable—please do not be afraid. I assure you that my resurrection is short-lived. I will soon return to my rightful place among the dead, and you will not see my face again.

"You might be wondering what has prompted this unusual visit. My purpose here is to fulfill a brief but important mission. I'm certain that many of you saw my last film, *The Rebellious Winter*. Well, it wasn't until after my death that I discovered . . . my little film is actually a terrifying prophecy. My mission, on this first day of the winter season, is to forewarn you all that every horrific scene in *The Rebellious Winter* will come to pass. Indeed, I predict that before this broadcast is over, the first plague will have already begun to unravel."

All hell broke loose. Finney's posthumous appearance on national television cast fear into hearts across the country. The ghost's three-minute clip played repeatedly on every channel. By daylight, businesses and schools had resorted to emergency shutdowns. The millions who had watched Finney's last film were gripped by panic as they realized the film's scenes could become real at any moment.

A grave silence descended on the country as people confined themselves indoors. Hour after hour, they monitored the TV news. A pretty newscaster reported the latest updates on the impending crisis.

"Good morning. This is *BBC News at Ten*. I'm Barbara Harrison. As we continue to probe into the Finney Phenomenon, as it has come to be called, researchers are still uncertain whether this so-called prophecy is something to fear, or, as some believe, nothing more than an elaborate hoax. At present, the vast majority of citizens fear the worst—that our nation should prepare to endure an imminent end-times biblical prophecy.

"On the panel to uncover the truth, and here to share their insights on the details of this mystery, are two of our nation's renowned religious leaders: Cardinal Frank McCartney, representing Father John McClain, who is currently in Rome, and Reverend Raymond Balls of New Jerusalem Church. Welcome, gentlemen."

"Thank you," Cardinal McCartney replied.

The reverend smiled. "It's a pleasure."

"Not to deviate from the topic," Barbara said, "but I'm surprised to see you both so calm, even though I understand that you are men of God. Since learning of the grave weather predictions, our nation has been on the brink of chaos for months and plagued with anxiety. But neither of you appear overwhelmed or particularly troubled. Can you tell the viewers your secret?"

"There's no secret to my calm spirit, Barbara," Cardinal McCartney replied. "I live by the word of God, and by faith. The Bible states in Second Timothy, first chapter: 'God has not given us the spirit of fear, but of power, and of love, and of sound mind.'"

Reverend Balls chimed in. "And David says in the Book of Psalms, 'For I will not be afraid of the arrows by day from the hands of my enemies, nor the terrors by night.'"

Barbara nodded, their words of courage appearing to calm her. "I believe both of you watched the late Albert Finney's live broadcast this morning, yes?"

"We have, of course," the cardinal answered.

"Well," Barbara continued, "many are wondering if this phenomenon could be interpreted spiritually. Can you weigh in on this, Cardinal McCartney? Do you believe this nightmare could be linked to an end-times biblical prophecy?"

"Well, there's no place in—"

"Did you see the movie, Cardinal?" Barbara interrupted.

"Yes, I did," McCartney replied. "As a matter of fact, I've watched *The Rebellious Winter* numerous times. As I was saying, there is nothing in the scriptures that suggests an end-times prophecy being announced by a ghost. There is absolutely no passage in the Holy Book that describes such an incident."

"So," Barbara said, "if this prophecy is to be fulfilled, what can be done to abort it? Under what circumstances could this blood bath be avoided?"

"The answer is simple," the cardinal responded. "It will take God's divine intervention, his miraculous power. But unless that happens, I see no hope."

Barbara turned to Reverend Balls. "What's your opinion, Reverend?"

"Barbara, I can't offer any deep insights. What I do believe is that this crisis is a mystery our mortal minds can't possibly conceive of. Only by the help of God can our eyes open, in order to grasp the mastermind behind this madness."

Barbara pressed on. "Why would God allow such evil to destroy us all, just like that?"

The reverend drew a breath and pondered. "Let us not conclude that evil, or the forces of darkness, will utterly prevail. God can, in a split second, avert the situation. He can intervene in an instant."

"Do you believe we saw a ghost today?" Barbara asked the reverend. "Do you believe Albert Finney rose from the grave to announce impending doom?"

"Finney is a dead man, we all know that. His body has no place in living society; a ghost is not human. To put this idea in the right perspective, I will say that his manifestation in human flesh is some sort of satanic revelation. This is evil at its worst."

Barbara Harrison's expression dimmed. "Are you saying that the person we saw this morning on the weather channel was not actually Albert Finney, but rather a demon spirit posing as the dead filmmaker?"

"This is beyond the scope of my knowledge," the reverend replied, "and beyond my human imagination, as well. Can a demon manifest itself in a dead man's body? I simply cannot say."

Barbara turned her attention back to Cardinal McCartney. "Those folks who didn't see the movie, or don't know who Albert Finney was, think that this horror is based on a myth and not to be taken seriously. What's your view on this?"

"Let me just say that those people probably don't know the true definition of 'myth,'" he said. "'Myth' is simply defined as something imaginary. How can a ghost's appearance on national television be imaginary?" The cardinal straightened in his chair. "No, this is not a myth. It's real. And the only thing we can do as a nation is pray. This is not the time to be overcome by fear. I truly believe that if we pray, sincerely, God will move on our behalf and save us from nature's devastation."

"Thank you, gentlemen."

"It's been a pleasure, Barbara," Cardinal McCartney replied.

Reverend Balls nodded politely. "You are most welcome."

Barbara faced the camera. "I have been chatting with Cardinal Frank McCartney and Reverend Raymond Balls. Stay tuned in the next hour as we keep you updated on the Finney Phenomenon. Until then, I'm Barbara Harrison. Thank you for watching."

BOOK ONE
The Rebellious Winter

Chapter 1

Day Two
15 degrees below zero

Midmorning on the second day after the ghost's announcement, forty-four-year-old priest John McClain landed at Salisbury Regional Airport aboard his Citation X. The priest had been hosting the Soul-Winning Crusade in Rome. McClain was far from completing his mission when the looming nightmare at home forced him to abandon the crusade and return to England.

As he disembarked the aircraft, McClain sensed the dark shadow of dread in the air. His outward appearance remained untroubled, but deep within, he was panic-stricken like everybody else.

From the back seat of his Jaguar, McClain gazed balefully at the city and discovered something strange: in a little more than twenty-four hours, Salisbury had become a ghost town. Only a few cars traveled the silent streets.

The Jaguar rolled to a stop in front of the Salisbury Cathedral, and McClain hurried through the severe weather, the wind whipping his overcoat. Inside his warm office, McClain dropped his briefcase behind the desk and stepped to the window to open the blinds. For a while he stared down at the neighborhood that looked quiet as the grave, hearing in his mind the silent cry of terror. It suddenly dawned on him that England was on the verge of collapse.

The priest glanced at his Rolex. He was anxiously awaiting the arrival of his two clerical counterparts, Cardinal Frank McCartney and Reverend Raymond Balls, who were now fifteen minutes late. He had decided to host an emergency meeting with his colleagues to share with them the revelation he had received from God concerning the real enemy—the mastermind behind the evil crisis.

McClain sighed and flipped open his briefcase, reaching for his personal VHS copy of *The Rebellious Winter.* He set the tape on the desk and paced the floor.

A knock at the door interrupted his trance-like state. "Welcome, men of God," he uttered with a smile as McCartney and Balls entered the room. He greeted his colleagues with handshakes. "Thank you for coming on such short notice." He directed them to take a seat on the couch. "Before I forget, I want to thank you both for the views you expressed in the BBC interview yesterday."

"I did my best to reassure the people," Reverend Balls said.

Father McClain nodded. "I watched the interview from my hotel room."

"You did?" McCartney asked with surprise.

McClain nodded again and sank into the chair behind his desk, staring at the VHS tape sitting before him. "I was probably the only one who wasn't awake when that ghost made his public appearance," he said. "But I will tell you that God, in his divinity, has embarked on a dark journey of deep revelation concerning the entire phenomenon. You won't believe the series of sinister events that have unfolded in the spirit world. The vision was so horrifying, it was only by the power of God that my eyes could withstand glimpses of the tragedy that threatens to destroy this country." He paused, pondering the divine vision. "I never dreamed I would be a vessel for such a vision." He rose up quickly and sat on the edge of his desk. "Gentlemen, as I speak, we are already dead. We already dwell in the spirit world—every single one of us."

"What are you saying, Father?" the cardinal asked.

"I'm saying," McClain replied, his voice rising, "we are dead, and it's only a matter of time before the nightmares foreseen in the realms of the spirit manifest in our world." He trembled as he spoke. "The vision came to me on the last night of the crusade, right in the middle of my sermon, while I was preaching in the sold-out Coliseum. I could barely contain myself—the experience was that disturbing."

"You must have had a—"

"Now," McClain said, interrupting the cardinal, "let us bear in mind that the film is indeed a prophecy . . . however, not from God, but from Satan himself."

McCartney and Balls exchanged a puzzled glance.

"Here is the situation," McClain continued. "In the Devil's tireless effort to dethrone our Lord God and inflict his evil judgment on the world, he has branded England a satanic empire that shall be governed by the powerful demonic spirit Jezebel, who is the crowned Queen of Hell.

"Her legions of dark angels, or demons, are under encampment in the abyss of the Bermuda Triangle as we speak. Any moment now, Jezebel will be unleashed to lead a mass invasion. The annihilation of every living soul is her only means of inheriting the emperorship."

"How is it possible to wipe out millions of lives?" the reverend asked.

"The evidence is in the movie," McClain said, gesturing toward the tape on his desk.

"But the movie is about natural disasters," Balls argued, "not demons."

"Yes," replied McClain. "And what forces do you think make up the origins of those horrible plagues?"

The reverend arched an eyebrow. "Demons?" he replied hesitantly.

"Right."

Balls nodded in shock, slowly coming to agreement with McClain.

McClain drew a deep breath to compose himself. "Let us examine the Finney Phenomenon from a *mystical* standpoint. My question to you both is this: In the film, what happened after millions of innocent lives were wiped out? What happened after the souls of an entire nation were lost in the massive flood caused by the tsunami?"

The cardinal and the reverend stared at McClain thoughtfully. They knew that the story ended with the tsunami that drowned the population of an entire country, leaving not a single survivor. But they reasoned that the question McClain asked was an avenue the priest had used to unearth another mystery. Having no clue what the answer could be, however, they were left hanging.

Awaiting their response, McClain walked to the window and gazed out at the intensifying storm.

Reverend Balls was the first to speak. "I assumed the story ended there," he offered, unsure of his own judgment.

"And you, Cardinal McCartney?" McClain asked.

The cardinal shrugged. "As the reverend said, that's where the film ended. What else occurred after that? Nothing."

McClain returned to his desk and gave his fellow clergymen a stern look. "The story did not end there. Indeed, the end of the movie was only the beginning."

"What exactly are you trying to tell us?" the reverend asked.

"*The Rebellious Winter* begins where it ended, gentlemen," McClain boomed. He sat back on the edge of his desk. "The aftermath of the disasters and deaths—this is where the Lord came in and took me on a journey of revelation. He showed me scene-by-scene footage of the invasion."

"So what happens next, after we all perish?" the cardinal asked, overwhelmed with fear.

"The answer to your question, Cardinal, finalizes

everything," the priest said confidently. "Here is the evil plot: Jezebel, the Queen of Darkness, and her demons— millions of them—have marked the mortal bodies of every living soul, which they hope to possess in pursuit of an earthly existence.

"You see, without our mortal bodies, the demons cannot survive the earthly realm. In order for their plan to succeed, they must first bring forth the great annihilation—the destruction of every English citizen. And that's where Queen Jezebel, the mastermind of this dark crisis, comes in. She intends to inflict our nation with various natural disasters . . . plagues so deadly, they have never before been recorded in the history of mankind. Once we have all perished, the demons will incarnate our bodies, and we will once again live—but resurrected as demons in human form."

An eerie silence engulfed the room. McClain couldn't help but ponder the vision he was vividly experiencing all over again. Finally he said, "I saw the reign of our Queen Elizabeth come to a bloody end. I watched every moment of her untimely death."

"You saw what?" McCartney asked, frightened.

McClain's eyes locked on the cardinal's. "She is Jezebel's prime target. The body of Queen Elizabeth is the demon's prey. This demon marked our queen's body to reign in as emperor."

The cardinal crossed his legs nervously and drew a ragged breath. "Is there any possibility that God, in his divine power, will destroy this Queen of Hell?" he asked. "Or is he going to let the souls of this nation perish by the Devil's wrath?"

"I'll come to that in a minute," McClain said calmly.

"No hope?" the reverend chimed in. "Not a single survivor?"

"Absolutely none," McClain replied. "You've seen the

movie, gentlemen. It's a powerful testimony. But I've got good news, too, and that's the ultimate reason we are gathered here this morning." He glanced toward the door. "In private."

"At the end of the vision, after the catastrophe, God commissioned me into battle to redeem England. Although he told me that the Kingdom of Darkness has an excellent chance of prevailing, he also told me that we have just as good a chance. If a few men of strong faith were to join forces in prayer, we could triumph."

The reverend and the cardinal eyed him skeptically.

"I know it sounds impossible, gentlemen, but we must take God at his word. And remember, with him, all things are possible."

"I do not wish to doubt the word of God," the reverend said, "but how would that be possible? The demons are countless, and we are but a few mortal men."

"The power of God is not measured in numbers, Reverend. Think about it. God used the least to perform great miracles. For example, he used Moses's rod to drown Pharaoh and his Egyptian army in the Red Sea while they pursued the Israelites. He merely calls on us to act on our faith as we've never done before, and he'll do the rest."

This piqued Cardinal McCartney's curiosity. "Are you saying that the survival of this nation relies solely on our faith?" he asked, gesturing to himself and his colleagues.

"Exactly," McClain said, feeling truly hopeful for the first time since learning of the prophecy. "Now, if you both agree to join forces with me in hourly prayer and intercession, which of course you will, we will tap into a whole new realm of faith."

"It seems like an insurmountable challenge, Father," the reverend said.

His colleague's doubt annoyed McClain, but he maintained his composure. "It certainly is," he replied. "But

God assured me that if I fear not, and arm myself with unwavering faith, he will slay the forces of evil."

"Why is this faith so important?" McCartney asked.

McClain was growing impatient. "Because our prime adversary, the Queen of Hell, is using her ultimate weapon—fear. Without faith to conquer fear, she wins the battle."

McCartney stood, growing more courageous. "What does this Queen Jezebel look like? Is she the Beast, the dark princess that is supposed to rise from the sea?"

"She is a dreadful being," McClain said, "with features of both a crocodile and a dragon—though she can stand upright, like a human."

"What about a tail?" asked the reverend. "Does she have one?"

McClain gave his colleague a quick nod and grabbed the video tape off the desk. "This is my copy of *The Rebellious Winter*," he said, heading to the television cabinet. "Before I bring this meeting to an end, I would like for us to view together specific excerpts from the film."

McClain felt his colleagues' eyes on him as he inserted the tape into the VCR. "I hate to have to do this," he said, "but I want you to have a broader, clearer picture of this nightmare. Let us refresh our memories of these scenes— not to be entertained, as we all were before, but with our thoughts on the reality we're facing."

He snatched the remote from the top of the television, stepped back, and pressed *play*. When the credits appeared, McClain forwarded the tape to the beginning of the spiraling disasters that struck the land. It was the beginning of the end.

The scene showed the densely populated city of Nineveh at the stroke of midnight. The city was in a deep freeze— eighty below—and experiencing deadly gusts of wind and thunderstorms as lightning streaked across the sky. A transformer caught fire, activating a fire that didn't cause an immediate power outage, but spread rapidly across the city's neighborhoods. By the time residents became aware, the fire was roaring out of control.

As the fire intensified, thousands of displaced residents, trapped out in the deadly cold, fled toward neighboring Kadesh. They were still several kilometers away when, one by one, each of the residents froze to death.

Father McClain paused the tape. "From my observation," he stated, "this movie has no hero or antagonist. The characters are all victims fighting to survive nature's wrath. We must anticipate the reality of everything we've seen here, gentlemen."

He fast-forwarded the tape and pressed *play* again. The movie continued from the third week of the winter season, when the whole of Nineveh had been ravaged by fire. Millions across the country were evacuating to bordering Damascus in response to an emergency alert about an approaching tsunami. McClain fast-forwarded through the long evacuation scene. He stopped as the tsunami began to overtake the country. It was late in the evening when the ocean began swirling vigorously. Within minutes, a thousand-foot wave spiraled into the air and viciously swept hundreds of kilometers inland. Multistory buildings standing tall in the city square, crowded with evacuees, were buried in the blink of an eye beneath hundreds of feet of water.

McClain forwarded to the end of the film. The three men watched in awe as Nineveh, a once beautiful city, was at last plagued by the reign of ceaseless darkness, with the massive flood of the Mediterranean Sea covering the entire land.

McClain again pressed *pause* and drew a deep breath before speaking. "Here we are, gentlemen. Imagine London, one hundred thirty kilometers west of us, buried beneath a massive flood. Millions of innocent lives trapped on the Atlantic floor."

McClain turned off the television and quietly laid the remote control on the desk. "I've played these excerpts because I'm trying to get a point across—to watch them from a spiritual viewpoint this time, and not for entertainment purposes. Before the premiere of the film, during the weeks of previews on numerous channels, the thing that really struck me was when the announcer said, 'The most devastating event in history is about to occur . . . ' Those words have always troubled me, right up until today. Now those words are set to become a reality." McClain looked at his colleagues inquiringly. "Any fresh revelations, gentlemen?"

Balls and McCartney sat together in silence. Viewing excerpts from the movie had hindered their ability to see beyond the immediate aftermath. Understanding that the prophecy could be fulfilled at any moment, they each attempted to battle their fears before contemplating how they could possibly fight the demons.

Father McClain patiently watched the two men in their struggle to come up with a response. "Anything at all, gentlemen?" he asked. He continued to eye his colleagues, hoping they would come to accept the strategy he believed would halt the crisis, perhaps even before it struck.

The cardinal was the first to break the silence. "What's the point of having faith if we're all destined to die?"

"Sounds to me like you're dwelling on the problem rather than the solution, Cardinal McCartney. I have no idea the exact nature of God's plan to avert the crisis. I'm only doing what he has commissioned me to do. The rest is his to take care of."

The cardinal nodded with partial approval, trying to resist the constant attack of his inner fears. After several moments, the wisdom of the idea of using his faith as a weapon began to sink in. As his courage grew, his face lit up.

McClain grinned. The cardinal's newfound resilience delighted him. "Think about your families, gentlemen," he said. "Think about your children, your wives. The little babies—you don't want them all to die. You don't want this evil prophecy to invade this beautiful country of ours. So I sincerely encourage you, in the name of God, to stand firm on the promise of faith. Take this warfare very seriously, gentlemen, and leave no room for fear and doubt."

The reverend finally spoke up. "I guarantee my commitment," he said assuredly.

"Well, then," McClain replied, "with that said, are there any final questions or comments before we close with a word of prayer?"

"No questions here," Reverend Balls replied.

Cardinal McCartney concurred. "No further questions, Father."

Father McClain bowed his head. "Father God, thank you for the divine insight you have given me, through which the mystery of this evil prophecy has been unveiled. Merciful Father, not only have you shown us the revelation, you have given us wisdom, and have endowed each of us with the supernatural power to conquer our enemies. As we walk through the valley of the shadow of death, we will fear no evil, because your divine protection supersedes everything else. And so, heavenly Father, my prayer to you at this moment is that we, your faithful few, can rise in faith and in prayer and in meditation of your holy word, which breathes life and power—power we will use hand-in-hand with the only weapon that can conquer the wrath of evil. We refuse to succumb to our prime enemy—fear—and we rebuke the reign of death. Most of all, you have given us confidence that this nation will rise up and once again live in freedom and liberty. Amen."

Chapter 2

Minutes before midday, the White House staff was interrupted from their routine when an urgent memo was distributed from the Office of the president. The commander in chief reminded his staff and the media that at twelve o'clock noon, he would be making an address to be broadcast worldwide via satellite.

At exactly twelve o'clock, the president of the United States approached the podium in the East Room. Grief spread across his face as he gazed upon the cameras. "Three days ago, at approximately six a.m., the people of England received devastating news: that a prophecy of destruction is set to be fulfilled and will decimate their entire country. The United States and the rest of the world are deeply concerned by this disturbing turn of events, this so-called prophecy that threatens to wipe out the existence of millions of innocent citizens. This disaster, when it erupts, is predicted to take the form of the worst natural disaster ever to occur in human history. Standing at this podium, I hear the cries of England and feel the fear of the millions of citizens trapped in their struggle to escape the wrath of Mother Nature.

"This looming catastrophe is of deep concern to our nation. Although we do not possess the power to fight nature, the United States will take the initiative to come to the aid of the English people—to do everything in our power to save as many lives as possible.

"To ensure that the people of England have ample opportunity to escape to safety, an emergency rescue team will be dispatched within forty-eight hours. Their mission: to launch a speedy evacuation aboard a fleet of humanitarian jetliners that will bring the citizens of England back here to the US." The president paused, his expression serious yet confident. "As the president of the United States, in identifying with the grief and fear of the people of England, I hereby declare a state of emergency.

"In closing, on behalf of the American people and myself, we extend our heartfelt sympathy to the queen, the royal family, the prime minister, Parliament, and all the citizens of England. Thank you."

~~~

England
5:10 p.m. Greenwich

The president's quest to evacuate England took the country by storm. The prophecy could be fulfilled at any minute—any second—and its magnitude was fiercely anticipated. Dark clouds hovered ominously over the country. This was no joke. It was real. People understood that the Finney Phenomenon was not to be taken lightly.

English citizens seized the opportunity to flee. Bags were packed hurriedly as thousands and then millions of people journeyed toward Heathrow Airport. By six o'clock in the evening British time, less than an hour after the US president granted a state of emergency, city streets, highways, and freeways were jammed with cars. Tens of thousands of those without vehicles tramped on foot. Fear took over, and the situation spun out of control as horrific images of Finney's movie replayed in the mind of every citizen.

By late evening, the cities of England had become ghost towns.

~~~

Day Four

By twelve o'clock noon on the fourth day, Heathrow Airport was crowded beyond capacity. Tents lined the roads leading into the terminal for eight kilometers out. The fight for one's life became the only thing that mattered.

~~~

3:00 p.m.

Father John McClain, barely wavering in the face of this turmoil, remained in solitude. After three straight hours of prayer and intercession, he broke from his prayer and rested momentarily. From his living room window, the priest was shocked to discover that the neighborhood had become a ghost town. He recalled seeing his neighbors scrambling down the streets hours earlier, and only now realized that they'd abandoned their homes entirely and disappeared.

He closed the blinds and sat on the sofa, his mind reeling in disbelief. The sudden disappearance of the residents troubled him deeply. But McClain refused to allow the dire situation to crush his faith, truly believing that the threat of evil would bow before divine intervention.

McClain's instincts told him that people had fled in search of refuge. Eager to confirm his suspicions, he dressed warmly, pulled his winter coat from the closet, and grabbed his keys from the coffee table.

A ferocious gust of wind nearly knocked him off his feet as he stepped outside. Head down, he treaded across the lawn and stood at the edge of the pavement. As McClain studied the abandoned streets, his eyes peering in every direction, he was unable to spot a single soul.

He opened the garage door and reluctantly slipped in behind the wheel of his car. For several long moments, the priest contemplated pulling out into the narrow street. Perhaps he wasn't alone. If he could find just one person who hadn't fled to safety, that would be enough to give him hope.

At last he exited the garage and slowly made his way through the streets of his four-square-mile neighborhood. Like a police officer patrolling a high-crime area, McClain made the rounds, carefully gazing upon one house front after another. Empty driveways, open garages, not a single parked car to be seen. Not one soul to be found in this once vibrant neighborhood. By now, the fleeing of the residents was no longer strange to the priest. But the pressure of being the only one left behind mounted.

Holding out little hope, McClain stopped at the house of his friend Martin Summerfield. After stepping out onto the street, he hurriedly made his way to Martin's front door. He anxiously rang the bell and waited, hoping to be surprised by a response or to catch someone peeking out the window. After several moments and no answer, he pounded on the door. Nothing.

McClain noticed the empty garage, the door left wide open. His friend seemed to have left with all the others. But maybe not. Perhaps Martin was running an errand and the children were inside waiting for him. McClain knocked again. No answer.

"Hello?" he called out. "Martin?" But silence engulfed the air, his voice echoing through the neighborhood. "It's me, Father McClain. Is anybody in?"

Silence.

When the priest finally accepted that the family had fled, he backed away from the door and returned to his car. Anguish set in as the abandoned neighborhood threatened to steal his faith. Three hours of prayer hadn't changed a thing, and to his eyes, the situation was worse than before.

McClain arrived home, profoundly discouraged, and shuffled to the couch in shock. As he lay back, he wrestled with the same fears that had forced his friends and neighbors from their homes. He allowed himself only one moment of panic before he turned back to God for direction, reminding himself that it was too early to give up.

The crushing dread eased when the reverend and the cardinal surfaced in the priest's mind. The thought of his brethren calmed him, instantly casting away the panic and fear.

~~~

Reverend Balls, his wife, and their two teenage boys were the last family to depart their neighborhood. Several blocks into their journey, having remembered he'd left his wallet on the bed, Balls made a sudden U-turn and raced back toward home.

Balls pulled the car into the driveway and dashed into the house. As he scurried toward the bedroom, the jarring sound of the telephone ringing halted him in his tracks. He stared at the phone hesitantly; he knew it was the priest trying to touch base with him. But the reverend had no intention of picking up the receiver. He knew the nature of McClain's call, knew that the priest expected him to stand with him against the dark forces of evil.

After several rings, the phone fell silent. Balls sprang to action and grabbed his wallet from the bedroom. But as he reached the front door, the telephone began ringing again. He paused in agony, caught between his duty to his family and the promise he'd made to the priest. He wasn't in any condition to have a conversation with McClain right now. But he knew the priest and knew the man would persist until he managed to track him down. The reverend had made a promise, and his conscience gnawed at him.

Balls stood paralyzed just inside the front door. He stared at the phone, wracked with guilt for having betrayed the priest's trust—in a life and death situation, no less. His wife honked the horn, distracting him momentarily from the incessant ringing. She called to him, asking why it was taking him so long.

In those few seconds of distraction, the ringing stopped. The reverend took a step toward the threshold. But before he could step out onto the porch, the phone rang again. The priest was not giving up.

Raymond Balls was growing increasingly agitated— nearly frantic—with the dilemma of whether to answer the priest's call or sprint to the car and flee with his family. His guilty conscience weighed on him as he wrestled with the thought of abandoning his promise, of turning away from God's request. But what about his family? Didn't he have a sacred duty to them, too?

For the third time, the telephone ceased ringing. The reverend stood, glued to the floor of the entryway, and waited.

Ring.

His wife honked the horn a second time. "Honey," she called urgently. "Hurry."

Ring.

"Come on, Ray. Let's go."

Ring.

Unable to endure the mounting pressure, Reverend Balls stepped to the phone and lifted the receiver. "Hello?"

"Reverend," the priest blurted breathlessly, "Father McClain here."

The reverend swallowed hard. "What can I do for you, Father McClain?" he asked, doing little to mask his irritation.

By the sour tone in the reverend's voice, McClain sensed that Balls' faith was wavering. "Well, nothing in particular. I called to find out how you and your family are getting along, and—"

Balls interrupted. "Father McClain, how many times did you watch the movie? How many times have you watched *The Rebellious Winter* from a prophetic standpoint?"

McClain was taken aback by the reverend's harsh tone.

He knew his colleague was getting at something but couldn't imagine what. Perhaps the reverend had a hidden agenda.

"Are you still there, Father?" the reverend asked after several moments of silence.

McClain drew a deep breath. "Three times," he replied.

"Good. So what scene in *The Rebellious Winter* depicts the moment we are all now experiencing?"

McClain sighed, deflated. "I know. It's the mass evacuation of the people of Tyre, just before the tsunami hit."

"Yes, that's exactly it. Meaning that this evil prophecy has already begun to unfold." His hands trembled, the phone nearly slipping from his grasp. "The movie predicts that we'll all perish, and there's nothing you or God can do to stop it."

"So that's the position you've taken?" McClain asked sternly, hearing the fear in the reverend's voice.

Reverend Balls glanced out the living room window and toward the car, where his family waited for him. "Yes, Father. Right now, as I'm talking to you, it's just me and my family left in our entire neighborhood. Everyone else has left . . . and we're leaving, too. It would be foolish to remain here and perish."

"And where do you suppose you're going to go?"

"You know exactly where I'm going."

"The States?"

"You've answered your own question."

"I thought we were supposed to be in this thing together."

The reverend sighed impatiently. "I'm sorry to have to say this, but you're in deep denial."

"Where is your faith, Raymond?" the priest asked, his voice quavering.

Reverend Balls, sensing McClain's desperation, softened

his tone. "Bather, I believe your faith in a miraculous intervention is rather . . ." He paused, struggling to find the right word. "Naïve."

"I unveiled to you and the cardinal a secret," McClain uttered, clearly hurt. "A secret that will save us all from this evil massacre."

The disappointment in the priest's voice chipped away at the reverend's resolve.

"I trusted you," McClain continued. "Yet you didn't hesitate to betray that trust."

"How much worse does this chaos have to get before you realize there's nothing God—much less you—can do to prevent it?"

"Are you saying you no longer trust God, Reverend?"

"No. I've simply realized that God has no control over the evil hand we've been dealt. This prophecy was meant to be fulfilled. And it is being fulfilled, Father—before our very eyes."

"You no longer sound like a man of faith," McClain said sadly. "I can't begin to imagine how terrible that must feel."

"You think keeping my family out of harm's way is somehow an affront to my faith? Then prove me wrong. Prove to me that you're right to stay here, hanging onto to some . . . some *vision*."

The priest ignored the reverend's icy tone. "The fourth day of the prophecy is nearly behind us. It was said that Mother Nature would strike with as much force as she has, but here we are on day four, and aside from some severe weather, we haven't yet seen anything of a catastrophic nature. Is this not evidence that God has the situation under control? We both know, if it wasn't for his divine intervention, today would have been an entirely different story. We wouldn't even be having this conversation."

"Millions are crowding the airport, seeking survival.

With all due respect, we're not talking about some vain hope here. We're talking about reality."

"Are you walking by sight or by faith?" McClain asked.

"I thought we, as men of God, were supposed to be wise, not just spiritual."

"For Christ's sake," the priest said, exasperated, "I shared this revelation with you, a revelation I received from God himself. The *wise* thing is to fulfill your mission, and that is all. Block out the turmoil around you and focus, man."

Reverend Balls continued to plead his case. "Maybe you haven't been monitoring the news lately. Have you even bothered to learn of the intensity of this . . . this nightmare?"

"The news? Forget the news. Have you forgotten that this crisis, from God's perspective, was not created in the natural world? I am moved by revelation. In spite of the dramatic circumstances, I see hope for restoration. I see millions coming back home and returning to life as usual. And I see our children living happily with their parents again."

"Father, you have a deep faith and a pure heart, and I applaud your choice to stay and fight. But I've made my decision—I will not remain here and perish. I pray that you live to see God's miraculous power prevail against the evil of Satan." Without giving the priest time to respond, Reverend Balls hung up the phone and hurried to his car.

~~~

Deeply disappointed, McClain stood with the phone in hand for several long minutes. After finally accepting that the reverend was a lost cause, he reluctantly replaced the receiver, trudged across the room, and sank down onto the couch.

It bothered the priest that his clerical counterpart could be so naïve—and actually accuse *him* of being naïve. How could the reverend not see, not share his faith? He had walked away from an opportunity to witness God's greatness with his very own eyes. He had turned his back on an opportunity to serve God and the people of England by using his mortal body to reverse the curse.

McClain, exhausted from the agony of betrayal, lifted the remote from the end table and pressed the power button. The TV screen lit up with the BBC News in progress. A live broadcast of the evacuation aired in the upper-right corner of the screen as a middle-aged female newscaster, seated at the news desk, reported:

"With a current temperature of negative thirty-eight degrees and gusting winds up to eighty kilometers per hour, millions of evacuees from all walks of life are traveling to Heathrow International Airport in response to the state-of-emergency assistance granted by the United States.

"As the rest of the world watches a disaster on the verge, citizens of all ages are flooding the streets and overwhelming the roadways in pursuit of safe haven. Tens of thousands of homes have been abandoned, transforming our once busy cities into ghost towns, exactly as Albert Finney's film predicted.

"As of this broadcast, Heathrow Airport is crowded beyond capacity, and a mass encampment of evacuees extends at least seven kilometers beyond the airport terminal. In response, we've just received word from the United States that their fleet of humanitarian jumbo jets, called the Apollo Twelve, will launch the first phase of their mission effective midday tomorrow. Approximately twelve thousand evacuees are expected to be airlifted to American soil by the day's end.

"We will continue to keep you posted as information becomes available. Theresa Kidman, BBC Breaking News."

McClain hastily switched off the TV and drew a deep breath, trying to force down his rising panic. The report seemed overly dramatic, almost theatrical, with the events described in direct opposition to what he'd anticipated. He closed his eyes and hung his head in prayer, fervently and silently pleading with God for guidance. He prayed for courage in the face of evil, to stay strong as the events taking place around him threatened to rob him of his faith.

But fear interrupted his conversation with God, and panic rose up and swallowed his resolve. His faith waned beneath the weight of the images of men, women, and children fleeing the country in desperation.

The revelation slowly replaced the unsettling images in his mind. The demon, the Queen of Hell, was using her ultimate weapon—fear. In the absence of faith, the priest reasoned that he could wind up defenseless, vulnerable prey to his adversary.

Suddenly and confidently, McClain lifted his head heavenward, walked to the phone, and dialed Cardinal McCartney. The phone rang several times with no response. Finally, an automated voice came on the line: "The party you are calling is not answering. Please hang up and try again later." McClain hung up, presuming that the cardinal, too, had abandoned his promise and had run to safety.

It suddenly dawned on McClain that God had chosen *him* for this mission—that he alone had been asked to serve, to help conquer the Queen of Hell. It was time for him to accept his role as a one-man army, selected by God himself, to battle an entire legion of dark angels.

Still deeply troubled by the betrayal of his trusted colleagues, McClain folded his arms tightly across his chest and paced the living room floor in silence. The priest had set about the overwhelming task of battling his fears when the silent voice of God interrupted him. God ordered

McClain to confine himself to seclusion in the sanctuary of Salisbury Cathedral.

His commute from home to the cathedral usually took thirty minutes, but not today. The heavy traffic heading toward the airport continued, making car travel nearly impossible. He did his best to navigate through the thousands of people flooding the roads, but it soon became clear that his thirty-minute trip would take several hours, if not half the day.

Chapter 3

The president's urgent mandate to evacuate England shut down normal operations at JFK Airport indefinitely. CNN, as well as several other mainstream news networks, crowded the runway, providing twenty-four-hour live coverage of the humanitarian effort. Operation Apollo Twelve was preparing to dispatch the first jumbo jets, each to carry five hundred passengers from England back to the States as the world looked on.

Millions of early-morning viewers watched in awe as the shocking events unfolded. Most could not comprehend the pandemonium that would ensue after another country's entire population flooded into the United States.

The US Emergency Aid Team, dressed in gray jumpsuits, boarded the planes. Shortly afterward, the pilots fired up the engines and headed for the runway.

CNN reporter Jeff Roberts, dressed in a gray leather tailcoat and matching turtleneck sweater, reported:

"Today, citizens of America are witnessing a deeply unsettling event—perhaps the saddest event ever to occur in human history. Here at John F. Kennedy Airport, normal flights have been suspended indefinitely. In approximately twenty-four hours, the airport will be receiving the first British refugees. Over the course of the next several days and weeks, the US is set to receive hundreds of thousands of refugees.

"Many are asking, how is this possible? The truth is, it's difficult to determine just how far-reaching the effects of this operation will be on our own resources. But keep in mind that, as I speak to you right now, the situation has reached a critical stage. The desperate need for refuge has plunged the citizens of England into deep despair. Millions of families have already abandoned their homes and have crowded into an over-burdened Heathrow Airport.

"The clock of disaster is ticking. As English citizens begin to pour into the US, millions around the world will be watching—live—as the mystery unfolds. When a giant tsunami wipes England from the map, as predicted in the film The Rebellious Winter, the entire world will witness the devastating catastrophe.

"The question is: How quick is quick enough? Will Operation Apollo Twelve be able to evacuate the first group of refugees before disaster strikes? There is no definite answer to this question. For now, as the emergency crew sets to embark, the rest of us can only wait and hope. This is Jeff Roberts, reporting for CNN in New York."

~~~

Father McClain arrived at Salisbury Cathedral at seven-thirty the next morning. He entered the sanctuary feeling deeply discouraged. The vast departure of citizens hoping to be rescued troubled him deeply. He couldn't ignore the fact that the surreal events unfolding around him were eerily similar to the film. It was becoming more and more difficult to retain his faith that the prophecy could be reversed.

He turned on the sanctuary's large television monitor. The twenty-four-hour news coverage continued, discouraging him further as he stared mutely at the giant screen. The BBC news network captured a live, panoramic view of a Heathrow International Airport terminal, now crowded beyond capacity with tens of thousands of displaced citizens. Even more frightening were the approximately two million citizens camping in the surrounding areas, shivering as the country plunged further into a deep freeze. The expressway leading into the airport was jammed with cars that hadn't been able to move in days.

McClain switched off the TV and battled to remain faithful to the task, to the ordeal. He was certain that, by now, a powerful tornado or hurricane had ravaged half the country, destroying lives in the thousands. Worse, the impending plague of permanent darkness that the movie had foretold could have, by now, taken hold.

The priest conceded that the signs of England caving into ruin at any moment were there. Mother Nature had already begun the cycle of severe weather. Disaster could certainly strike any second. The discouraging thoughts prompted McClain to act as never before.

"Merciful Father," he cried in desperation. "I pray this day that the purpose for which you have called upon me brings victory and glory to your kingdom. You initiated a covenant when you said that no weapons or attacks of evil raging against your people shall ever prevail. Dear God, I pray with a sincere heart that this covenant, during this darkest of seasons, sees the light of day and will result in victory for my fellow citizens.

"To fulfill my duty, I willingly render my body unto you. Use me as a weapon to sabotage the threats of the army of darkness and the reign of death. God, on that sunny day when you drowned Pharaoh and his army in the Red Sea, so shall that same power drown Jezebel and her demons before they can implement their plot of destruction. With your divine power of protection, which has been bestowed upon this land, I decree that England be liberated from this dark terror. As I stare into the face of death, I decree that normal life be returned to this soil once again. Amen."

~~~

3:00 p.m.

The aircraft of Operation Apollo Twelve crossed the Atlantic Ocean and entered England's airspace exactly at the top of the hour. The first phase of the evacuation mission was forty-five minutes from gliding onto the runway of Heathrow Airport. If the wrath of nature, which loomed in the distance, didn't strike by four p.m., six thousand English citizens would be evacuated immediately.

When the lead aircraft was approximately ninety kilometers from the airport, the pilot radioed the air traffic control tower. "Good afternoon, Heathrow Tower. This is Captain Adrian Cox, Apollo Twelve, Aircraft One. We are completing our journey across the Atlantic and flying at an altitude of thirty-eight thousand feet."

"Roger that, Aircraft One," replied the tower chief. "You are cleared to land. Please be aware, however, that we are currently experiencing strong winds out of the north. Use extra caution on your approach."

"Thank you, sir," said Captain Cox.

Just as the air traffic controller predicted, powerful winds suddenly swept up from the north, causing severe turbulence. None of the pilots had ever experienced anything like it. Hundred-mile-an-hour gusts battered the planes relentlessly. Three jets toward the back of the fleet spun when the wind hit them and crashed violently into the Atlantic.

As tension mounted in the control tower, one of the crew looked toward the approaching planes to discover that the remaining aircraft were scrambling through a pitch-black funnel cloud. The tower crew erupted in a frenzy of activity as they tried to make sense of what was happening. The earlier clear sky had vanished mysteriously and given way to a dark and raging storm.

~~~

Father McClain was fervently praying at the altar when a powerful feeling of fear jolted him from his conversation with God. He bolted down the middle aisle of the sanctuary and out onto the front steps of the Cathedral. Panic rose in his throat as he gazed heavenward and caught a horrifying glimpse of the Apollo Twelve emergency. Stunned, McClain tried to comprehend the horrifying image: three planes going down as crushing winds hurled the jets into the Atlantic. The sight of it was so vivid, as though he were experiencing the disaster himself.

He stepped back into the church, trudged down the aisle in a daze, and sank down onto the front pew. He breathed deeply, attempting to calm himself, but this offered him little relief. His heart pounded wildly as he tried to wipe the shocking image from his mind.

The priest discerned that the dark angels behind the prophecy had successfully launched their destructive mission and had begun aborting the US rescue operation. He knew it was only a matter of time before the entire Apollo Twelve fleet was catastrophically knocked out of the sky. Convinced that his suspicions were correct, he felt the pressure mounting. Father McClain had to do everything in his power to help God ward off any further crisis.

~~~

The air traffic controllers continued their intense effort to bring in the remaining planes. They had expected to be signaling the jets for landing by now, but instead had lost radio communication with the pilots. Moments later, they could no longer locate the planes on the radar screen.

As the crew began to give up hope, the radio beeped.

The chief controller hastily snatched up the receiver. "Apollo Twelve, this is Heathrow," he announced. "You are cleared for landing."

"Heathrow, this is Apollo Twelve, Aircraft One. We—"

A burst of static interrupted the transmission. Nevertheless, the chief had detected the panic in the pilot's voice. "Aircraft One, are you still with us?"

"It's pitch black up here," Captain Cox answered. "We're trapped in some sort of giant storm cloud. We can't see a damned thing, can't see our way through. The high winds are battering the plane. I'm barely keeping the aircraft from spinning out of control."

The controller's heart pounded. "Stay on the line, Aircraft One," he said, unsure of his next move. He set the radio receiver on the desk. "Gentlemen," he called to the crew, "we need to take another, more careful look at those radar screens. Aircraft One is still out there, but they've lost their way. They're fighting the battle, but it doesn't look good. We may very well lose the entire operation."

Executing the chief's order, the crew monitored the radar screens for any signs of aircraft. Just as they were about to give up, two signals appeared on the screen. The high winds had swept the planes 120 kilometers off course. Worse than that, the radar showed the planes spinning out of control. The chief struggled to reestablish contact with Captain Cox.

"What the hell's going on here?" asked one of the controllers. "How did we lose them so suddenly?"

The chief tried the radio again. "Aircraft One, come in," he said into the receiver. "Are you there, Aircraft One?"

No response.

"Aircraft One. Come in, Aircraft One."

But it was no use. Once again, he'd lost communication with Captain Cox.

His subordinates, realizing the severity of the situation and the mounting pressure on the chief, gathered around their boss. There was no denying it: the situation was beyond their control.

"No response?" a controller asked, already knowing the answer to her question.

The chief shook his head. "Apollo Twelve has mysteriously vanished."

"You're sure?" another controller asked. "You're absolutely sure?"

The chief looked at him, defeated. "Come on, people. It doesn't take a rocket scientist to figure out what became of the Apollo Twelve mission. Just minutes ago, those planes entered our air space, and look." He gestured to the radar screen. "We've got only two on the radar now, both of which are spinning upward and onward to God knows where."

~~~

Above the Atlantic, the vicious winds swept the jets far above their normal flying altitude. Still spinning out of control, Aircraft One collided with Aircraft Five, and in the blink of an eye, both planes exploded in flames.

Trapped in a ferocious spin cycle, the left wing of Aircraft Eight ripped through the fuselage of Aircraft Four, and two more planes were lost. The funneling clouds of fire mingled with the powerful wind and chased the remaining two jets at lightning speed, setting them ablaze.

~~~

"Almighty God," McClain prayed, more desperately than ever. "I pray that you will endow me with your supernatural power in every measure of my faith, which is being put to the test. Lord, please grant me the courage to remain steadfast in my promise to slay the evil Queen Jezebel and her dark angels. You know I am up to the task, Lord. Use me to conquer our enemy and—"

Alarmed by a foul smell wafting into the sanctuary, McClain was forced to cut his prayer short. Within seconds, the church was polluted with the odor of aluminum and burning rubber. McClain hastened to one of the side windows and quickly threw it open. Thick, dark smoke rapidly rolled through the air, the sky becoming darker and darker as the seconds passed. Less than a minute later, though the clouds of smoke partially obstructed his view, the priest spotted what appeared to be some metal objects scattered a short distance away in the church parking lot. Upon closer inspection, he saw what he presumed was fallen debris from the ill-fated jets.

~~~

The airport terminal was crammed beyond capacity. Not a single inch of room remained for even one more person to push his or her way in. The mass exodus of the country's citizens had spiraled out of control.

As would-be passengers anxiously awaited the arrival of Apollo Twelve's rescue jets, they dreamed of the miracle of rescue. To their horror, they instead witnessed the first truly horrifying event of the prophecy. The crowd could only look on in despair as thick clouds of black smoke filled the atmosphere, saturating the air around them with the stench of burning metal and burnt flesh. Hordes of jam-packed citizens stood in the terminal, stunned, groping to understand what had just happened.

The public address system chimed, followed by the quavering voice of the chief air traffic controller. "May I have your attention," he said urgently. "This is Richard Powers, chief of air traffic control. My staff and I regret to inform you of the tragic loss of the entire Apollo Twelve operation. The twelve humanitarian jets en route to Heathrow were approximately fifteen minutes out when our radar signaled the tragic explosions of each aircraft. We are still trying to understand what happened. The reasons for the accident are yet to be determined.

"The smoke you're seeing is the aftermath of the destroyed planes. For your safety, we must advise that everyone depart the airport premises as quickly as possible and return to their homes. The atmosphere is polluted, unstable, and extremely dangerous. Also, please be mindful of falling debris. Thank you for your cooperation."

Chapter 4

He who dwells in the secret place of the Most High shall abide under the shadows of the Almighty.
Psalm 91:1

Day Eight

The disaster of the Apollo Twelve Operation automatically concluded the US state-of-emergency mission. Even more horrifying, permanent darkness was inflicted on the citizens of England that same day, as prophesied.

McClain secluded himself in solitude. Likewise, people throughout England hid indoors, terrified of the "Reign of Darkness." The fulfillment of the prophecy laid out in *The Rebellious Winter* convinced the priest that the unimaginable nightmare was coming to pass. His thus far unsuccessful quest to save England from the evil prophecy, to annihilate Queen Jezebel and her demons, had taken a profound toll on his faith. He was certain that if he'd more readily risen to the task, evil wouldn't have inflicted itself on England at this level. For days, he isolated himself, zealously adhering to the sacred oath that unlocked the supernatural power that was to conquer the forces of evil.

Darkness, however, plagued his country, casting fear and panic throughout the nation. For four days, the priest had interceded passionately, battling to avert the pending massacre. But his efforts seemed to no avail. If anything, the situation had worsened. Was his faith being tested? Or could it be that, in order for God to come forth with his miraculous intervention, McClain must first endure and conquer his fears?

Despite the temptation to succumb to defeat, the priest rose from his prostrate position on the altar. With pleading eyes, he yearned for the promised divine intervention. His face flushed, his body stiffening with increasing strain, Father McClain reluctantly climbed the stairs to the balcony and leaned against the railing. He gazed out at the bronze crucifix above the altar, bowed his head, and prayed.

"Merciful Father," he began, "as your love and mercy shower the universe, the burden you've given me to deliver this nation from destruction, from the wrath of the evil Jezebel, is unbearable." McClain swallowed hard, trying to keep his desperation from taking over. "I know it's time for me to take another step of faith. I can hear the millions crying out for mercy, desperate for miracles from your throne. As you've commissioned me to undergo this ultimate sacrifice, grant me the power to orchestrate signs and wonders on your behalf.

"God, I understand that only you hold the power to contain the dark plagues of evil. By the precious blood of Christ, who was once nailed on the cross to redeem the souls of this world from death and destruction, use this evil terror to manifest your purpose—the purpose of aborting the plans of our adversary, the Queen of Hell.

"Almighty God, because life is so precious to you, I know it is not your will to allow demons to wipe out the very existence of humanity, to imprison our souls and corrupt our mortal bodies. This evil that plagues our country has never existed in your perfect plans for this world. We will not perish. The dark army of Satan will not be allowed to annihilate your purpose for this nation. Amen."

~~~

Brighton: London by the Sea

By 10:00 a.m. on the eighth day, a silent vigil consumed the nation. Pitch-black skies brooded ominously over the people of England as grave silence plagued the length and breadth of the country. Already gripped by terror, people understood that the worst was yet to come. In the face of hopelessness, citizens mourned their own inevitable deaths.

In an odd turn of events, the citizens of the city of Brighton managed to rise above the bleak circumstances, having quickly grown numb to the looming evil. The massacre that promised to drown England in utter desolation had prompted the people of Brighton to seize their final moments and enjoy to the fullest what was left of their lives.

Seemingly fearless, Brighton residents passionately indulged themselves in ways they had only dreamed of: parties, gambling, shopping, and willfully engaging in degrading lifestyles. You name it, they were doing it. In less than a week, Brighton had transformed itself into a veritable Sin City. It was fast becoming evident that England was doomed. Since not a single soul was destined to survive the crisis, why live one's last days in panic and despair?

The inevitable coming of the tsunami, which had initially weighed heavily on their minds, became an excuse to embrace death by way of excessive indulgence. Nightclubs, bars, casinos, restaurants, and even shopping malls reopened and operated around the clock. As the darkness continued, Brighton crowds overwhelmed the entertainment establishments. Those who didn't frequent the various businesses threw wild parties in their homes at all hours of the day and night. People were literally wining and dining themselves toward their imminent deaths.

Debauchery and decadence spiraled out of control. Governing laws vanished overnight. Churches and courtrooms performed endless marriage ceremonies. Tens of thousands geared up for last-minute shopping sprees, buying anything and everything their hearts desired. Now was the opportunity to get what they wanted and make use of it, before death took them to the grave.

Some wondered if Brighton's sudden departure from the gloom and doom seizing the rest of the country could have anything to do with Queen Elizabeth's scheduled visit to address the nation from Brighton's Royal Pavilion. Others pondered whether the horrifying obliteration of the Apollo Twelve air rescue mission had simply driven the people of Brighton to madness.

Chapter 5

Day Nine

At 10:30 a.m., Queen Elizabeth was preparing for her trip to the Royal Pavilion of Brighton. This nightmare deeply troubled her, more so than it did any of the millions of citizens, perhaps because the queen of England knew that she had more to lose than most. She conceded that her reign had ended abruptly on the morning of the first day of winter, when the ghost of filmmaker Albert Finney had announced to the country that England was doomed to the same fate as the country portrayed in his terrifying movie. Effectively stripped of her royal power, the queen soldiered on as if she still held the title.

A young maid wheeled the queen's attire into her master suite on a miniature clothing rack, rolled it to the foot of the bed, and excused herself.

Moments later, the queen's thirty-year-old makeup artist, Cynthia, armed with her beauty kit, stepped into the room and made her way to the queen's dressing table. She removed several items from the case and placed them carefully on the table. Cynthia's mind drifted to the troubling thought that the service she was about to perform could very well be her last. She was convinced that the queen wouldn't live to see the end of this day.

The queen suddenly appeared in the room, having finished her shower. Cynthia inclined her head and curtseyed. "Good morning, Your Majesty."

"Good morning, Cynthia," the queen replied, managing a slight smile. She drew a ragged breath before sitting on the stool in front of the mirror.

"Is everything okay, ma'am?" Cynthia asked.

For a long moment, Queen Elizabeth silently regarded her own face in the mirror. Tired, vacant eyes, ghostly pale complexion—she was almost beyond recognition. Her deep concern for herself and her people had drained all of her usual vivacity. Finally she spoke. "All my life, I've never experienced the devastation of fear. I have heard many unfortunate stories in which people have succumbed to their fears. I know people who have suffered nervous breakdowns. For me, fear has never been an option. But today, now that I've come to realize that these moments are perhaps my last, I have come to know fear. It's all around me; I cannot escape it. I am hopelessly caught in its web, with seemingly no way of breaking free."

The queen's hairdresser, Anna, a middle-aged woman with golden-blond hair, quietly entered the room and exchanged a worried glance with Cynthia.

"For days on end," the queen continued, "our country has been plagued by this reign of darkness." She pondered for a few seconds before continuing. "I am of the opinion that God has irreversibly cursed this country."

"What have we done to deserve such a fate, ma'am?" Cynthia asked.

The queen sighed heavily. "I haven't any clue, Cynthia. What I do know is . . . we are doomed." The queen closed her eyes as Cynthia applied some light blue shadow. "Of course, everyone already knows that."

After Cynthia had completed her task and exited the room, Anna stepped up to the dressing table and curtseyed. "Good morning, Your Majesty."

Queen Elizabeth regarded her servant thoughtfully. "Before you start, Anna," she said, "I'd like to tell you something."

Anna's mind began to work overtime, wondering why the queen would choose to tell her, a servant, something in confidence. "What is it, Your Majesty?"

Queen Elizabeth paused for a long moment and uttered miserably, "If . . . if I die . . . and I certainly *will* die, I would like to die a peaceful death."

Stunned by her frankness, Anna gazed steadily at the queen in the mirror.

"Death, just the thought of it, can be very painful. Knowing that you're perhaps hours or minutes away from . . ." The queen hesitated, agony spreading across her face as tears streamed down her ashen cheeks.

"Oh, ma'am," Anna soothed, her own eyes filling. "Please calm yourself." She wanted desperately to relieve the queen's despair. "It'll be okay. Everything's going to be just fine."

The queen looked at Anna and smiled through her tears. Though she knew the kind young woman's words held little truth, she felt genuinely consoled by her reassuring gesture. "Thank you," she said, reaching for a tissue. The queen gently dabbed her eyes. "Can I trust you with a secret?"

The question sent a jolt through Anna's body. "A . . . a secret, ma'am?" she asked. "I don't know if trusting me with something of that nature is a good idea."

"I know, Anna," the queen replied. "A simple yes or no will suffice. I wish to share a secret with you, and I need to know whether I can trust you. I will reveal the secret only to you and the other party involved. You cannot share what I wish to tell you with anyone, not your fellow workers, family, friends, the press . . . not even the prince."

The queen sounded desperate. What other choice did Anna have? "Okay, ma'am. You can confide in me. You can trust me to protect your secret."

The queen smiled politely before her expression turned serious. "Promise me, Anna, that this secret will die with you."

Anna nodded. "I promise, ma'am."

"Good," the queen said. She straightened on the stool and looked directly into Anna's eyes. "What I want is to die by way of suicide. I wish to take my own life."

Anna's heart raced. "Oh ma'am, you can't be serious," she replied, her eyes filling again.

"Oh, but I am serious, dear," the queen said confidently. "If all goes well, immediately after my final speech—my death speech, if you will—I will return here, where my doctor will be waiting, and die a peaceful death."

"But . . . but how, ma'am?" Anna stammered.

"Poison," the queen stated matter-of-factly. "With an injection needle. Doctor Wallenberg promised to render the service without bearing the torment of guilt." She turned on the stool and gazed at the bed.

Anna eyed the pajamas lying at the foot of the bed.

"My death bed," the queen declared. "The pajamas you're looking at? The clothing I shall wear when I quietly embrace my exit from this world." After a long moment of silence between them, the queen spoke again. "Do you wish to know why, Anna?"

Anna nodded slowly, not certain she really wanted to know.

"I am doing this," the queen said, "so the world will believe that my death was innocent. And peaceful."

Anna hung her head, attempting to hide her disapproval. Feeling as though she might collapse, she gripped the edge of the dressing table. Finally she found the courage to speak. "But ma'am, suicide?" she asked grievously. "Do you not understand that such an act is a sin? That people might not regard your death in the way you hope them to?"

"I understand all of that, Anna, but I'm willing to take that chance. Do you have a problem with me taking my own life? Either way, I'm going to die. I simply wish to go out on my own terms."

"Of course I don't have a problem with it, ma'am," Anna

lied, still hiding her disdain for the queen's decision.

"Good." The queen smiled. "Now it's time to style my hair for the last time. Let's make it extra special."

~~~

11:20 a.m.

The royal convoy of seven cars lined the front lawn of Buckingham Palace, ready for the thirty-mile journey to Brighton, but signs that the delegates would safely make the trip to and fro didn't seem promising enough to risk their lives.

Queen Elizabeth was seated beside her son, Prince Andrew, in the back seat of her car. She felt highly unpleasant, battered by worry that something treacherous would cut the trip short. By the time the convoy exited the M45, goose bumps covered her entire body.

When they were approximately ten kilometers from Brighton, a tornado appeared suddenly on the lonely highway, whirling toward the motorcade. The powerful wind swept the cars off the highway and sent them flying in all directions.

A Special Security Service vehicle veered off the road and crashed into a light pole, overturning onto the side of the road and falling down a steep embankment. Seconds later, the wind pulled another nearby light pole from the ground and thrust it across the expressway. A car, sliding out of control, tumbled over the top of the pole and flipped several times in the air before crashing onto the pavement. The queen's car slammed sideways against the concrete barricade dividing the highway.

A WWN News van, veering away to avoid a collision with another vehicle, overturned, all four wheels still spinning as the car slid along the pavement upside down, until the wind swept the van off the road and down the steep embankment on the side of the highway.

~~~

Father McClain snapped out of his intercession, interrupted when the sanctuary's stained-glass windows blew open. Before he had time to react, the church was in chaos. Candles, their holders, Bibles, and hymnals flew up from their places and swirled about the great room.

The crucifix above the altar swung violently above him. As he descended the steps of the altar, he lost his balance and stumbled. The wind was on the verge of sucking him from the sanctuary and thrusting him out into the darkness. "In the name of God," he cried, "I command you to cease. Now!"

Miraculously, the tornado subsided, and silence returned to the cathedral. For the first time in days, a glimmer of hope flickered inside the weary priest. As he surveyed the ransacked sanctuary, a powerful wave of calm rippled through his body.

Father McClain sensed something happening outside the building. He walked gingerly toward the wall of opened stained-glass windows and peeked out, his eyes widening in surprise. A radiant light beamed from the heavens and streamed down onto the premises of the cathedral like a protective shield.

McClain stood, astonished, trying to take in this indisputable act of God. He immediately understood that his command to stop the tornado had unleashed the power within that God had bestowed upon him, manifesting itself as this mysterious light. The priest was more certain than ever that he possessed the supernatural capacity to avert the evil prophecy. Moreover, aborting a tornado destined to wreak great havoc enhanced his faith and his courage, and ultimately convinced him of his ability to prevent the tsunami.

But what about the reign of permanent darkness? If he was able to stop the tornado, why was England still immersed in pitch black?

~~~

12:40 p.m.

The Royal Pavilion of Brighton sat high on a hill, overlooking the coast approximately a half mile away. The current scene at the pavilion was like no other political event ever hosted there. Security was particularly tight. A chopper hovered low, directly above the pavilion's roof, dropping another band of Special Forces troops. On the grounds, along the gated fields, the troops lined the premises. Heavily armed and wearing their night-vision goggles, the soldiers covered the lawn in the deadly cold, under the pitch-black midday sky. They held tight to their automatic assault rifles and machine guns, fingers clenched on the triggers, ready and waiting to open fire on any trespasser.

An hour after her scheduled speech was to take place, Queen Elizabeth's badly dented car pulled up in front of the pavilion, followed by what was left of her motorcade.

As the queen and her entourage headed into the building, a Special Forces soldier positioned on the roof of the pavilion spotted the black faces of multiple unidentified figures scattered across the surface of the iced-over sea. Consumed by terror, the soldier stared through his night-vision goggles, struggling to identify the creatures. They had seemingly emerged out of nowhere. While scanning the area just minutes earlier, the soldier had noted that the icy waters were calm and clear.

The Queen of Hell was only moments away from rising up from the Abyss. It seemed Jezebel and her minions were well aware of Queen Elizabeth's scheduled speech.

The soldier glanced right and then left, attempting to alert his comrades, but hesitated before saying anything. His fellow soldiers were aiming their weapons at the sea as well, but it soon became clear that only he could see the dreadful creatures. When he realized they were here to target the queen, he advanced his weapon. Seconds later, the soldier spotted something in the distance that he hadn't seen before. Fiery-red eyes had formed in the creatures' once-empty sockets. "Holy Mother of God," he exclaimed, ripping his night-vision goggles from his face.

~~~

A pavilion attendant escorted the queen and her entourage from the pavilion's State Room to the Grand Room. As was custom, the attendant shared bits of history about the structure as he guided the group through the building. "The Royal Pavilion of Brighton is a John Nash version of an Indian mogul's palace," he began. "It's quite unique, as I'm sure you've all noticed—ornate and exotic. Over the years, it has been subject to the devastating wit of English satirists and pundits. But today we can examine it more objectively as one of the outstanding examples of the Oriental tendencies of the Romantic Period of England.

"I sincerely hope that you all have had a wonderful time touring the pavilion state rooms," he concluded.

The royal officials applauded politely.

~~~

Jesus Christ, thought the soldier. *What in this God-forsaken world is going on?* He hadn't made any attempt to pass along the information to his comrades-in-arms. He'd continued to monitor the icy waters, and all he could see now was a sea of fiery red eyes glaring out from the darkness. The shadowy, reddish flames glowed in the frigid air, partially lighting up the atmosphere—fire and brimstone raging on the sea.

The demons, having sensed that someone could see them, though they lurked in an unseen realm, began monitoring the soldier's every move.

The soldier quickly realized he was being targeted, and trembled as fear set in. "Damn," he exclaimed, when the strange entities shot fire through the sky from their eyes.

Seconds later, the dark sky cleared of flames and the demons' eyes returned to normal.

Suddenly paralyzed from his shoulders to his feet, the soldier collapsed. He was no longer able to form words, his head heavy on his shoulders. He felt his organs shutting down, one after the other. His head snapped back and his rifle dropped to the ground, alerting his comrades.

~~~

The royal dignitaries applauded unenthusiastically as Queen Elizabeth stepped up to the podium. She placed the notes for her speech on the podium and stared intently at her audience. Cameras snapped and flashed from every angle as the queen nervously slipped her reading glasses onto her face.

"Citizens of England," she began grimly, "today marks day nine since this great country of ours plunged deep into doom. Unfortunately, as predicted, it is a tragedy that promises to sweep us all to our deaths, without a single survivor. The wrath of Mother Nature has, in her mysterious way, targeted us for annihilation. It is a calculated massacre; none like it has ever occurred in human history. Indeed, it will be a ghastly extermination of innocent human lives that God, in his divinity, does not seem to possess the power to reverse.

"As I stand here, I see the millions of lives trapped in harm's way, including myself, who have no choice but to face the cold hands of an untimely death. Who would have thought, over past centuries, that evil could invade at such magnitude—beyond our human imaginations? Whoever thought, living in a generation of dreamers, the wrath of Mother Nature would plunge England into utter desolation?

"Seeing that this dark crisis has spun beyond our control, I sincerely believe that this part of the world is coming to an end. This is our judgment day."

~~~

The Special Forces soldier positioned next to the victim dropped his weapon, removed his night-vision goggles, and scooted to his comrade's aid. He looked upon the fallen soldier's features and was horrified to see that his friend's eyes had begun sinking into his face. He was barely breathing, but was alive enough to give his fellow soldier some idea about what had caused his mysterious collapse.

"Talk to me, Lewis," he screamed, shaking his comrade back to consciousness. "What happened?"

Lewis tried to form words, but couldn't.

"Tell me," his comrade insisted, "what's going on? Did you see something?" He continued to shake his friend to keep him from losing consciousness.

Mustering the last of his strength, Lewis raised his arm and weakly pointed to the frozen sea. His comrade snapped his head in the direction Lewis was pointing, but saw nothing but an empty, frozen sea. He looked back at his dying friend. "I don't see anything."

"Look . . . again . . . ," Lewis croaked. "Army . . . of demons . . . can't . . . fight them."

Lewis's comrade looked out to the sea a second time and, stunningly, the sight of the demons spread across the sea unveiled before his eyes. "Oh my God." He turned to the others. "Men," he shouted, pointing. "Look."

The troops responded immediately, positioning themselves along the edge of the roof. Their eyes on alert, they aimed their weapons toward the encampment of strange figures and waited for their next move.

The men watched as a monster, the scariest of them all, burst through the ice and swooped high into the air. Using its giant eagle-like wings, the creature soared directly toward the rooftop. Like a swarm of locusts flooding the sky, the hordes of fiery-eyed demons stormed out after their leader.

~~~

Queen Elizabeth was a few lines from concluding her speech when the sound of gunfire interrupted her. She stood at the podium, mute and trembling. Shots rang outside the pavilion, echoing in every direction. Camera operators and news reporters abandoned their posts and dropped to the floor. The dignitaries, initially paralyzed with fear, quickly followed suit.

~~~

While in deep meditation, Father McClain glimpsed a vision of the horrific events raging at the Royal Pavilion of Brighton. Unnerved, he hastened down from the altar and paced the center aisle.

He managed to calm himself, but the thought of Jezebel and her dark angels emerging and capturing the city of Brighton filled him with dread. Reasoning that his faith was being tested, McClain knew he had to act quickly.

~~~

Demons stormed out of the iced-over sea en masse, possessing the bodies of giant seahorses. With wings like flying dragons, they streaked the blackened sky like sharks swarming in the ocean. The Special Forces troops intensified their heavy artillery assault against the demonic army, to no avail. The shots merely bounced off the demons' bodies.

Jezebel swooped down and pounced on the back of the commander of the troops, positioned on the pavilion's rooftop. With her claws drilled deeply into his skin, she swept the commander from the roof and high into the air. She shredded him to pieces, his tattered body parts plummeting to the ground.

~~~

A security guard rushed into the Central Room in horror. "Security breach," he announced to the small group of bodyguards protecting the queen. The guards escorted her out of the room to a more secure location.

"Your Majesty, I advise you not to leave the hall," one of the guards warned. "It's extremely dangerous out there—very risky. You can't even imagine how bad it is. There are too many predators."

"What's going on?" the queen asked the guard, terrified.

"It's a demon invasion, ma'am," he replied nervously. "And they're seemingly indestructible."

"What are we going to do?" asked one of the other security guards.

"I suggest that we stay tight in here," the first one replied. "It's not safe to even go past these doors. This room is the safest place right now." He paused. "I watched one of those horrible beast-like creatures destroy the entire troop guarding the roof."

~~~

Gunfire echoed from the premises of the Royal Pavilion, sending nearby residents into a panic. The community soon discovered the multitude of strange, horrifying creatures inundating the dark sky. Before any of the residents could identify that the creatures were demons, Jezebel's forces seized the entire city of Brighton.

Great terror erupted, upending the devil-may-care attitude of the residents of Brighton. Panic-stricken people froze in the face of the brutal attack. Within minutes, the city began shaking. The crowds of people still indulging in last-minute escapades abandoned their activities and fled to their homes in fear for their lives. They had expected to be taken by the massive tsunami, but acknowledged that their fate had changed as they beheld the sinister flying seahorses, their fiery-red eyes gazing upon the people like scarlet laser beams.

Cars raced aggressively through the streets as people fled home. Thousands rushed on foot, screaming hysterically, as fear and dread flooded the air. The huge, boisterous crowds that had once filled the town dispersed, leaving the streets and alleyways nearly empty. In the space of ten minutes, Brighton had become a ghost town.

~~~

After feeling God's power penetrate every fiber of his being, McClain looked heavenward with courage. "God of Light," he called out, "Ruler of the Universe, your written word declares: life and death lies in the power of the tongue. By the same word, you spoke the heavens and the earth into existence. By the power of your word, you birthed each and every living creature on the face of this earth. I believe with all my soul that your inscribed word is still alive today, and powerful, too.

"With these testimonies at heart, by the power of my voice, in the name of Jesus, I will erase the death verdict and decree that not a single soul shall die. By your divine power, I will seize and destroy the evil spirit of death."

~~~

The monster sprang ferociously into the second floor lobby of the pavilion. The Special Forces troops guarding the area fired shots from close and distant ranges. Like the speed of lightning, Jezebel sprung from wall to wall, diving from one level to another, dodging the speeding bullets. In swift succession, she pounced on each of her attackers and set them ablaze with the fire that spewed from her nostrils.

Queen Elizabeth and her dignitaries lay flat on the floor of the hall, trembling in panic. They soon realized that the heavy shooting sounded throughout the building, casting another vast wave of fear over them. The armed bodyguards remained on hair-trigger alert, their weapons aimed in all directions, anxiously waiting to open fire upon any creature's entrance.

The group was taken off guard by a momentary cease fire, unaware that a demon had already rampaged the building, wiping out the troops stationed in the lobby. Without warning, a burst of smoke spewed from the ceiling.

The group looked up just as the demon materialized through the smoke, swooped low, and began circling above them. The guards opened fire on the predator.

Jezebel dove from wall to wall, expertly dodging the speeding bullets. She managed to upend one of the guards with her tail, coming face-to-face with the man as she hovered above him in midair. All the while, bullets from every direction bounced off her skin.

"Oh my God," Queen Elizabeth screamed, shielding her head with her hands.

"I am a spirit," Jezebel declared in a British accent, with the voice of a middle-aged woman. "I am indestructible." She set the upended guard alight with fire from her nostrils and flung him violently through a plate-glass window.

Another guard, horrified by the gruesome death of his comrade, dropped his weapon and threw himself out the window after his friend.

The demon ascended, hovering close to the ceiling. When she realized the assaults on her were diminishing, Jezebel ceased dodging bullets. She extended her mighty wings to their full span and struck the gunmen with spears launched from under her feathers, instantly killing them all.

An eerie silence fell over the room as the demon gently and quietly fluttered above Queen Elizabeth, sneering at her primary target, her prey.

From out of nowhere, a javelin, ablaze with fire, flew into the hall and struck the demon square in the forehead. She growled angrily and vanished without a trace.

Chapter 6

For the weapons of our warfare are not carnal, but mighty through God to the pulling down of strongholds.

2:00 p.m.

The fiery javelin thwarted Jezebel's mission to assassinate the queen of England, causing the demon to flee to the Tower of London in search of the intruder in question.

Jezebel's strong powers of intuition suggested that the hand of God had intervened and aborted her mission. But she sensed in her gut that a human force was also involved—perhaps the mastermind behind it all. Her powerful instincts whispered louder than her intuition. What she knew for sure was that the weapon had severely wounded her brain and destroyed half of her power.

She swiftly flew from the Tower of London and landed in the large suburban district of Bromley. She prowled the streets and city square on a vicious rampage, in pursuit of her adversary. When it occurred to her that her fate rested solely on the capturing and killing of this adversary—even if the adversary happened to be God—Jezebel grew desperate. She took to the air and continued to soar in search of her enemy.

Approximately eighty kilometers from London, Jezebel spotted a giant stream of light beaming down from the heavens. It looked to be shielding a huge cathedral several kilometers away. She picked up speed and landed on a mountaintop approximately two kilometers from the site.

Jezebel was annoyed to find that the mysterious light safeguarding the sacred domain showed signs of being divinely fortified. The structure was well protected from her evil plot—her invasion.

Using her satanic powers, Jezebel scouted a clear view through the cathedral's stone walls. Inside the sanctuary, astonishingly, she located her adversary, the mortal who had thwarted her campaign to take Queen Elizabeth's life. Was he a cardinal? A priest, perhaps? Yes, of course. It would have to be a priest. But what made this mere mortal so special? Why had God chosen this man to be his vessel here on Earth? The Queen of Hell gazed upon her enemy for several long moments, pondering her options.

Her profound wish was to storm the cathedral and attack the priest, but she immediately thought better of such a plan. God had bestowed this man with supernatural power. She acknowledged again, while regarding the light surrounding the church, that he was protected by external power, as well. Deep in thought, she strategized how to best enhance her power in order to slay her adversary.

Less than a minute later, a smile spread across her face as a seemingly perfect plan formed in her mind. The only way to destroy the priest would be to drown him in the massive flood caused by the tsunami—the tsunami she had the power to inflict at will.

~~~

Seconds later, the deafening roar of violent rushing waters—ocean waves gushing beyond their boundaries—alarmed the masses. The waiting and wondering was over.

The tsunami had begun.

~~~

Residents of cities far and near to Brighton heard the rage of the rushing water as it drew near. Before people had time to react, ocean water gushed violently into their homes.

"Mother, I think we should flee to Ireland now," Prince Andrew suggested, "before it's too late." He swallowed hard, his terror rising as the creatures relentlessly pursued their motorcade.

"It's too late, son," said the queen. "We should've fled two days ago."

He drew a sharp, deep breath. "How is it too late?" he asked, his eyes widening. "Instead of heading back to the palace, don't you think we—"

"No, son," she said sternly. "Don't you understand what prophecies are? The film predicted that every single soul would die, including you and me. And that's what is bound to fulfill."

"Maybe we should . . ." He paused. "What's that noise?" he asked, hearing what sounded like a rushing river close by. "Oh my God," he exclaimed. "Mother, look."

Through the front windshield, the queen spotted a monstrous wave the height of a telephone pole as it came rushing toward their vehicle. She screamed hysterically, alerting the other passengers. They all watched in horror as the tsunami crashed down on the motorcade, lifting their car from the pavement and pulling it under its enormous weight.

All over England, in a sudden sweep, the tsunami buried countless cities and residential areas, leaving millions of people trapped under its raging waters.

~~~

"The Lord is my light and my salvation. Whom shall I fear? When dark enemies encamp around us, God Almighty shall hide his people under the shadows of his wings. Yea, though I walk through the valley of the shadow of death, through this wrath of Satan, I fear not their threats. The whole armor of Jehovah Almighty . . ."

McClain was zealously reciting passages from the Book of Psalms when he heard the roar of the tsunami streaming closer. No longer able to hear the sound of his own voice, the priest dashed to a nearby window and peered out at the glowing premises through the stained glass. His heart pounded wildly as he listened in shock to a wave he thought was less than two kilometers away. His body shaking, Father McClain feared that the powerful wave was only minutes away from drowning him, like it had millions of others.

Wearily, the priest backed away from the window, his eyes still peering at the beaming light outside as he made his way back toward the altar. He shuddered at the thought of drowning in a flood amongst a brood of ravenous vipers.

His faith wavered at the sound of the approaching tsunami. Could it be that his divine mission to avert the evil prophecy had failed? Death seemed only a heartbeat away. The priest hung his head in defeat, reasoning that his fervent prayers, even his faith, could not save him now. He stood, feet glued to the sanctuary floor, as a two-hundred-foot wave plowed up against the building and crashed over the roof. He stared in awe as the powerful rushing water crushed the vaulted ceiling and the roof came crashing in.

The priest shrank in fear, gawking at the mountainous wave through the stained-glass window. The waters rose swiftly past the windows, making the church appear like a sinking ship. It struck him then, when he spotted the tsunami's multitude of victims drifting beneath the flood water, that his fate was sealed. The shocking presence of the dead bodies drained what little faith Father McClain had left.

A loud smashing sound turned his attention to the stained-glass window in the balcony. He looked up in time to see the wave crashing through the enormous glass wall, scattering multicolored shards in all directions. Water gushed over the choir loft and down into the center aisle, flowing directly toward the priest. Less than a second later, the violent wave swept the priest off his feet and sucked him under.

The entire sanctuary flooded within seconds, water rapidly spiraling up toward the ceiling. The contents of the chapels, offices, and bookstore—all down below on the crypt level—floated up past the ceiling within minutes. Water gushed from the exits.

Chapter 7

At three o'clock on that pitch-black afternoon, the tsunami ceased just as quickly as it had begun. From the cliffs of the Chesapeake tower standing five hundred feet above, Jezebel stared in triumph at the massive flood she'd inflicted on the country. In the catastrophic aftermath, the demon was impressed by her evil power to transform England into the Atlantic Ocean. Once the entire population had drowned, only her legions of demons could be heard, hissing in victory as they whirred in the sky above.

Jezebel ascended from the tall building, taking to the sky. From above, she surveyed the ruins of Salisbury Cathedral and monitored the priest intently as he lay among the pews, trapped beneath the water. The satisfied smile on Jezebel's face suddenly disappeared as her adversary's eyes popped open.

~~~

Father McClain, revitalized by the icy water, had regained consciousness. He stared straight up, in shock, mystified by this miraculous act of God. He soon realized that he could breathe normally under the water, just as if he was on land. Seemingly unharmed by the vicious wave, the priest rose from the floor, gazing in awe through the gaping hole in the ceiling. Powerful radiance beamed upon his face, rays of bright-white light shining down into water surrounding him.

~~~

A horrified Jezebel watched in fury as the priest floundered beneath the water and managed to make his way up to the balcony stairs. For a long moment, she stared on in bewilderment as her enemy gasped for air, taking obvious comfort in the warmth and relative dryness of the balcony.

Seeing the miraculous survival of Father McClain—a sure sign of his indestructibility—Jezebel circled the sky on a rampage.

~~~

McClain leaned against the banister, gazing at the water which had filled the cathedral to within six feet of the balcony. It occurred to him that the prayer he'd rendered two days ago had been answered. He had prayed fervently, with unwavering faith, asking God to unleash his divine power to abort the raid of death. Amazingly, he had marched, unharmed, out of a pool of deep water which should have drowned him instantly.

The priest grew certain that the citizens of England, trapped in the belly of the tsunami, were alive as well. He reasoned that mortals were not made to exist under water and that they had only moments to live. If he didn't act quickly, their souls would be lost forever.

McClain understood that the stakes were higher than ever. He had survived only to face intense chaos. The flood waters had imprisoned him in the balcony. With no food or water, he could die.

His mind shifted back to the big picture. The people of his country were plagued by the flood, and only he had the power to save them. He gripped the banister railing tightly, his face flushed. His jaw muscles stiffened as he threw back his head. He raised his hands heavenward and snapped his fingers once.

As divine power surged through him, McClain locked his gaze on the dark sky. Lightning bolts streaked above him, the clouds turning a fiery red.

~~~

Jezebel was still furiously soaring above when a slap of severe heat scalded her body. She looked up in horror. The fleeting clouds above, now a fiery red, were raining balls of fire down onto the flood waters. After managing to dodge and swoop her way through the flaming showers, Jezebel gazed below to find the intense heat sucking her legion of demons into the ocean of fire, melting them all instantly.

~~~

The raining flames ceased abruptly, leaving a raging wildfire in their wake. Father McClain refused to move an inch from where he was. Then the miracle erupted before his very eyes. From his place in the balcony, he gazed in awe as blankets of fire mysteriously glided from the four corners of the great room below. The flames united, spiraling up into a pillar in the center of the sanctuary. He gaped at the spectacle as the fire sucked up the remaining flood water, rocketed through the remains of the ceiling, and vanished.

McClain backed away from the banister, stunned, and walked gingerly down into the sanctuary. His eyes widened in disbelief as he staggered through the aisles, unable to detect any water damage. The church looked pristine, as though it had never been plagued by the deadly flood. He found no traces of moisture. Everything seemed to be in perfect order, the sanctuary miraculously restored to its former glory.

The priest reached down and lifted a Bible from the front pew. As he gently turned the pages, McClain grinned. Not a single page was ruined. He sank down onto the wooden bench, leaned back, and closed his eyes.

~~~

McClain awoke with a start, the dawn's light warming his face as it streamed in through the windows. He rose quickly, hastened to the front entrance, and threw open the doors. The shock of daylight was almost too much for his tired eyes, but the priest rejoiced in the return of the light that had vanished nine days ago. He cast his eyes cast heavenward, stepped into the sun's glow, and immersed himself in its warmth.

Distracted by the miracle of light, McClain had failed to notice the bodies. As he tore his gaze away from the heavens, the priest drew a sharp breath. Victims of the flood lay everywhere, scattered on the fields and along roadways. Like a brutal massacre, the flood had ravaged the lives of an entire country. McClain saw far and near, the countless victims of the tsunami lying about, exposed to the elements, unconscious.

McClain walked for several blocks up and down the streets near the cathedral. Victims lay in the streets and alleys and all throughout town. Rows of countless bodies stretched on for kilometers.

~~~

As a mild wind kicked up and blew from the west, victims of the tsunami awoke from their comas. One by one, they rose from the ground. They stood, gazing in awe at the glaring sunlight, trying to comprehend how they could have survived the tragedy.

~~~

Day Twelve

After pondering a verse of scripture, Father McClain slapped closed his Bible. Seconds later, the hair on the back of his neck rose.

He wasn't alone.

He caught movement from the corner of his eye—a sudden and strange appearance of someone or some*thing*. He looked up from the elevated marble pulpit to find that Jezebel had secretly entered the church. She had climbed atop the banister of the balcony, her claws digging into the railing. Her wings flapped slowly as she eyed the priest, ready to pounce.

McClain backed away from the Bible, staring up at the demon with hostility. "Welcome to the House of God, Queen Jezebel," he said fearlessly. "Or do you prefer the 'Queen of Hell'?"

Jezebel growled.

"Lucky to be alive, aren't you?" the priest continued. "Since the wrath of God hasn't devoured you yet, perhaps it's about time for you to give this matter some serious consideration."

The demon growled again—this time louder.

Emboldened, McClain pressed on. "Your evil prophecy has failed, as well as your mission." He stepped out from behind the pulpit. "And now look at you," he scoffed, "nothing but a wounded, vulnerable beast. Whatever are you going to do now?"

Furious, Jezebel stretched her tail, wrapped it around the chandelier dangling above the balcony, and ripped it from the ceiling.

"You might be able to destroy me," he said, descending the altar, "but you will still have God to contend with."

Jezebel swooped from the balcony, attempting to attack her adversary. Halfway across the sanctuary, a multitude of broadswords, kindled with flames, suddenly appeared from an unseen realm. The fire-laden weapons pelted every part of Jezebel's body, setting her ablaze.

McClain watched in triumph as his adversary plummeted down into the center aisle, immersed in fire. Anxious to see the demon destroyed, he leaped the last three steps of the altar and gazed upon his now hysterical enemy as she withered among the flames, gradually melting away.

Chapter 8

McClain drew a victorious breath as the mysterious fire annihilated the Queen of Hell. But seconds after the foul smoke of the demon's remains cleared the sanctuary, the priest found himself transported to a strange wilderness. In a flash, the church around him had vanished, leaving him to wander about in a dreadful domain.

Although not entirely dark, the wilderness was dimly lit, making it difficult to assess his surroundings. Bolts of lightning flashed above him in rapid succession, rippling across the clouds. Mystified by his curious and sudden displacement, fear crept into McClain's bones. He wanted to believe this was God's doing, that he hadn't been spirited out of the sanctuary by some other powerful being, but that his instincts failed him in the face of fear.

Haunted by the thought of an untimely death, McClain's fear escalated. Panic-stricken, he felt on the verge of collapse.

"Father McClain."

The voice, soft but powerful, echoed through the gray light. The priest discerned that it was the voice of God.

"Father John McClain!"

His eyes darted nervously to the clouds, hoping to glimpse some physical feature of God, if that was even possible.

"Calm yourself, Father."

A peaceful feeling came over him. His hands and face, which moments earlier had been drenched with sweat, dried instantly. "Where are you, Lord?" he asked.

"*Why ask such a question, John,*" God replied gently, "*when you know that I am everywhere?*"

"Is it okay to ask where I am?" McClain asked tentatively. "Have I defeated the enemy, only to be snatched by death?"

"*Who said you are dead?*"

McClain sighed in relief. He was convinced that he had died. "Then . . . where am I?"

"*Where you are is not important,*" God replied. "*Bear in mind, your existence in my holy presence is a mystery—a mystery I beseech you to solve.*"

McClain tilted his head. "A mystery?"

But God did not elaborate and instead changed the subject. "*Well done,*" He said. "*Your conquest of the Queen of Hell has deeply impressed me. I am grateful for the extreme sacrifices you have endured. When all hope vanished, you remained faithful, and conquered. Congratulations, my son. You have won the battle, as I anticipated, but the war has yet to begin.*"

McClain swallowed hard. "War?" he asked, his voice cracking. "You mean, this is not the end? There is now a war to fight?"

"*Yes,*" boomed the voice of God. "*I have spoken. There is but one more enemy—one more powerful than Jezebel. He must be destroyed!*"

For a long moment, McClain remained silent, hesitating to respond. He finally summoned the courage to ask, "And who might that be?"

"*The enemy is inhuman, but* not *immortal,*" replied God. "*He is as old as the universe, and existed long before I breathed the gift of life into this world.*"

A shiver snaked up the priest's spine. "I'm confused," said McClain. "If he's not human, nor immortal, what exactly is he?"

"*He is a spirit.*"

The priest tilted his head. "This is highly inconceivable," he replied. "How can I possibly confront an adversary that I cannot see with my natural eyes? Who has no physical identity? How do you propose I conquer an enemy whose existence I cannot conceive of?"

"*Where is your faith, Father McClain?*" asked God. "*Do I have to remind you that we fight not against flesh and blood? Shall I remind you that the enemies of mortal souls can only be defeated by faith? Who else can I trust? No one but you.*"

"You have proclaimed that this adversary is unlike the Queen of Hell," McClain said. "But I need you to give me some clue as to what I am to face."

"*The dark princess.*"

McClain's eyes widened, and his heart pounded wildly. "Now—"

"*A prominent woman will carry a pregnancy presumed to be mysterious,*" God continued. "*The child, while still an embryo, will be predestined by Satan himself to reign as the dark princess. I anoint you to take custody of this child immediately after her birth. The infant must reside under your roof from the outset of her life, as early as possible, no later than four weeks of age.*"

McClain nodded.

"*The quest for the enemy lies solely in the adoption of the dark princess.*"

"I understand."

"*Your bond with the dark princess will point you to the spirit. It is a fate you cannot repudiate. More importantly, the conquest of this adversary will not only save the world from the wrath of the dark princess, but will also fulfill the prophecy of the apocalypse.*"

"What's his name?" McClain asked.

"*His name is feared by the entire human race—even my angels fear him. For this reason, I will refrain from revealing his identity. But at the appointed time, you shall know.*"

BOOK TWO
Annabelle

Chapter 9

St. Ann's Convent

The reverend mother sat patiently at the head of the long dining table, quietly watching as the small circle of nuns sat down for breakfast.

"Surprised to see you up and about so early today, Reverend Mother," said Sister Ellen gleefully.

"Are you implying that I am usually late?" the reverend mother replied. "Though I am not always the first to get here, I assure you, I am always on time."

The nuns glanced at each other and smiled.

The reverend mother eyed the empty seat to her left. "Where is Sister Annabelle?" she asked.

The nuns shrugged.

The reverend mother glanced at the clock. "Nine o'clock mass begins in twenty minutes. Sister Sarah?"

Sister Sarah straightened in her chair. "Yes, Reverend Mother?"

"Please go to Sister Annabelle's room," the reverend mother ordered. "Check to see if she's okay."

"Um, Reverend Mother?" Sister Sarah replied sheepishly. "Sister Annabelle, she's . . . um . . . using the restroom. That's why she's running a bit late."

"Does she not usually arrive before the rest of us?" the reverend mother asked.

"Yes," the nuns replied in unison.

Sister Margaret spoke up. "Indeed, she is always the first one to get here, Reverend Mother," the old nun said. "She has never once missed a day here without being the first."

Their conversation came to an abrupt end when Annabelle appeared in the doorway and took a seat at the table.

"Sorry for keeping you all waiting," she said quietly.

The reverend mother gazed questioningly into Annabelle's hazel eyes; she detected that the twenty-two-year-old nun was troubled in some way. Although she made an effort to disguise her discomfort, her face wore a decidedly gloomy expression—one the reverend mother couldn't ignore.

"You don't seem quite yourself, Sister Annabelle," she said, concerned. "Is there a problem?"

"No, Reverend Mother," Annabelle replied timidly. "There is no problem."

Sister Margaret glanced at the reverend mother and raised an eyebrow. The faraway look in the girl's eyes was enough to suggest that something was troubling her; Annabelle seemed almost grief-stricken. She turned her attention back to the young nun. "Are you sure everything's okay, Sister Annabelle?"

"Of course, Sister Margaret," she replied, her voice quavering. She looked on the verge of tears.

The other nuns eyed each other nervously.

"Just the same, Sister Annabelle, I wish to see you in my office immediately after mass."

"But Reverend Mother, I don't think it's necessary. I'm just fine—"

The reverend mother flashed the girl a stern glance.

"Yes, Reverend Mother."

"Well, then," the reverend mother said, smiling gently at the troubled young nun, "since you kept us waiting this long, you can lead the blessing."

"Yes, Reverend Mother."

~~~

Sixty-four-year-old Father Ryan watched from the pulpit

as a dozen elderly parishioners trickled into the sanctuary for midweek mass. Shortly afterward, the small group of parish nuns hurried up the aisle and took their seats. The priest, surveying the congregation, looked questioningly at the reverend mother. "Where is Annabelle?"

The reverend mother, startled by the priest's inquiry, glanced up and down the pew where the group had settled. But the troubled young nun was not sitting among them. She and Sister Margaret stood and scanned the sanctuary— still no Annabelle. Alarm bells went off in the reverend mother's head. Annabelle had managed to slip away from their group while en route to the chapel.

"Is Sister Annabelle attending mass today, or not?" the priest asked, his voice conveying concern. "Shall we wait for her?" Father Ryan cared for all of the nuns, but young Sister Annabelle was his favorite. He saw the worry in the reverend mother's eyes and knew immediately that something was amiss.

"I . . . I don't know, Father," the reverend mother replied hesitantly. "We all walked from the convent together, as we always do, right after breakfast. I thought she was with us. Somehow I must have lost sight of her."

~~~

Annabelle sneaked out of her room and closed the door quietly. Wheeling her suitcase behind her, she crept into the family room, dropped her luggage, and hastened to the window. She pulled the draperies aside and peeped down at the front entrance of the parish, a block away from the convent. She could see that mass was in progress and reasoned that she had a moment to fulfill her hidden agenda.

She lingered by the window, unable to resist the intense morning glow of the autumn sun. The trees planted along the drive were nearly bare, piles of rusty leaves covering the ground below. Her heart ached. She already missed the convent and St. Edward's Parish, though she hadn't yet left their beautiful grounds.

She glanced at the two paintings on the far wall. The replicas of *The Last Supper* and *Jesus's Crucifixion* saddened her. Every single day for two and a half years, she had taken the time to behold these paintings. They were as much a part of convent life as praying and attending mass. She pulled her eyes away from the portraits, picked up the phone, and dialed the number for a nearby cab company.

"Blue Bird Cab," the receptionist on the other end of the line answered.

"Yes, how far are you from St. Edward's Parish?"

"What's the address?"

"2278 Mills Bourn Road," Annabelle blurted.

"I can have a car there in approximately twenty minutes."

"That fast, you're sure?"

"I'm positive, ma'am."

"It's just that—I'm in a terrible rush, and . . . can the cab pick me up in front of St. Ann's? It's the convent behind the parish, just a block or so."

"Yes, ma'am. Shall I send a car then?"

"Yes, thank you," she replied breathlessly. "I appreciate it."

~~~

Annabelle entered the chapel quietly and sat in the last pew. She had missed the Liturgy of the Word and the Homily, arriving just before the Eucharist. She knew that her reason for leaving would cause grief among the nuns and clergy of St. Edwards, and her inability to explain her reasons for leaving would seem highly suspect to the Church. Leaving without notifying the others seemed the only viable option.

Tears filled her eyes as she looked at the nuns sitting several rows ahead of her. She would miss them all dearly.

~~~

Father Ryan looked solemnly upon his congregation. "Please stand for the singing of the hymn, 'Blessed Mary.'" As the parishioners and nuns slowly got to their feet, Father Ryan spotted Annabelle in the back row. She seemed to have appeared out of nowhere, her face awash in an expression of shame. Though she clearly sought to camouflage her guilty feelings, there was no mistaking their presence. He knew her too well to be fooled.

The singing voices of the congregation faded into the background as Father Ryan monitored Annabelle as closely as he could. His instincts told him that the young nun was struggling with something serious—perhaps even dangerous. Whatever the nature of her problem, the faraway look in her eyes suggested that her devotion to her life as a nun had somehow diminished.

After the congregation's rendering of "Blessed Mary," Father Ryan found himself distracted, burdened by whatever trouble Annabelle faced. As he walked behind the communion table, he wondered what could have possibly happened to weaken the spirit of his favorite nun. He resolved to speak with her immediately after mass.

He turned his attention back to the congregation. After the altar server placed the wine and the bread on the communion table, he began the exhortation: "Pray, brethren, that my sacrifice and yours may be acceptable to God, the almighty Father."

The congregation responded: "May the Lord accept the sacrifice at your hands, for the praise and glory of his name, for our good, and the good of all his holy Church."

~~~

Annabelle rose quietly and crept out of the church, unnoticed. She hurried down a short flight of stairs and out the back door. As she reached the convent's front steps, she spied the taxi steering through the compound's gateless entrance and making its way to the front door of St. Ann's. She looked at her watch. *Right on time.*

At exactly ten fifteen, the cab driver dropped off Annabelle at the crowded Fulham Train Station. Dressed in her habit, her luggage beside her, she stood by the curb for several long moments. A wave of relief washed over her now that she was finally away from the church. The religion to which she had been so devoted for the past two years had begun to feel oppressive in the face of her dilemma.

~~~

Thirty-six hours earlier

The nuns, exhausted, filed out of the family room after watching a two-and-a-half-hour movie on the life of Christ.

"Cecil B. DeMille's version of the life of Jesus is phenomenal, don't you think?" the reverend mother asked the others.

"I agree one hundred percent," Sister Claire, a middle-aged nun, replied enthusiastically. "It's as though hundreds of secret cameras filmed Jesus's every move."

"Makes me wish there were actually cameras back in Christ's day," chimed in Sister Betsy, "so that we wouldn't merely have to accept the director's imagery of our Lord and Savior."

Annabelle turned to the group before heading down the corridor. "Goodnight, sisters."

"Why the hurry, Annabelle?" asked the reverend mother, winking. "It's not even bedtime yet."

"It's almost seven o'clock, Reverend Mother," Annabelle replied shyly.

"Of course," said Sister Catherine. "You know every evening around this time Annabelle retires to her studies."

"Oh, of course," the reverend mother said. "Forgive me, Annabelle. I must have gotten carried away by the film."

Annabelle smiled at the reverend mother and nodded at

her fellow sisters. "Goodnight, everyone," she said before hurriedly making her way to the convent library.

Annabelle walked into the cavernous room, fatigued. The long, intense film had left her feeling drained. She decided to cut her usual three hours of study in half, perhaps even shorter, if necessary. She pulled a book from the shelf and laid it beside her Bible on one of the tables. Before opening either book, she knelt beside her chair, closed her eyes, and began to pray.

Only a few silent words had escaped her lips when a chill crawled up her spine. She quickly opened her eyes and scanned the room—nothing. But she couldn't shake the feeling that she was being watched. Sensing movement above, she lifted her eyes to the ceiling and froze in horror, her gaze fixed on the intruder: the shadow of a ghost hovering directly above.

Annabelle murmured in panic as she scrambled to her feet. She peered around the room, holding her breath, as the library vanished and was replaced by a strange, unearthly paradise. The young nun lifted her eyes heavenward and, to her great alarm, spotted seven moons arranged in a perfect circle.

Annabelle wondered if she was hallucinating as the towering pillars of clouds and rays of moonlight engulfed her. Perhaps she was caught up in a vision, that supernatural encounter with God she'd longed for since taking the vow. As Annabelle stood, transfixed on the moons above, it dawned on her that her wish had finally come true. She managed to calm herself, subduing the terror that threatened to overwhelm her. The clouds parted and an angel descended from the heavens, hovering only a short distance in front of her.

For minutes, Annabelle stared mutely at the angel. A gentle breeze blew through his snow-white form, capturing her attention in a way she could never have imagined.

"Who are you?" she asked.

"I am Angel Michael, the messenger."

"You're an angel? An actual angel?" It had never occurred to her that an angel's voice would sound like a human's, but, astonishingly, angel Michael sounded perfectly human. She even detected a Scottish accent. "I can see you're an angel, but your voice . . . it doesn't sound like I thought an angel's would." She felt her face getting hot when she realized how silly it was to be questioning such a trivial thing when a genuine angel hovered before her. She released a nervous giggle. "I'm sorry," she said, surveying the surroundings. "I'm just a little overwhelmed right now."

Michael smiled. "Don't be. It is simply unwise for angels to convey the message of God to his chosen ones in our own language."

Annabelle grinned. "Of course. That makes perfect sense. So, may I ask . . . why am I here?"

"A worthy reason, I assure you," he said. "This is a sacred encounter with the giver of life that is bound to shape the course of your destiny forever. Make no mistake, you are in the presence of God. A sign of a divine mystery has been bestowed upon you."

"A divine mystery?" she asked, deeply curious. "What do you mean?"

"The Lord has anointed you to fulfill a mission for his heavenly kingdom, a divine mission only you can bring to fruition. Annabelle, you are destined to give birth to a special child, both human and divine. When your baby comes of age, she will rule the world as a princess. She will be the light that points the human race to the coming of Christ into our world. And when he comes, the princess will redeem the human race from the wrath and judgment of God."

"How would that even be possible?" she asked,

incredulous. "I'm a nun, a virgin. I was made to believe that it is God's will that I remain childless."

The angel landed softly, grazing his feet on the cloud beneath. "Wrong," he snapped. "Deception is a sin—a sin that must face the full weight of destruction. Woe unto him who has burdened you with such lies."

Taken aback by the angel's passionate display, Annabelle pondered the mission God wished her to fulfill. A divine privilege had been handed her, one she didn't feel she deserved. "But I'm a nun, devout in my sacred vows. Why would God choose me for such an important task?" She paused, hesitating to ask the obvious question. "Might it seem a bit strange to the rest of the world? Nuns are married to God, and God only."

"Don't you see?" Michael replied. "That's precisely why he chose you, Annabelle. It is through the seed you shall bear that Christ will look upon and pardon the sins of a generation of souls—souls condemned to his eternal wrath."

Her apprehension subsided, giving way to a joy deep within. A smile slowly spread across her face. "My eyes have been opened to the light of his glory and power."

"Good," Michael said, smiling. "Now, this may seem unrealistic, but you must accept it. Remember, Jesus, the son of God, was not conceived in a palace. Oh, he could have been, had the heavenly Father wanted it so, but our Lord and Savior, Jesus Christ, was born in a place where animals were kept. With this in mind, God orders that you release yourself into the world by sunrise."

Puzzled, she asked, "Is he suggesting that I live a secular life?"

"Exactly. You must understand that the real world will never discover the light inside you if you live in isolation." He paused, eyeing Annabelle intently. "There is one thing God will hold you accountable for."

"What?" she asked, her eyes locked onto Michael's. "What is it?"

"The secret."

"The secret?"

The angel nodded, his expression serious. "The fate of the Lord's vision, and the destiny of this child to be born, lies in you burying this moment deep in your heart."

She sighed heavily, her brow furrowed. Annabelle was anxious to share this amazing news, especially with her mother. She was terribly disappointed to discover that the privilege divinely bestowed upon her came at a price—her silence. She wasn't sure she could make such a promise, much less keep it forever.

Michael pressed on. "You must vow to God, Annabelle, that the mysterious birth of the princess will remain concealed. It is the Lord's dying wish that not a single soul gain knowledge of his promise to the world."

"What if, somehow, the secret gets out?" she asked, not certain she wanted to know the answer.

Michael eyed her sternly. "Any attempt to reveal the secret will immediately shatter God's vision for this world—and ruin your chances, as well."

Chapter 10

Susan was a widow in her mid-forties. A devoted school teacher, she was, above all, a devout Anglican.

It was a cool, breezy autumn evening. Susan's eighth-floor Westlake apartment, furnished with antiques, was warm and quiet. She adored the cozy, relaxed atmosphere of her flat this time of year. The early nightfall, however, prompted her to prepare supper a little earlier than usual. She hoped her longtime friend, Bill McCoy, might make a surprise visit.

She was reaching for a dinner plate when she heard a knock at the door. Susan turned away from the cabinet and hesitated, a wave of anxiety washing over her—a sense that something was terribly wrong. She drew a deep breath, attempting to slow her racing heart. Her instincts were rarely incorrect.

A second series of knocks broke Susan's trance. She walked to the door and cracked it open, her eyes widening in surprise. There, on the other side of the door, stood Annabelle, her one and only daughter, waiting to greet her.

Annabelle burst through the door and threw herself into her mother's arms. "Good evening, Mother," she greeted her cheerfully.

"Good evening to you, my lovely daughter," Susan replied, still in shock. She hadn't seen her daughter since she'd entered St. Ann's convent two years before.

After a long embrace, Annabelle reached for her suitcase and headed down the hall. Susan closed the door and watched her daughter wheeling her luggage behind her.

Moments later, she heard the door to Annabelle's room close.

Annabelle's unexpected return raised her suspicions. Despite her daughter's cheerful demeanor, she sensed that something was terribly wrong. Suddenly remembering her dinner still cooking on the stove, Susan scurried back to the kitchen.

~~~

The familiar scent of a girl's room greeted Annabelle as she entered. Although she missed the sisters terribly, she embraced the feeling of freedom at having liberated herself from the prison of religious convocation. For the first time in her life, she relished the opportunity to spread her social wings and embrace the worldly lifestyle she'd once shied away from.

Annabelle kicked off her shoes and pulled back her veil, revealing straight, shoulder length, dark brown hair. She stepped in front of the dresser and scrutinized her image in the mirror. She had nearly forgotten what she looked like. It seemed that her appearance was no longer important once she had taken up residence at St. Ann's. From the day she'd taken the vow to live as a servant of God and remain a virgin for the rest of her life, she never imagined living any other way.

The self-satisfied smile on her face disappeared as an intriguing thought surfaced. Seemingly out of the blue, Annabelle's mind stumbled upon a particular career that would undoubtedly place her before the eyes of the public, and perhaps even force her to confront the pressures of her past that she had once escaped.

~~~

Susan flinched when the door to Annabelle's room suddenly banged open and slammed shut. She stepped away from a sink full of dirty dishes and grabbed the towel from her shoulder. She was still drying her hands when she peeked around the kitchen doorway.

Susan's eyes widened, and her mouth fell open. The dish towel dropped to the floor. Her daughter, the nun, was strutting up the hall wearing tight jeans and a plain white, see-through T-shirt—her midriff exposed, belly-button and all.

Annabelle eyed Susan's shocked expression with obvious amusement. "Everything okay, Mother?"

For a long moment, Susan stood silent, lacking the ability to form words. She finally managed to pull herself together. "What is going on with you?" she asked, her voice rising. "Have you turned yourself into some kind of tramp?"

"Mother," Annabelle exclaimed, insulted. "What kind of thing is that to say about your daughter?"

Susan's mood swiftly escalated from shock to anger. "Look," she said, "you show up here, unannounced, without so much as a phone call, and in the space of twenty minutes, have transformed from a habit-wearing Anglican nun to . . . to . . ." She gestured toward her daughter's bare midriff. "This." Susan drew a deep breath and exhaled. "I deserve an explanation, Annabelle."

Annabelle bowed her head. "You're right, Mother," she replied. "I'm sorry."

Susan stepped into the kitchen and spooned two ladles of chili into a bowl. She returned to the dining room and set the bowl on the table in front of her daughter.

Annabelle pulled out a chair and sat. "So," she said, smiling sheepishly, "do I at least get a 'welcome home'?"

"Not yet," Susan replied flatly. She shuffled back into the kitchen, poured a glass of mineral water, and grabbed a dish with a baked potato on it. She brought the items to the table and sat down across from her daughter.

Annabelle could see that her mother was profoundly unhappy. She had been so caught up in the ecstasy of her divine path that she hadn't stopped to consider how her mother would feel about her sudden about-face—her mother, the devout Anglican, who had been ever so proud the day Annabelle took her vow. She thought about Michael's warning: that no one must know about God's plan for her. She sighed and picked up a spoon, her earlier delight giving way to mixed feelings. Not being able to share the amazing turn of events with her mother made them less appealing. But she had made a promise to God— one she intended to keep.

"So," her mother began, "tell me why you're here, and, more importantly, why you're *not* at the convent."

"I know I should have discussed my leaving with you first," Annabelle replied, evading the question. "But I was afraid."

"Afraid?" her mother asked, her brow furrowed. "Of what? Me?"

"I was afraid it might upset you. My leaving St. Ann's. I didn't want you to talk me out of it, I suppose."

Her mother regarded her suspiciously. "I don't understand. You were so happy there. What happened? Annabelle, did you break your vow?"

"Yes, I did."

Susan searched her daughter's face for some kind of remorse, but found no clue as to Annabelle's motivation for breaking her sacred vow. "No, Annabelle," she cried. "No. Please tell me you're joking. How could—"

"Mother," Annabelle interrupted. "Please."

"Don't," Susan barked, her eyes filling with tears. "Just, don't." Her jaw quivered in anger.

For several long minutes, they sat in silence.

When she finally regained her composure, Susan asked, "How in the world could you denounce your faith? How do you just wake up one morning and decide to be something you never wanted to be? Who's influencing you,

Annabelle? Because I know this couldn't have been your idea."

"No one influenced me, Mother."

"Then why? How could you be so foolish? There had better be a justifiable explanation for all of this."

Annabelle looked at her mother and sighed. The tension between them grew, and silence once again filled the room. But Annabelle remained hesitant. She knew she couldn't reveal her divine mission, but she had never before lied to her mother. She hadn't the first clue as to how to even go about it, much less come up with a plausible explanation. She bit her bottom lip and bowed her head.

"I'm waiting, Annabelle."

"Mother, I'm twenty-two years old—an adult. I have the right to change my mind about my future."

"This hasn't got one damned thing to do with age," Susan replied, annoyed with her daughter's naiveté. "You've walked away from God. Who knows what kind of consequences you will reap for dishonoring your vow to him."

"I knew you wouldn't understand," Annabelle said, defiance rising from some unknown place deep within.

"Understand what?" her mother countered. "What's to understand? You've told me nothing. You've compromised your devotion to God. You've gone back on your sacred vows, and you won't even tell me why." Susan straightened in her chair. "My feeling is, if you had a good reason for doing this, you wouldn't be so afraid to tell me what that reason is."

"Maybe living as a nun just wasn't for me," she offered lamely.

"Since when?" Susan shot back. "Your entire life, this is what you wanted. And now you've just changed your mind? And just when did this change of heart strike you, anyway?"

"I don't know," Annabelle replied hesitantly. "About two days ago."

Susan sighed, her deep disappointment showing on her face. "Annabelle, you made a choice. Since you were a young girl, you had a burning passion to serve God. When you took your vow, anyone could see that it meant everything to you." She paused, locking her eyes onto her daughter's. "That vow can't be broken under any circumstances."

"I know, Mother, but I just . . . I'm not destined to be a nun. I wish I could explain it to you, I truly do. All I can tell you is that I'm not perfect. I mean, everyone makes mistakes. I just happened to make one about what I wanted for my future. It's not unheard of. People switch careers all the time."

"Careers? Being a nun is a career now? Funny, I thought making a choice to devote your life to Christ was a little more than a career. Do you realize what you've done?"

Annabelle's face fell. "Don't make me feel like I've committed some terrible sin, Mother."

"But that's exactly what you've done. You're an outcast." Susan tried to get a hold of herself, but rage had taken over.

"Sisters have left the order before," Annabelle countered. "It does happen, you know."

Susan stood and brusquely walked into the living room. She gazed out the window, agony swirling inside her. "Two years of your life—wasted."

"Mother," Annabelle replied softly, "I'm still young. I've got my whole life ahead of me."

Susan spun around, a stinging barb on the tip of her tongue. But seeing Annabelle, her shoulders slumped, her head hanging over her dinner, she knew it was time to let it go. She exhaled, allowing her anger to subside. "Well, now that you're here, let's make the most of it." She paused and smiled at her daughter, who lifted her head and turned to meet her gaze. "I can't tell you I understand, but my sense is that your reasons for leaving are equally as passionate as those you had for taking the vow. Am I right?"

Annabelle let out a relieved sigh. "Yes."

"So you've obviously given this a great deal of thought. What is it that you want to do?"

Annabelle swallowed hard and blurted, "I want to pursue an acting career."

Susan froze. "Acting?" she asked, incredulous. "This is the reason for leaving the order? To be some . . . some movie star?"

"Well, what I really want, eventually, is to be a family woman. I want to marry, have a husband like you had. I want to have babies, experience the joy of raising a family. But it's not like I can just go out and become a wife and a mom. And acting seems like fun. I was too shy to try out for plays at school, but I secretly always wanted to."

Susan stepped into the dining room and stood beside Annabelle, her arms folded across her chest. She peered at her daughter skeptically. "All these years, you've never once mentioned this," she said. "It's never even crossed my mind that you'd be interested in such a thing, much less have any acting skills embedded in you."

"I was never in the habit of doing anything outgoing, Mother," Annabelle reminded her.

Her mother continued to watch her, unconvinced. Annabelle had to come up with something to convince her before she did the unthinkable and told her the truth. Then it hit her. Her heart raced as the lie formed in her head. "One night, while the sisters and I were watching *The King of Kings*—you know, that stunning old film about the life of Christ?"

Her mother nodded.

"Well, while we watched, it hit me. I couldn't stop

thinking about it for days—the beautiful and talented Dorothy Cumming as Mary . . ." She allowed her voice to trail off dreamily. She hoped she wasn't overdoing it. "Well, the inspiration just came to me. I knew then and there that I had found my true calling." She searched her mother's eyes for signs of approval.

A slow smile spread across Susan's face, and she shook her head. "What to do with you, Annabelle? What to do?"

Annabelle smiled back. Maybe she had some acting skills after all.

Chapter 11

Susan set a platter of spaghetti and meatballs on the dining room table. "Lunch is ready," she called. She spied Annabelle making her way up the hall. "What are you doing in your room this time of the day?" she asked. "Mourning?" A mother could hope, right?

An irritable sigh escaped Annabelle's lips. "I am not in mourning, Mother."

"Sorry, my mistake." Susan decided to go another route. "So how was the audition?" she asked as she dished up the food.

"I did the best I could."

She detected a note of self-doubt in Annabelle's voice. "You know something? I wouldn't trade a solid devotion to God for something that will not bring him glory."

Before Annabelle could respond, the doorbell rang.

"You expecting someone?" her mother asked.

Annabelle jumped up from the table. "No, but I'll get it." She hurried to the door and opened it.

"Certified mail for Annabelle Smithson," the letter carrier said, smiling.

"I'm Annabelle," she said excitedly, guessing the contents of the letter.

"Would you sign this, please?" He handed her a green card he'd torn from the back of the envelope.

"Sure." She signed her name. "Thank you."

As Annabelle closed the door, the phone rang. Susan dropped her fork onto her plate, walked into the living room, and reached for the receiver. "Hello?"

Annabelle, meanwhile, rushed back to the table, ripped open the envelope, and began reading the one-paragraph letter.

Susan placed her hand over the receiver. She watched as Annabelle eagerly read the letter, her face glowing. "It's for you," she said grimly, handing Annabelle the phone. A knot formed in the pit of Susan's stomach. The man on the other end of the line had introduced himself as some script writer, an executive producer working for Septum Network. She gently laid the receiver on the table.

"I'm accepted," Annabelle gushed breathlessly. "It's a TV drama. The script will be here in two days. Shooting starts in four weeks."

Susan grinned, sincerely relishing this moment along with her daughter. "Congratulations, honey. I'm happy for you, but . . ." She pointed to the phone lying on the table.

"Oh," Annabelle said, giggling. "I almost forgot. Hello? Yes, this is Annabelle Smithson . . ."

Chapter 12

Annabelle came in just before midnight, exhausted. She hauled in a dozen or so shopping bags from the corridor outside her mother's apartment.

"It's eleven thirty," said Susan. "I was worried about you."

"Worried?"

"Of course. How do you expect a mother to feel when her only daughter left early this morning and didn't arrive home until now?"

"What if I was on the set?"

"Well, that's one thing, but I knew you weren't, 'cause if you were, you would've told me."

Annabelle sighed, smiling. "You're right," she said wearily, dropping down onto the loveseat.

"Well, somebody's tired," Susan said.

Annabelle closed her eyes. "I sure am."

Susan eyed the shopping bags in the entryway. "You must have had one hell of a day of extravagant shopping."

"More than just shopping, Mother. I had other things to take care of, too."

"With all that loot, you're going to need another closet."

Annabelle straightened. "What do you mean?"

"I'm saying," Susan replied, suppressing a giggle, "that there's not room enough in your closet to house all those new clothes."

"Don't worry, Mother." A sly smile formed on her lips. "It's all taken care of."

Susan regarded her daughter curiously. "What do you mean?"

"I bought a home today—a condominium. The master's got a walk-in closet the size of another bedroom. I'm sure it will house all of those things"—she gestured toward the bags—"and much more where that came from."

Susan's eyes widened as she stared at Annabelle.

"What's the matter?" Annabelle asked. "Are you okay?"

"Uh, I'm fine."

"You sure got real quiet all of a sudden."

"I just don't seem to understand you anymore, Annabelle."

"What's there to understand?"

"I didn't know you even had plans to move out," she said sadly. "And here you've gone and bought a home of your own without even telling me first."

"What's the big deal?"

"You don't see what's wrong with that?" She was fast beginning to realize that she no longer knew her daughter. This person sitting across the room from her was little more than a stranger. "Remember, you're still a nun, regardless."

"All right, Mother," Annabelle relented. "I get it. I'm sorry. I didn't mean to upset you. Things aren't as crazy as they seem." She sighed, realizing that, once again, her enthusiasm had gotten the better of her. "The condominium I bought is still under construction. I don't have any immediate plans to move out. I bought it in advance because I didn't want to risk losing it."

Susan calmed a little. Her pained expression gradually disappeared. "When will you be moving out?"

"About a month after construction is complete," Annabelle replied. "I want to add a few finishing touches before moving my stuff in. Then I can settle into a place of my own before shooting for the next series begins."

"Yes, but when exactly will that be?"

"The third week of September."

Chapter 13

Annabelle's debut was a huge success. She never dreamed this kind of fame and fortune would cross her path. The overwhelming love she had earned from millions of fans for the role of Dr. Ellen Whitaker in the inspirational television drama *The Prodigal Doctor* took her breath away. For two years running, she won the Emmy Award for Best Actress.

But, despite her many accomplishments, Annabelle battled the void lurking within. The mysterious secret embedded in her heart haunted her, causing her to perhaps overly relish the joys of her success.

Annabelle woke up feeling uneasy. She ought to be excited—joyful beyond her imagination. She was roughly five hours away from signing a twelve-million-dollar contract with Time Warner to star as "the secretary" in the blockbuster hopeful *The Secretary*.

She grabbed the remote from her nightstand and pressed the *power* button. The big-screen TV at the foot of her bed came to life. Thirsty and craving orange juice, Annabelle swung her legs over the side of the bed and stood. She hesitated before making her way to the kitchen; something on the screen had caught her attention.

Channel thirty-four was airing a telecast of Father John McClain. The religious broadcast was unfamiliar to Annabelle. Having avoided her devotion for over two years, McClain's sermon had a mesmerizing effect, capturing her full attention. Her guilt-ridden dismissal of all things having to do with the order somehow compelled her to listen and absorb McClain's message.

Trapped in an internal battle to regain true happiness, Annabelle felt hopeful for the first time in years. As McClain's sermon went on, she felt revived. The misery she harbored inside melted away. Sitting at the edge of the bed, she fixed her hazel eyes on the giant screen, undistracted, silenced by the level of edification and healing. She began to sense a reconnection to the Holy Spirit, the bond with God she'd turned away from over two years ago. Within minutes, she was completely entranced by the priest's message.

The message was getting to her; the conviction of her devotion reanimated in a powerful way. Annabelle never dreamed she'd feel like this again, that she'd be able to repair the brokenness inside of her.

The camera angle switched from the congregation back to a close-up of the priest. Annabelle sat on the end of the bed, staring face-to-face with Father McClain as though he was preaching directly to her.

"There is a young woman out there watching me as I speak right now."

Startled by his eerily timed words, Annabelle stepped up her already rapt attention. She marveled at Father McClain's graceful yet stern delivery.

"If I may," the priest said, "I would now like to unveil a word of prophecy to this young woman, as I am led by God to do." He paused and cleared his throat. "The road to fame and wealth, as you know, is narrow and difficult. Achieving overnight success beyond your wildest dreams is quite unlikely for most. Let me be clear. This revelation is not meant to scare you or divert you from your great achievements. But the high price for achieving it all will end up costing you dearly. So if this—"

Annabelle switched off the TV and stared at the blank screen, anxiety washing over her. The priest's words of prophecy brought back her sense of unease in full force. She finally understood the fear that constantly haunted her: the fear of what would happen if she, by accident, revealed the secret that she would someday give birth to a divine princess.

Annabelle paced her room. She couldn't get Father McClain's words out of her mind. She instinctively suspected that the prophecy he spoke of was linked to her, but she had to find out for sure. A knock at the door disrupted her reverie.

"Good morning, my lovely, *loyal* daughter," Susan said, barging into Annabelle's condo. "What an honor to see you. I mean, it's only been three and a half months since we last saw each other."

Annabelle noted the sarcasm in her mother's voice. "Yes, I know, Mother," she said apologetically. "Please understand that I have very limited time, even for myself."

"So why are you even here, then?" Susan asked. "I'm surprised you don't have somewhere important to be."

"Mother, please," Annabelle replied wearily.

"Okay, okay."

Her mother seemed wholly unaware of Annabelle's distress as she reached into her bag and pulled out the latest issue of *Vanity Fair*. "Look," she said, bursting with pride. "I can't believe *my* daughter is on the cover of one of the most reputable entertainment magazines in the country. I can't tell you how proud I am of you, honey."

"Thanks for your support," Annabelle replied flatly, plopping down onto the couch.

Susan dropped the magazine on the end table and sat down next to her daughter. "When are you going to break the big news?"

"What news?" she asked irritably.

"Annabelle, don't play coy with me."

"I'm signing the contract later today. The movie will

take four to six months to shoot."

"Well, now that you're officially a screen actress, I figured you'd want to share all this success with your loving mother."

Annabelle was growing more and more annoyed. "Oh, is that so?"

"What's gotten into you?" Susan asked, regarding her daughter curiously.

Annabelle sighed. "I've been having funny feelings lately."

"Oh no. Don't tell me it's one of those tragic stories about the so-called glamorous life of celebrities, how you appear to be living the life everyone dreams about, but behind closed doors you're deeply troubled, inflicted with all sorts of dark issues. You're not one of them, are you?"

Annabelle rolled her eyes.

"Then what could it possibly be?"

"Mother, you've been a devoted Anglican for a long time. Has there ever been a time when you had a sacred encounter with the unseen world?"

Susan's jolly expression faded instantly. "What do you mean? Like seeing God?"

"No, not exactly . . ."

"Me, personally? No. But a sister once shared her personal testimony with me, several years ago now, about how she had a near-death experience."

"And what did she say it was like?"

"Peaceful," Susan replied.

Annabelle pondered for a moment and drew a long, ragged breath. "How often do you watch Father McClain's weekly telecast?"

"Regularly," Susan replied. "He's a powerful man of God, he is. He reaches millions, worldwide, every week."

"You caught his recent telecast, then?"

Susan nodded. "I listened to the radio broadcast on the

way over here."

"Okay, then bear with me. I've been wrestling with some mighty strange feelings lately, and his sermon today kind of got to me."

Susan searched Annabelle's eyes. "Is that what's bothering you? The prophecy?"

"Yes."

"Oh, don't be so naïve, Annabelle. Do you have any idea how many millions of women around the world watch that telecast?"

"I know, Mother, but it felt like he was saying those words directly to me—only to me. And since then, I—"

"Oh, don't be silly. Think about it: Are you the only woman in this entire world who's ever amounted to anything?"

"Of course not, but—"

Susan smiled. "Well, there you go."

Chapter 14

Bob Goldman's *Wealth Building* seminar was set to resume in mere moments, at six o'clock sharp. The event attracted successful business owners from all around the world who were currently seated in the ballroom of the Hilton Hotel. The audience of business tycoons applauded the event manager as he stepped up to the podium.

"Thank you," the event manager called out enthusiastically. When the applause subsided, he continued. "I want to begin by thanking you all for taking the time to be here and for making this year's wealth building seminar a big success. As many of you may already know, this year marks the sixth anniversary of Bob Goldman's seminar—a seminar that unveils the wisdom and strategy behind building wealth. Over the years, this conference has grown tremendously in its attendance and in creating more and more successful business owners."

The audience interrupted him with another round of applause.

"Speaking of tremendous growth, please allow me to share this philosophy: *wealth is never satisfied*. That said, it is my distinct honor to introduce to some and present to others, the man himself: billionaire Bob Goldman."

The audience stood and applauded the forty-one-year-old multibillionaire as he greeted the event manager and enthusiastically took the podium.

"Thank you," he said above the adoring applause. "Thank you very much."

The clapping gradually subsided, and the attendants took

their seats.

"Good evening and welcome, my fellow business partners."

"Good evening," the audience responded in unison.

"Before I go any further," Bob said, "I want to take this opportunity to thank you for attending this year's *Wealth Building* conference. As I stand before you tonight, it is very important that this be said: without your attendance, my dream of enriching your lives wouldn't be alive today."

A rousing applause erupted again, subsiding only after Bob gestured politely with his hands for the attendees to hush.

"Now since my ultimate goal, my mission, is to unravel the secret of making you a million or more dollars richer by the time this conference is over, I'll start off by asking: How many of you have realized that dream since last year's conference? Please stand so I can see you."

Business tycoons, by the tens, began standing in almost every row. Bob's spirits were bolstered by the seemingly unusual level of success in the past year. The *Wealth Building* seminar must really be helping people.

"Now, give *yourselves* a round of applause."

After the applause died down, Bob continued. "Most of you can now attest to the principles of our seminar. As you all know, I always like to start off with a familiar statement. So here it goes; here's the secret. The passion to pursue wealth must first start with a vision. With that vision at heart, you have to search within yourself, reign in those creative ideas. Sometimes it's a simple act of creativity. Or it could be a God-given talent embedded deep inside of you. Whatever the source, the drive to achieve wealth ultimately stems from a simple idea. Whether big or small, it is simply an idea that will, in the near future, launch you into your financial destiny—that millionaire or billionaire status you've always dreamed of.

"The idea that I discovered at the young age of six, was that I simply adored all kinds of telecommunications. Yes. Telecommunications. Living with this vision for the rest of my teenage years and up to adulthood paved the way to making me who I am today—the proud owner of the largest telecommunications network in the world. And not to mention," he said, winking, "the richest man in all of Europe. So for many of you who are striving to reach this goal in whatever business venture you are currently pursuing, I assure you that you are at the right place and the right time." The audience applauded wildly for close to a minute.

"And now with those thoughts," Bob continued, "I am delighted to share some of my plans for expanding modern telecommunications, not just in Britain and Europe but globally, as well.

"Six months ago, I had a vision to extend my wireless communications network to Africa, the second largest continent in the world, with a population of one billion. It will require approximately three point five billion dollars to make this vision a reality."

The curtains behind him slowly opened, revealing a huge projector screen lit with a display of tens of satellites orbiting in outer space.

"In our recent studies," Bob explained, "we learned that, geographically, Africa is divided into five regions: North, South, East, West, and Central Africa. These satellites will orbit over each region, transmitting clearer signals to the hundreds of installed towers. These devices, as you see, will eliminate the embarrassment of dropped calls and secure the use of modern technology via wireless communication.

"Now here is the really big news. By the year 2022, Eurocom Wireless anticipates a dramatic growth of our wireless users on that continent—up to thirty million carriers of our phones."

~~~

Bob Goldman carefully steered his Bentley into a space in the parking lot of the French Renaissance Restaurant. At least two evenings a week, Bob could be found in the VIP lounge at the Renaissance, having grown accustomed, over the years, to its upscale wine-and-dine atmosphere. It had been less than a week since he'd hosted his sixth *Wealth Building* seminar. He couldn't wait to relax with a glass of wine and dine on the best food in town.

"Good evening, Mr. Goldman," the hostess greeted him as he breezed through the front doors. "Wonderful to see you. Your usual table?"

Bob nodded, taking a quick glance around the VIP lounge. It was early in the evening, and only a few patrons dotted the dimly lit room. Out of the corner of his eye he spied a woman seated alone at a booth beside the front window—dark brown hair, long legs. She seemed more interested in the smooth jazz playing on the restaurant's sound system than with whatever story she was reading in the newspaper that lay in front of her.

"On second thought, Connie," Bob said to the hostess, "I think I'd like a booth by the front window this evening."

Connie smiled knowingly. "Of course, Mr. Goldman. Your wish is my command." When they reached the table, she added, "We have a wonderful new Napa Valley cabernet. Can I interest you in a glass?"

"That sounds lovely, Connie," Bob replied. "Thank you."

Connie nodded politely and hurried off toward the bar.

Bob slid his burgundy briefcase onto the seat next to him and set his hat on top. While unbuttoning his coat, he noticed the lovely scent of the woman's perfume wafting over to greet him.

"Here you are, Mr. Goldman," Connie said as she placed

the glass of wine in front of him. "Henri will be by in a few minutes to take your order."

Bob reached for the glass and took a sip. "Very nice. Thank you, Connie." He set the wine down and picked up his menu.

"Mr. Goldman?"

Bob looked up from his menu, expecting to see Connie again. His eyes widened in surprise as he beheld the beautiful creature standing next to his table.

"I'm sorry to bother you," she said, smiling politely, "but I happened to notice you when the hostess seated you here in the booth next to mine. I recognized your face from last month's *Forbes* magazine cover."

Bob couldn't believe he hadn't recognized her before. "You . . . you're Annabelle Smithson."

Annabelle offered him a shy smile. "Yes, that's me."

Bob was overwhelmed by her grace, her smile threatening to carry him away. *Get a hold of yourself, Bob. You're a billionaire, for God's sake.*

"I don't mean to interrupt your dinner, Mr. Goldm—"

"Please, call me Bob." He felt like a teenager, his stomach doing flip-flops. *The* Annabelle Smithson, right here at *his* table.

"Okay, Bob." She smiled again. "As I was saying, I didn't mean to interrupt your dinner, and I hope this doesn't sound too forward, but your story in *Forbes* was just so fascinating." She paused, blushing. "I . . . I saw that you happen to be alone here, and I . . . well, I wondered, would you like to join me for dinner?"

Bob smiled, a feeling of warmth washing over him. "I would be honored."

"I assure you, Mr. Gol . . . Bob," she corrected, "the honor is all mine."

The waiter arrived with Annabelle's dinner as Bob was transferring his briefcase, hat, and coat to her booth.

"Thank you," Annabelle said, handing the waiter her empty glass. "May I have some more iced tea, please?"

"Of course," Henri replied. "Right away." He turned to Bob. "Are you ready to order, Mr. Goldman?"

"I'll need a few more minutes, Henri, thank you."

Henri gave a short nod and quietly stepped away.

Bob was fascinated by Annabelle's beauty. He had watched her just two weeks ago on television, winning her Golden Globe for her role as Princess Lydia in the romantic epic *The Princess of Egypt*. Even then, he was captured by her beauty and grace. She was capable of rubbing elbows with any rich man in the world, and here he was, sitting across from her in his favorite restaurant—and she had approached him. He assumed she knew, since she mentioned reading the *Forbes* article, that Bob was among the top five billionaires in the world.

~~~

Annabelle was fascinated by Bob's success story. That he happened to be incredibly good-looking was a bonus. Despite her own fame and fortune, she couldn't help but be somewhat intimidated by his vast wealth. She wondered if he had any real friends—he'd come in alone, after all. *It must be hard to know who your real friends are when you have that much money,* she thought. Of course, being famous, she understood all too well how that felt.

Did he have a wife or a girlfriend? She couldn't remember the article mentioning either. If he did, she probably wouldn't be too happy that he'd accepted Annabelle's dinner invitation. Annabelle wondered if there was potential for this relationship to lead to romance. She hoped so, because she was attracted to Bob Goldman like no other man she'd met before.

Bob was hopelessly taken in by Annabelle's charm, her smile, and the glow in her sparkling hazel eyes. He felt intoxicated by the scent of her perfume. "That's a lovely fragrance you're wearing," he said.

"Thank you."

The waiter arrived with Annabelle's iced tea, set it on the table, and turned to Bob. "Have you made a decision this evening, Mr. Goldman?"

Bob realized that the excitement of enjoying time with the stunning Annabelle Smithson had stolen his appetite. "I'll just have a house salad with oil and vinegar, Henri," he replied. "Thank you."

After Henri scurried away to the kitchen, Bob noticed Annabelle's extravagant meal. "Looks like you have a love of seafood," he said, smiling.

She tilted her head and regarded him curiously. "Not really."

He sipped his wine. "Well, that's strange." He gestured to the lobster sitting in front of her. "I've never heard of someone ordering lobster who didn't like seafood."

She placed a small piece of the shellfish into her mouth. "Oh, this," she said, giggling softly. "This is the *only* seafood I like."

He nodded. "Ah, I see."

Annabelle reached for her glass and took a sip, her eyes never leaving Bob's.

"I haven't seen you in here before," Bob said. "First time at the Renaissance?"

"Yes. I must have heard about this restaurant a dozen times. You're a regular, I take it?"

"Twice a week, for years."

"Well, I can see why you like it so much," Annabelle said, her eyes scanning the elegant room.

"What can I say?" he replied, locking his eyes onto hers. "I like fine dining, especially restaurants that cater to the rich and famous." Annabelle's face was hard to read; he wondered if she knew he was trying to flirt with her.

"I can appreciate that."

They were sharing a quiet smile when Henri arrived with Bob's salad. "Here you are," he said, placing the plate of mixed greens in front of Bob. "Anything else for you, sir?"

"Not right now. Thank you, Henri."

"Enjoy your meal." Again the waiter slipped quietly away from the table.

Annabelle glanced at Bob's plate. "Are you a vegetarian?" she asked. "Trying to be. Eating healthy is the number one way to maintain a healthy body." He looked down and grimaced. "Actually, my doctor recommended I eat more vegetables."

Annabelle laughed—this time loudly, the sound of her infectious giggle rippling over the conversations of the other diners. Bob was positively smitten.

"What about your wife?"

Bob's stomach lurched—the inevitable question. He sighed. "I'm not married. Well, not anymore." Bob thought he detected a hint of a smile forming on his dinner companion's face.

"So, you're divorced then?"

"Yep. Does it surprise you?"

"No, not really. I . . . I'm actually sort of relieved."

Bob set his fork on the table and raised an eyebrow. "Relieved?"

"It's silly . . ."

"No, please elaborate."

Now she'd really gone and done it—said too much too soon. Now that he'd put her on the spot, what choice did she have but to be honest? "I figured a man like you had to be married. And then it occurred to me that if you're married, you could never be interested in me. Well, that or you *might* be interested in me, but then, why would I want to get involved with someone who was married?" She paused, realizing she'd revealed way too much. Her face flushed. "I'm sorry, though, about your divorce."

He grabbed his fork and stabbed at his salad, his expression grim. "It's a long story."

"I guess it must be hard, losing someone you love."

Bob looked up. "All I can say is that sometimes love can't be trusted. One only has to look at the current divorce rate to see that's true."

Annabelle looked down, feeling sheepish. "I don't mean to probe into your personal life—"

"Oh, I don't mind, really."

She wasn't sure she believed him, but decided to take his reply at face value. "So, if you don't mind me asking, what happened . . . with you and your wife?"

"Ex-wife," he said, pushing a tomato to the side of his plate. "Insecurity, I guess."

"Insecurity?"

"Yep." He looked at her, shaking his head. "Life is full of strange surprises."

"Strange surprises? I don't understand."

"Well, as horrible as my divorce was, if I hadn't gotten divorced, I wouldn't be sitting here with you." He took a sip from his glass and carefully set it back on the table. "As to my marriage, well, we've all made mistakes when in the throes of romantic love, haven't we?"

"Actually, I can't really relate," Annabelle replied. "I've never been in love before. In fact, I've never even dated."

Bob drew back, his eyes wide, surprised by Annabelle's stunning revelation. The beautiful and talented Annabelle Smithson had never been in love before? Had never even dated? How was that possible?

"You?" he replied. "*You* have never been in love before? Have never even been on a date?"

"You don't believe me," she replied.

"No, it's not that. I'm just . . . it's nothing."

"I can see by the look on your face that you're not convinced. Either that, or you're just plain horrified." An uneasy smile formed on her lips.

He was still trying to grasp the full meaning of what she was telling him. "You mean, your whole life, you've never had a single date? Not even a date to the prom?"

She shook her head.

"Annabelle, are you"—he leaned in close and whispered—"a virgin?"

"Yes, Bob," she replied matter-of-factly, "I'm still a virgin."

He leaned back against the booth. "You've got to be kidding me."

"I'm not kidding you."

"I'm sorry, it's just that you're so . . . well, look at you. You're beautiful and talented and famous. I never thought it possible that . . ." He stopped himself before he said anything that might upset her. "Forgive me. I'm acting like a jerk."

She smiled shyly. "It's okay." Then she added, winking: "It's a long story."

He laughed. "Touché."

Annabelle took another bite of her lobster.

"Wait a minute," he said jokingly. "You're not trying to investigate what it's like to live a celibate life, are you?"

She rolled her eyes. "No. Like I said, it's a long story."

Deeply curious, Bob pressed on. "Okay. Why? How?"

Annabelle dodged his question. She could still see traces of doubt and disbelief on Bob's face. "Why is this so hard for you to believe?"

"Look at you. You're a gorgeous woman. Wouldn't you be surprised if you were me?" He smiled and took her hand. "But seriously, you must possess a great deal of self-control and patience."

She smiled. "It's a gift. Everybody thinks and feels differently." Annabelle was desperate to change the subject. "We've strayed from the original subject here," she said, eyeing Bob intently. "What's your long story?" She didn't want to admit it, but she was deeply curious about why his marriage had ended.

"Are you suggesting that I attempted to evade telling you the reasons why I'm divorced?"

"You said it, not me," she said playfully.

He chuckled. "Oh, you're good."

"So how did 'insecurity' end your marriage?"

"My dream, for one. It was too intimidating for her. She couldn't handle it."

"I don't get it. What woman in the world wouldn't want to be married to an ambitious, successful man?"

"My old man had a philosophy: life is full of fairy tales."

Before she thought to stop herself, Annabelle blurted, "And sometimes those fairy tales are filled with dark miseries."

Bob set down his fork and stared at her. "You have a point."

"Your divorce hurt you very badly," she said, sensing the pain in his voice.

"It did. Since you've never been in love, you don't know what it's like when the one you love betrays you."

"It's never occurred to me to be insecure," she said. "I imagine, in a relationship, it spells emotional disaster."

"Yes, and trust me, the art of deception is very real."

"Deception? Did it go that far?"

"She got addicted to psychic readings," he explained. "It perverted her ideas about what makes a successful marriage."

"Psychic readings? Like tarot cards and all that?"

"Yep."

Henri appeared at the table. "More wine?"

"No, thank you, Henri," Bob answered. "Just coffee." He looked at Annabelle, and she nodded. "And for Ms. Smithson, as well."

"Right away."

Annabelle couldn't help but be intrigued. "So, she foresaw the future or something?"

"Maybe. Let's say she did. What I want to know is, what was so horrible about our future together that made her wake up one morning and file for divorce?"

Annabelle smiled sympathetically and took another bite of her lobster.

"You're not interested in marriage, are you?" Bob asked, casting a curious glance her way.

"Oh, I'm interested," she replied, perhaps too eagerly. "I definitely hope to marry someday. So, any kids?"

"Nope."

"As wealthy as you are?" she said, surprised. "Raising heirs wasn't part of your dream?"

Bob looked down at the remains of his salad and batted another tomato to the side of his plate. "Medical problems," he said quietly.

Annabelle's heart sank. "You? Or your wife?"

Henri arrived with the coffee and set it on the table, along with a small pitcher of cream. Annabelle was waiting on pins and needles for an answer to her question. She smiled tensely at the waiter, who seemed to understand. Henri slipped away from the table even faster than usual.

Bob reached for the cream. "It was her."

Annabelle breathed a silent sigh of relief.

"We'd been trying for nearly three years when the doctors diagnosed her with endometriosis. We never even had a chance to discuss fertility treatments and, well, by that time, she had already started all the psychic mumbo-jumbo." He sighed heavily. "This so-called psychic turned her against me, made me believe that, years down the road, I would betray her somehow. I kept asking her to tell me how exactly I was going to do this, and all she would tell me was that I would do whatever I had to do to have the children I wanted, and since she couldn't give me children, well . . . you get the picture, I'm sure." Bob was more than ready to change the subject. "So what do you do in your leisure time?"

She chuckled. "Leisure time? Such a time does not exist for me."

"You can't be serious. None at all?"

"A busy actress hasn't the time for pleasures," she replied. "Very seldom, anyway. And then there's the media. It's difficult to go out and have fun when I'm constantly being followed."

"You know something, I haven't felt this way in a long time. I feel like I'm alive again."

She smiled and glanced down at her watch. "Oh, my goodness," she cried. "I had no idea it was so late. I'm so sorry, but I really must be going. It was wonderful meeting you in person, Mr. Goldman, and such a pleasure chatting with you." She grinned widely, unable to mask her joy.

"What's your schedule like next Friday?" he asked.

Annabelle pondered for several seconds. "I'm not sure. I have that day off from shooting. I was hoping to do some shopping in the afternoon."

"What about the evening, say, around this time?"

The twinkle in her eye suggested she was going to say yes. Bob's heart leapt.

"Well, I usually reserve my Friday evenings for down time," she said, "especially when I'm not on set."

Bob was surprised by her noncommittal answer. But he wasn't about to give up. He reached into his coat pocket, pulled out a business card, and slid it in front of her. "Nine p.m.," he said. "I'm addressing some local business executives at the Marriott. There's a reception immediately following. I'm quite sure you'll enjoy yourself."

"I'm an actress, not a stockbroker," she said, taking the card.

"Well, if not for the seminar, come for the food. It's guaranteed to be delicious. I'll even have the caterer prepare something with lobster, just for you."

Annabelle suppressed a giggle. Her genuine delight in his joke was hard to miss.

Bob smiled. "If you would be my guest at the reception, it would be a true honor."

Annabelle slipped the card into her purse. "I'll think about it and give you a call."

"Not if I call you first," he said teasingly. "I mean, what if you forget?"

Their eyes met. "Okay," she said.

Bob was over the moon. Annabelle Smithson was going to give him her personal phone number.

"Wait, uh, no," she stammered. Before she even knew what she was doing, Annabelle had unwittingly agreed to give Bob Goldman her number, which was strictly against her usual policy. "I mean, I don't give out my phone number."

Bob could see by her expression that Annabelle wasn't going to make an exception, even for him. He was surprised how deeply her rejection affected him. He thought they'd had such a great connection, especially when she said she was relieved that he was divorced. But now, as they were parting, she was giving him mixed signals. He wondered if she was even interested in him at all.

Chapter 15

Annabelle entered her lake-view Winchester mansion at exactly ten o'clock.

"Meow."

"Hey, Snowball," she said, reaching down to pet the all-white Persian rubbing against her leg. The entire drive home from the restaurant, she hadn't been able to get Bob Goldman out of her mind. She made her way to the bedroom, kicked off her shoes, and plopped down on the bed. She drew a deep breath, a smile instantly forming on her face. The thought of Bob sent warm, gentle shockwaves through her body.

She spied herself in the mirror across the room. She couldn't remember ever being so happy, and couldn't believe her good fortune, having unexpectedly spent an entire evening with such a charming and powerful man.

Annabelle's mind was awhirl, savoring over and over every detail of their intimate dinner conversation. It was worth every second of her precious time. She felt like she already knew this man—the sparkle in his eyes, his playful demeanor. She knew the instant they set eyes on each other that something special was happening, that her feelings for Bob were real.

Throughout her long and lonely drive home, Bob Goldman had clung to every strand of her imagination. He was so friendly, so open about his private life. They shared an instant bond which resonated deep within.

She unfastened the diamond necklace around her neck. Annabelle's mind flashed back to their cozy booth at the restaurant—how confident Bob was, how he knew all the restaurant workers' names, how polite he was to her and to everybody. Even watching him take a sip of wine ignited her feelings. Love had blown her way suddenly, when she had least expected it.

Love? Am I in love?

Annabelle wasn't certain if the handsome billionaire was sent by God as her true soul mate, but she dearly hoped that he was. Bob Goldman had to be the man God had chosen for her, to father the princess of the world. He had to be.

Since she had launched her acting career, Annabelle had grown more and more anxious, had even worked herself into a frenzied state from time to time, over the issue of the man destined to take her hand in marriage. Now that signs of the child's imminent birth loomed, Annabelle had to be meticulous about choosing her spouse.

This baby would be conceived and born into the world as part human and part divine. Annabelle believed that the man with whom she conceived this child, the man whose last name the child would bear, must well deserve the honor.

She rose from the bed and laid the necklace on the dresser beside her makeup case. She gazed at herself in the mirror and thought again of her amazing evening with Bob Goldman. Her memories of wining and dining with Bob filled her with a sense of incredible joy and peace.

Annabelle smiled, remembering Bob's great sense of humor. He was surprisingly down-to-earth for a man so rich and powerful. Her guess was that he didn't show that side of himself to everybody, only to those who got to know him personally. From the article in *Forbes* she'd learned that he was not only a business tycoon, but also a firm believer in God. For her, that was what mattered most. Minutes ticked by as Annabelle stared dreamily into the mirror. She simply couldn't escape the excitement stirring inside her. She

imagined Bob Goldman proposing to her. She wondered
what else there was to learn about him. What had she yet to
discover about the rich and charming Bob Goldman? He
seemed very intelligent and sensitive, not to mention honest
and faithful. He obviously had a great deal of integrity, too.
To top it all off, he seemed to have strong feelings for her,
as well. Annabelle realized she was experiencing the joy of
falling in love for the very first time, and with one of the
wealthiest men in the world. How blessed she would be, as
Bob's wife, possessing everything the world had to offer.

Annabelle reached for her purse on the chair beside the
dresser and opened it. She gently pulled out Bob's business
card and set it on the dresser. She would surprise him and
call him in the morning, perhaps even before breakfast.
Somehow she knew he wouldn't mind, even if it was still
dark or he happened to be catching his last minutes of
sleep.

Annabelle slipped off her dress, drew a lavender
nightgown from the top drawer, and pulled it over her head.
After brushing her teeth, she crawled into bed and turned
out the light. As she lay back, praying for dreams of love
and marriage, she was suddenly jolted from her earlier
elation. The darkness of the room seemingly brought
darkness to her thoughts. Her excitement over meeting Bob
Goldman vanished when she remembered the secret she
was carrying. If he was her soul mate and they did marry,
how could she explain the special purpose for their child?
Again, she would have to lie to keep her promise to God.
But spouses weren't supposed to lie to each other. Bob had
already been deceived once before in marriage. How could
she do that to him, too? She curled up in misery.

She saw herself, in the future, shying away from public
appearances and events—avoiding the media. No talks at
local schools, no talk shows. Annabelle saw herself
declining all invitations, except for a select few. The

constant fear of inadvertently revealing her true purpose, or her child's true purpose, would force her into isolation. Since seeing Father McClain's sermon several weeks back, she had realized she'd already started shying away from public life. Of course, she hadn't been shy about approaching Bob Goldman. Now that she had found love, who knew what the future held?

Annabelle stared at the ceiling, miserable. What if Bob found out about her past as a nun? Worse, what if he wanted to know her reason for leaving the convent? She didn't think she could lie to him. But she would have to; she had made a promise to God. What if Bob sensed she was lying and rejected her?

Her love for Bob Goldman suddenly scared her to death. If she was unable to reveal her true calling to the man she loved, was her life not destined to become a horrible nightmare?

~~~

Annabelle stepped out of the stretch black limousine which had just pulled up in front of the busy entrance to the Marriott Hotel. A gentleman who introduced himself as Mr. Goldman's assistant approached her the moment she entered the lobby.

"Good evening, Ms. Annabelle," he said with a friendly smile. "I'm Jack Vermont, Bob's assistant."

"Good evening, Jack," she replied. "It's very nice to meet you."

"Mr. Goldman asked that I take you to his suite," he said, ushering her toward the elevator.

"He did? I thought we were meeting in the ballroom."

Jack cleared his throat. "I believe Mr. Goldman was hoping to have some privacy."

The elevator door slid open, and they stepped inside. She watched Jack push the button for the fourteenth floor.

"How long have you known Bob—uh, Mr. Goldman?"

Annabelle asked.

"Six years, ma'am. I started working for him around the time of his first *Wealth Building* seminar."

When they arrived at the fourteenth floor, Jack stepped out of the elevator and gestured to the door at the end of the hall, which had been left slightly ajar. She stepped inside the room to the sound of one of her favorite Elvis Presley songs. How could Bob have possibly known she was a fan of Elvis Presley? Bob Goldman, twelve years her senior and destined to win her heart, stood across the room, grinning widely.

Bob had already taken off his jacket and loosened his tie. He stood beside the leather sofa, glass of champagne in hand. He couldn't help smiling. When Annabelle walked into the room, he wanted nothing more than to pull her into his arms.

Annabelle stopped midway between the door and Bob to behold the lavish setting of the dining table. Bob was proud of the spread: buckets of ice with champagne, two bottles of red wine, and, as he had promised, lobster for two.

"You look surprised," Bob said, walking toward the woman of his dreams. He sighed. "Seeing you is like a prayer being answered."

Annabelle approached him but said nothing.

"I know you weren't expecting a private reception," he told her. "I thought it would be nice—surprise you with your favorites."

"This is more than just a private reception for two, Mr. Goldman."

"Well, what do you think?" he asked, unable to keep from admiring her low-cut, black velvet gown.

"This is a stunning and romantic display," she said, looking again toward the table. "Is it some kind of a setup?"

"I beg your pardon, Ms. Smithson," he said, stepping up close to her, "but I'd hardly want to 'set up' the woman whom I love and want to be a part of my life." He reached for her, but she backed away. Her exquisite appearance made it hard not to force the issue, but Bob decided it was best not to push. "Would you like some champagne?"

"No, thank you. Not right now."

"All right then, make yourself at home."

"Thank you." She sat on the loveseat across from the couch and gracefully crossed her legs.

Bob walked to the dining table for a refill and returned to the couch.

Annabelle watched him suspiciously. "So what on earth prompted you to create such a lavish display, this dream I had no idea I was walking into?"

Bob smiled mischievously at her and sipped his champagne. Annabelle felt herself getting impatient.

"Well, something must have inspired you. What was it?"

"I believe everything has its own magic."

"Magic? What is that supposed to mean?"

"We often don't see our true images—who we really are, our secret treasures buried within. Sometimes it takes the compliments of others to open our eyes to our own gifts."

"Hmm. Now you've really got me confused."

He sighed impatiently. "Annabelle, I arranged for this private dinner because, well, you know who we are, famous people living in the eyes of the media. If we met in public, our picture would be on the cover of every morning newspaper in the country. I just wanted a chance to get to know you, without paparazzi lurking in the bushes outside the hotel or in the lobby bathroom."

Annabelle smiled and nodded. "Well, when you put it that way, I suppose this was a smart thing to do."

"I'm surprised you need me to explain, given how sensitive you are to public life. As for seeing this as a romantic setting, well . . ." Mischief crept into his eyes again. "That's something I honestly never thought about."

She chuckled. "It is indeed a wise thing for celebrities to sometimes seclude themselves from everything and everybody else."

"Agreed. By the way, I can't express how fabulous it was joining you for dinner the other night."

"Oh?"

"It was one of the most enjoyable conversations I've ever had." He locked his eyes on hers. "You're a very special person, Annabelle."

"I didn't realize I was being held in such high regard."

"Exactly," Bob said excitedly. "This brings me back to the point I made earlier. Sometimes it takes the compliments of others to help us see ourselves for who we really are."

"I don't make a habit of feasting on compliments."

"Why not?"

"What if they're nothing but flattery?" she asked. "Don't get me wrong, I appreciate everything you've done here, it's just that I learned a long time ago that in my business, you can't believe everything you hear."

"But compliments can sometimes be genuine, right?"

"Of course."

"Then you can take all of this at face value, Ms. Smithson," Bob said, gesturing toward the table.

"Okay, I will." She smiled.

"So, now are you ready for some champagne?"

"To be honest," she said, feeling a little embarrassed, "I don't mean to discourage your kindness, but I'm not a liquor kind of girl."

The expression on Bob's face dimmed. "Really? A woman of your class not appreciating fine wine?"

"So we're back here again, are we? You don't believe me."

Bob looked skeptical. "What about those scenes in your movies, all the wine and champagne glasses between those lips of yours—"

"Mr. Goldman, have you really fallen for the tricks of filmmaking?"

"Call me Bob, please," he said. "It's just that I've never met a movie star who hasn't been at least a social drinker."

"Not all people are the same, Bob."

He nodded, staring into her hazel eyes. "So, what makes you different?"

"Well," she said hesitantly, "for one, I'm from a spiritual background, and I do try to maintain that part of my life. You see, once upon a time, I was a nun."

Bob tried to mask it, but Annabelle could see that he was stunned by her revelation. He stood abruptly. Annabelle worried that she'd just blown her chances of ever being with this man. Who wanted to date an ex-nun?

"Sounds good to me," he said.

Now Annabelle was taken aback. He may have been momentarily shocked, but he'd certainly gotten over it quickly.

"I believe I have something you'll like." He grabbed his champagne glass from the table and trotted to the dining area. In seconds he returned with a bottle of red wine in one hand and two wineglasses in the other. "This is something special, just for you," he said, setting the items down on the table. "It's a fine, non-alcoholic zinfandel."

She was overwhelmed by his thoughtfulness. "I appreciate that."

He opened the bottle and poured some into each glass.

"Thank you," she said, reaching for the glass he was offering.

He nodded. "My pleasure."

They raised their glasses and made a toast.

As Annabelle took a sip and set her glass on the table, a thought occurred to her. Bob Goldman hadn't only been successful in merely befriending her; he was clearly making her a part of his life.

Although Bob Goldman often indulged in fine wine, this was his first taste of the non-alcoholic type. *Not bad.* He looked at Annabelle, realizing that he was hopelessly drawn to her. *What is it about this woman?* When he leaned over to set his drink on the table, something leapt within—a part of him that had been dead for years came alive. It was a breath of fresh air when he had least expected it. *I'm in love with a former nun.*

"So, what motivated you to pursue an acting career?" he asked, genuinely interested. "Especially when you had such a pious background?"

Annabelle frowned, and Bob instantly worried that he'd offended her. As she sipped her wine, instinctively he knew that the tone of their conversation had taken a turn, hopefully not for the worse.

"What do you think?" she said, setting her glass on the table.

Bob wrung his hands, realizing he'd touched a nerve. "I can't imagine your reasons," he replied honestly. "That's why I asked."

"What do you think would drive a woman like me, a woman who once served a godly order, who vowed, at the age of eighteen, to never live a worldly life?"

Bob gazed at her thoughtfully. "I imagine that being an actress must have been a dream of yours, one you weren't willing—"

"It was more than a dream, Mr. Goldman," she interrupted him. "Far more than the pursuit of something that everyone thinks I'm so passionate about."

He noted that she had resumed calling him "Mr. Goldman." He straightened. "To be honest, I'm really not sure where you're going with this."

"Care to guess?" she insisted.

He grinned. "Not at all."

Annabelle was fiercely tempted to reveal the secret that haunted her, but he could never know about what had transpired between her and the angel on that cool fall evening of 1991. She realized that she'd allowed the conversation to drift dangerously off-course. She flashed him a radiant smile. "Just what are you insinuating, Mr. Goldman?" she asked teasingly. "That I'm playing some kind of mind game?"

He smiled and shook his head. "I knew it."

For all she knew, Annabelle might never lay eyes on the angel again, but she hoped Michael would show his face, if for no other reason than to clear her doubts and answer a crucial question she couldn't have known to ask on that fateful night. By God's wish, she had vowed to conceal the divine vision: the birth of a child destined to reign as the princess of the world. But she desperately needed to know if the prophecy involved the man destined to take her hand in marriage.

She believed, as Bob Goldman unwittingly colluded with her true calling, that God moved in mysterious ways. He was capable of intervening in any matter that threatened to avert her from fully expressing her feelings for the only man she had ever loved. For fear she might risk losing the privilege of giving birth to a divine princess, Annabelle decided to keep her calling hidden from Bob, but the problem was clear: though she could manage to isolate herself from the public, she couldn't shy away from Bob.

~~~

Since they had met two months ago, Bob and Annabelle had become deeply attached. Although getting to know Bob was the greatest joy of her life, she worried constantly that keeping her secret would shatter their relationship, at least at some point down the road.

When Bob whisked her away for a romantic weekend getaway to the Ritz Carlton Resort in the Caribbean, they took a romantic horseback ride on the beach. Annabelle tried to enjoy herself, but inside she was troubled. Her desire to speak again with the mysterious angel was taking a toll on her love life. Moreover, she could barely endure the torment of not being totally honest with Bob.

Bob obviously couldn't help noticing her grim mood. "Are you all right?" he asked.

She mustered a small smile. "I'm fine."

"Maybe this wasn't such a good idea," he said graciously, "coming here this weekend."

"Bob, you're making too much of this," she replied, more harshly than intended. "I'm fine, really. Just a little tired."

But Bob wouldn't let it go. "I don't think I am making too much of it, honey."

"Yes, you are."

"Then tell me," he ordered. "Tell me the reason for that look on your face, and why my suggestion that this was a mistake angered you."

"What look?"

"You seem so down. Like you're not happy to be here." He paused, choosing his next words carefully. "It seems like, overnight, your world has been somehow shattered."

"Really? That's what you see in me?"

He stared at her, his expression suspicious. Annabelle couldn't stand Bob's scrutiny one moment longer. She raced away from him and headed down the shore.

Chapter 16

Bob and Annabelle joyously shook their guests' hands as they exited the sanctuary immediately after their twenty-minute wedding ceremony. Out back of the cathedral, in an open field, a helicopter waited to whisk the newlyweds away to Bob's cruise ship, the *St. Gordon*.

Annabelle looked out of the helicopter's window in amazement, suddenly filled with intense joy over her four-week-old pregnancy. She had yet to surprise her groom with the news. A feeling of unease came over her when she thought too much about this baby being a gift from God and the important role her daughter would play in the world. For now, she chose to focus on how much Bob loved her and how happy she was being his wife.

She looked into his eyes, her face glowing with happiness. "I've never felt more blessed," she said. "I feel like the queen of England."

Bob pulled a bottle of champagne from the mini refrigerator beside his armrest. "The queen of England?" he repeated, popping the cork. "Well then, I am humbled in your royal presence, Your Majesty."

They shared a laugh.

"Sometimes I wonder . . ."

"Wonder what?" he asked as he poured the champagne into glasses.

"You're very thoughtful," she said. She pondered for a moment or two. "I just couldn't have conceived of any of this, never knowing what true love was. Until you swept me off my feet, that is."

Bob handed her a glass and made a toast: "To the beginning of many happy days to come."

"Here, here," she returned. "With all of my heart."

Bob took a sip of his champagne and looked into her eyes. "My resolution for this marriage is that we live together through eternity. For years I dreamed about this moment."

"What about the venue for the reception? Was that part of your plan, too?"

"Well, not exactly. But, being a man of vision, I predict that in the years to come, my *Wealth Building* conference will attract an enormous number of people. No conference hall in England will have the capacity to stage my events. So I've created a vision of a world at sea. And, as a bonus, our wedding reception will be the maiden voyage."

~~~

By sunset, nearly all the five hundred guests had arrived and were boarding the *St. Gordon*. Couples walked arm-in-arm, roaming the ship's grand lobby and chatting about the much-anticipated arrival of the bridal party. The ship's crew had worked around the clock, ensuring that the lavish reception would be a memorable one, the wedding Bob Goldman had always dreamed of.

The boarding attendant was posted in the entry lobby, taking full charge of checking in the invited guests. Bob had explained to Annabelle earlier that there might be people who attempted to board without an invitation and that he wanted to make sure this first cruise aboard the *St. Gordon* went off without a hitch. The boarding attendant had been warned: if the name attached to the photo ID didn't match the name on the invitation, entry was not permitted.

In line to board was a man approximately six foot five and dressed in a priest's formal attire. He had a kind face, and his curly, shoulder-length hair was white as snow. He reminded Annabelle of the portrait of Jesus that hung in the entryway of St. Ann's Convent. Aside from his white hair, the man didn't appear particularly old, perhaps mid-forties.

Annabelle felt inexplicably drawn to the man. As she watched him, patiently standing among the other boarding passengers, she wondered if it was simply his attire reminding her of her past. She thought of the angel she yearned to see and pondered whether this was her angel in disguise. He certainly had the face of an angel.

She watched as he approached the boarding attendant who, to Annabelle's eyes, appeared to look upon the priest skeptically. "May I see your invitation and boarding pass, please?" the attendant requested.

"Sorry to say, but I do not possess either," he said.

"You don't have an invitation or a boarding pass?"

"Exactly."

"I'm sorry, Father, but this is a private wedding-reception cruise. It's not open to the public. No one comes on board without invitation and boarding pass."

"I understand, but, respectfully, I am a close friend of the groom. Is he around anywhere so I can speak with him?"

"What?"

"As I said, I'm a close friend of the groom," the priest repeated. "Mr. Goldman requested that I be here to serve as chaplain for the *St. Gordon*'s maiden voyage ceremony."

"I'm sorry, sir, but I was not advised of this. Were you not issued a written note permitting you to board this ship?"

"Everything happened so fast. I just spoke with Mr. Goldman a few days ago. Perhaps he didn't have time to think of it."

From her place on the stairs above the lobby, Annabelle could see that the attendant was losing his patience. The mysterious man was holding up the line of passengers waiting to get in, and the lobby was growing more crowded by the minute.

"Okay, sir. I'll look into it. Please step aside until I can get word to Mr. Goldman so that we can straighten this matter out." The attendant hailed another crew member and asked him to track down Bob.

An older wedding guest climbed the stairs and approached Annabelle. "Oh dear, you look lovely. And I've never seen Bob happier."

"Thank you," Annabelle returned politely.

Their conversation was interrupted by a commotion down below.

The boarding attendant's eyes darted from one side of the lobby to the other. He looked increasingly nervous as he addressed the next people in line, a young couple. "Did you happen to see what direction the priest that was just standing here went?"

The couple exchanged a puzzled glance. "Priest?" they asked in unison.

"Yes," the attendant replied. "He was standing right here in front of you—tall, white hair, skinny."

"We don't remember seeing any priest," the woman said. "There was a middle-aged couple ahead of us—you just let them in."

The color drained from the attendant's face as he yanked his walkie-talkie from his belt. "Security," he barked. "I think we have a crasher. A man tried to board without an invitation or a pass—said he was a friend of Mr. Goldman's. I do not have a good feeling about this guy."

Seconds later, a band of security guards rushed into the lobby. By that time, the attendant's face had gone from sheet white to blood red. Annabelle felt sorry for him. She could tell he felt responsible. She made a mental note to tell Bob to go easy on the guy.

"Search the entire ship," he ordered security breathlessly. "He's tall—six feet five or so—middle-aged, white hair, and dressed as a priest, but I have a strong feeling he's really not."

At that moment, one of the reception attendants whisked Annabelle away from the scene. "Pardon me, ma'am, but you're wanted by your guests."

~~~

The Pacific Lounge on the A-deck, where the reception was being held, had been, at Bob's request, decorated to Annabelle's taste: lavish dinner settings, chandeliers, and vases of fresh flowers on every table.

Under shimmering lights, more than five hundred guests took their respective seats. Family, friends, and business associates were all dazzled by the stunning atmosphere. The murmur of chatting voices, mingled with laughter and the smooth-jazz background music, was surely a start to a memorable evening. The room was impossibly glamorous, and exactly how Bob Goldman had always envisioned this moment.

Before making their arrival at the reception, Annabelle, Bob, and the maid of honor retired to a private observation deck above the hall, where they drank champagne and chatted. When the best man arrived to join them, Annabelle politely broke away from Bob and strolled down to the far end of the deck. She remained there in isolation, balefully gazing at the sun as it gradually disappeared below the horizon.

Security was still searching for the mysterious wedding crasher, and though they looked to be leaving no stone unturned, they were following protocol to the letter. If they raised alarm, the guests might become panicked, making the situation ever more dangerous. They'd made a decision to move forward with the reception and do their best not to let the man's unsanctioned boarding ruin their guests' good time. But they also speculated that their cruise passengers could be in danger if the intruder was not caught and arrested as quickly as possible.

Annabelle couldn't help but be distracted. She'd felt drawn to the man, and she could only guess why. Despite the effort to keep the search calm and discreet, the tension on the boat was steadily rising. She looked on as a squad of security guards, led by the boarding attendant, entered the Pacific Lounge.

"May I help you, gentlemen?" asked the bartender.

The attendant spoke up. "We're searching for a priest—tall, white hair. Have you seen him?"

The bartender shook his head.

"Well, if he happens to come in here, call security immediately."

"Yes, sir."

"What do we do now?" one of the security guards asked. "How in the hell are we going to track this guy down on a boat this size?"

Another guard chimed in. "On top of that, how are we going to identify him? For all we know, he's already changed clothes and is acting as one of the invited guests. He's probably watching us right now, thinking we're nothing but a bunch of idiots."

"What are you guys suggesting?" the attendant asked. "Just let it slide? Do you realize there are hundreds of people on board whose lives could be in danger?"

"But we've searched the entire ship," said the first security officer. "What else is there to do?"

"Gentlemen," another security officer interrupted, "we're wasting our time standing here arguing. We have to do something."

"You know what I think?" the attendant said, gesturing to the first two officers. "I think the both of you are grossly underestimating the potential danger of this situation. We don't know this man or his agenda. We don't have a choice here. We keep searching until the sucker is found." He paused, a hint of fear creeping into his eyes. "I talked to this guy, and I can tell you something was not right about him. No invitation, no boarding pass, but, more than that, he was downright creepy."

The first officer smirked. "You're exaggerating."

"No, I'm not. I said it because . . . when this guy approached me, the hair on the back of my neck went straight up." He pondered for a moment and locked eyes with the doubting officer. "Know what your problem is? You didn't watch a man vanish before your very eyes. I barely looked away for a second when I called to the desk for help, and boom, this guy was nowhere to be seen. If you'd experienced that, it would creep you out, too."

~~~

The bride and groom followed the bridal party into the Pacific Lounge and made their way to the long bridal table as their guests welcomed them with a round of applause. In the midst of the rousing applause, another band of the security squad discreetly entered the reception hall. Fear showed in their eyes as they spread along the side aisles, monitoring the faces of every male guest. Thankfully the guests, distracted by the entering wedding party, didn't seem to notice anything unusual.

The guards maintained their calm demeanor as they surveyed the room. The reception hall was their best hope. If the wedding crasher wasn't there, where else could he be? The security team had only moments to conduct their search. The bridal party had taken their seats at the long table. The applause gradually quieted down, and the officers, having made a plan to exit the hall by the time the guests had stopped clapping, quietly filed out of the room.

~~~

The emcee stepped onto the stage with a cordless microphone in his hand. "Ladies and gentlemen," he said, smiling widely, "welcome aboard. You are all the guests of this prestigious couple sitting before me, two of the most prominent individuals in our society. Please join me in congratulating the marriage of business tycoon, Mr. Bob Goldman, and his bride, the lovely and talented Mrs. Annabelle Smithson Goldman."

The guests applauded enthusiastically as Bob and Annabelle shared a kiss.

The emcee cleared his throat. "The bride and the groom wish to welcome you all aboard and join them in celebration of this remarkable, once-in-a-lifetime experience: a wedding reception aboard the beautiful *St. Gordon* as she sails the Atlantic."

By ten p.m., the *St. Gordon* had sailed far out into the waters of the Atlantic Ocean, comfortably cruising as guests enjoyed the amenities of such a luxurious liner. People ate and talked as the waitstaff filled and refilled glasses of wine and champagne.

~~~

Outside, the atmosphere had taken a strange turn. The summer night had turned prematurely dark. Where moments before the sky had been lit with the setting sun, one could no longer see the hand before one's face.

~~~

The guests buzzed as Bob and Annabelle Goldman stepped behind the wedding cake. Cameras flashed from every angle, capturing the couple's every move. People held camcorders, taping the romantic scene as it unfolded. Bob and Annabelle sliced and sampled their wedding cake, and kissed sweetly before their adoring guests.

~~~

The third squad of the security team bumped into the chief of security on their way out of the VIP lounge. Usually a stoic man, even the chief was consumed by fear of the stranger who seemed to have vanished into thin air.

"Did you see the intruder among the guests?" he asked the guards.

One of the officers stepped up. "No, sir."

"You're sure none of the guests at the reception fit the man's description?"

"Absolutely sure, sir." There were plenty of tall men, but only a few with white hair. And those with white hair all looked to be well into their sixties or beyond.

"We conducted a thorough survey of all the male guests, sir," another guard spoke up.

"Okay then," the chief said. "At midnight, all entrances to the decks will be locked down."

"Do you really think that's wise, sir?" the first officer said. "Don't you think that it might cast fear onto the guests?"

"What damned choice do we have?" he shouted. "Besides, the passengers don't even know what's going on. What the hell difference does it make?" He paused, trying to regain his composure. "What the hell are we looking for here, anyway, a goddamned ghost?"

The first officer said, "Maybe we could trace the guy from the guest list."

The chief's face reddened. "Don't be stupid. The boarding attendant already said that the guy wasn't an invited guest—that he tried to board the ship without a pass or ID. So what makes you think you'll find him on the passenger list?"

"Well, it could be a trick. Maybe he knew exactly what he was doing. And if he is some kind of a ghost . . ."

"Are you saying that because the attendant lost track of this guy, he actually possesses some kind of power to disappear? Good grief, people, think. If he had the power to do that, why would he have joined the boarding line in the first place?"

"Well, he's not stupid," the officer responded. "He's managed to evade us so far."

~~~

Annabelle and Bob entered their honeymoon suite, still hand in hand as they had been since leaving the reception hall.

"Wow, Bob," Annabelle exclaimed. "It's beautiful." She stood in the living room, mouth agape, the plush carpet burying the heels of her sandals. A single French door led to the patio. As she continued to scan the rooms in awe, her eyes drifted through the bedroom door to where Bob had walked. She watched as he took off his tuxedo jacket and laid it on the king-sized bed.

"Do you like it?" he asked, removing his bowtie.

"Do I like it?" she asked. "Bob, I can't even describe the feelings I have about this place." She looked at him lovingly. "Thank you."

Bob stepped to the closet and slid open the door, pulling a single-breasted navy-blue sports coat from one of the hangars. Annabelle kicked off her sandals and headed out to the patio to enjoy a few moments of solitude. She leaned over the banister and gazed out onto the pitch-black Atlantic Ocean. A mild ocean wind blew her hair across her face.

"Honey?"

Annabelle turned to find Bob standing in the doorway, his shirt unbuttoned far enough to reveal his chest. She wondered how long he'd been standing there.

Bob beheld his beautiful new bride, her inviting silhouette sending a signal to his mind. He could sense her wish to feel the warmth of his arms wrapped around her.

"Looks like you're having a jolly good time," he said, leaning against the door frame.

"Are you going to stand there and let me watch the waves all by myself?"

He walked up behind Annabelle and wrapped his arms around her waist. "The moment I stepped into that doorway," he said softly, kissing her neck, "I knew you wanted these arms around you—to protect you from the wind."

Annabelle giggled.

The romantic tension building between them was impossible to ignore.

"Well, now my wish has been granted," she said. "Just when I needed a passionate wish fulfilled, there you were."

"I will always be there for you."

Annabelle faced him and smiled—the same smile from that fateful first meeting at the restaurant. "You know something?"

"Tell me."

"As much as I never ever dreamt of such a beautiful wedding, I've been asking myself lately: What will it be like after all this is over? What will it be like spending the rest of my life with the man who truly has my heart?"

"Just think of what it means when a man finds the woman who completes him," he said, squeezing his new wife a little tighter.

She turned away to look out at the sea. After several moments and no response, Bob turned Annabelle back to face him. He was surprised to see that her expression had darkened from her earlier happy mood.

"What would you think if . . ." Annabelle hesitated, bowing her head.

"If what?" Bob asked, anxious to understand why his wife's romantic mood had changed so suddenly.

Annabelle pondered for several long moments and looked up. "I'm considering rededicating my life to . . . to God. I'm thinking about reentering the convent."

Bob stared disbelievingly into Annabelle's eyes, an uncomfortable chuckle escaping his lips. His hands slid down her arms and dropped limply at his sides. If this was true, why would she have gone through with the marriage? Bob battled to keep his calm, refusing to give in to this grim reality. He struggled for the right words. "You're kidding, right?" he asked, his voice breaking. "You're not actually thinking about going back, are you? Why on earth would you marry me if this was going through your mind? It doesn't make any sense."

"Why are you acting like this is such a big deal, Bob?" she asked, seemingly irritated.

Bob felt his heart breaking. Where was the woman he married just hours before—the radiantly happy woman with whom he had exchanged rings? "You can't be serious, Annabelle."

"You don't understand," she said, her tone softening. "Look, I know—"

"Understand? I've invested my whole heart in you, in this relationship, only for things to come to this?"

Chapter 17

The guests walked into the ship's glamorous dance hall, greeted by a live orchestra. At the conclusion of their first number, the conductor bowed to rousing applause.

The emcee stepped onto the stage and stood next to the conductor as the applause came to a close. "Give it up one more time for James Lass and the James Lass Orchestra," he cried.

Enthusiastic applause filled the room.

When the clapping died down and a hush fell over the room, the emcee spoke again. "The first dance of the night is, of course, reserved for the newlyweds. Would Mr. and Mrs. Robert Goldman kindly report to the dance floor?"

The orchestra resumed playing as the guests gathered to witness Annabelle and Bob's first dance as husband and wife. The couple walked arm in arm to the middle of the floor and began dancing.

~~~

Bob did his best to hide the agony in his heart as he held his wife on the dance floor. But he couldn't help but feel betrayed. In the space of minutes, Annabelle had managed a complete about-face. He couldn't understand it, and so far, she hadn't offered an explanation that made any sense. "You mean all of this is in vain?" he whispered. "What evil has possessed you to turn your back on me, on our marriage?"

"Evil?" Annabelle echoed quietly.

Bob felt his patience thinning. "What else could it be?"

"How can devoting my life to God be evil?"

"This is not a spiritual matter, Annabelle," he replied, his voice rising. He took a deep breath and tried to calm himself. "This is about betrayal, about you agreeing to marry me and then pulling the rug right out from under us before we've even gotten started."

"You need to think beyond yourself, Bob."

"What is that supposed to mean?"

"What if God wants it so? What if he called me?"

"Then you damn well should have answered that call before walking down the aisle with me." Bob, catching the alarmed eye of an old family friend, smiled and lowered his voice. "Why would God call you back when you're so happy? That doesn't sound very godly to me. I don't know much about the Bible, but I do know one thing: no god in his right mind would make a woman inflict pain on the only man she ever claimed to love."

"Is that what you think I'm doing?" she asked. "You need to think again."

He drew back, locking his eyes onto hers. "So tell me, what's your real reason for marrying me, for going through with this wedding when you had no intention of staying married to me?"

"I'm pregnant," she confessed.

Stunned, Bob was unable to respond.

"There's more," she said. "I have a godly mission to fulfill: I am to give birth to a divine child. Don't you see? I couldn't possibly give birth to a child conceived out of wedlock."

Annabelle's shocking confession was still hanging in the air when their song ended and the guests engulfed the couple on the dance floor. For the moment, they continued pretending that all was as perfect as it had been just hours earlier. But they would speak again, and when they did, Bob intended to get to the bottom of this horrifying situation.

He studied Annabelle's face for a moment and pulled her close. He could see that she was determined, and perhaps driven by the passion of her past life as a nun. But she projected a callousness he'd never have thought possible.

Yet, as they held each other close, her chin gently resting on Bob's right shoulder, he wondered if there was at least a chance to make this work, to find some compromise. "What makes you think God is going to accept you back," he whispered into her ear, "after you've indulged in the sin of hypocrisy?"

Annabelle understood that Bob was hurting, but she was determined to hold her ground. "There is always room for mercy and forgiveness," she answered. "I know my heavenly Father—"

Annabelle's breath caught as she spied the man who had vanished from the lobby among the crowd of guests. When Bob realized that something was wrong, he gently wrapped his arm around her shoulder and led her to the side of the dance floor. "Annabelle?" he asked, trying to get her attention. "What's wrong? What did you see?"

She kept her eyes on the man, not wanting to lose him in the crowd.

"Annabelle, you were saying something," Bob persisted. "About the heavenly Father . . ."

Bob's words barely registered as she continued to follow the mysterious stranger's every move. It wasn't long before she realized that, in this room full of people, only she could see him. She peered at him closely, soon realizing that he was, indeed, the angel who had visited her those years ago—the angel she'd hoped would come for so long.

"Annabelle, what are you staring at?"

But Bob's words fell on deaf ears. She watched the man making his way through the crowd. She could see Bob in the corner of her eye, looking in the direction of her gaze, but he obviously saw nothing. She stared on in awe as the angel walked through peoples' bodies toward the exit and vanished from the dance hall.

Annabelle was convinced it was her angel, Michael. The instant she spotted him, something stirred within her. She remembered her encounter with the angel in the fall of 1991. She remembered, in particular, his snow-white hair.

"What are you staring at?" Bob repeated, sounding annoyed.

She flinched at the sound of his voice. "Nothing. Absolutely nothing."

"Annabelle, you're cold as ice," Bob said, rubbing her arm.

Annabelle pulled away and stood. "I'll be right back." She gathered the skirt of her dress and headed for the exit.

"Where are you going?"

"Just give me a few minutes," she called over her shoulder. "I'll be right back."

In the corridor outside the dance hall, Annabelle stopped and looked in each direction. But the hallway was empty. She walked gingerly down the corridor, hoping to at least get a sense of which direction Michael had gone. When she'd walked several feet, the hair on the back of her neck began to rise. As she continued to walk toward the A-deck lobby, an intense energy surrounded her, magically pulling her back toward the corridor's dead end.

~~~

Paul Hart slipped quietly into the men's restroom and, confirming that he was alone, locked the door behind him. He stepped up to the sink and regarded his monstrous image in the mirror. A sinister smile spread across his face. He was no angel, but he had managed to convince Annabelle otherwise.

Paul Hart was a Satanist and devout Anti-Christian, a loyal agent of the Devil himself. An occult Grand Master, Hart presided over a secret society called the Knights of

Beelzebub. The Knights were an elite group of dark angels who possessed human bodies and devoted themselves to destroying God's vision for the world by way of eternal wrath and damnation.

By the time Annabelle realized that the man she thought was an angel was actually acting on the Devil's behalf, it would be too late. He had already successfully lured her into his evil web. Even better, she was carrying a child conceived out of the art of deception.

Hart continued to gaze intensely into the mirror. His eyes grew weaker and weaker, as though he were on the verge of falling to sleep. His eyes closed and he raised his fists heavenward, unleashing the evil within. He ordered the immediate manifestation of supernatural power, chanting for the amount of power necessary to execute his mission. When he awoke from the ordeal—his eyes blood-red—a puff of smoke escaped his mouth and floated toward the mirror. When the smoke cleared, the image of a ship sailing the dark waters appeared in the mirror.

He remained at the mirror, monitoring the cruise ship on his supernatural radar screen. After closely studying the vessel, Hart shoved his hand into the pocket of his robe and pulled out a silver coin. He placed the coin to the upper right-hand side of the mirror, where his screen showed clouds. He stepped back as the coin melted into a silver-like liquid and mingled with the clouds. The melting silver appeared like veins as they traversed the image of the clouds. As the silver residue dissipated, powerful lightning bolts streaked the sky. The fierce impact of unrestrained electricity on several of the ship's decks caused the vessel to shudder violently.

Hart slipped his hand into his left pocket and pulled from it a handful of copper coins. He threw the coins one by one into the image of the sea on his screen until his hand was empty. Suddenly, a severe turbulence erupted, coupled with horrendous claps of thunder, and a powerful ocean quake ensued.

Paul Hart blew another puff of smoke toward the mirror. Seconds later, the crowded dance hall appeared on the screen. Hart watched, smiling, as hundreds of panic-stricken guests groped their way across the floor, having been tossed about by the raging storm.

~~~

Annabelle crawled back to the dance hall, terrified by the sudden and violent strike of Mother Nature. She arrived to find the dance hall in shambles and panic flooding the room. Bob spotted her and ran to her side. Scared and miserable, she immediately fell into his arms.

As Bob held her, Annabelle thought about having fallen victim to an evil plot. The guilt and shame surfaced, threatening to strangle her. Bob held her up with ease as she drowned in her distress. He looked into her eyes, alarm spreading across his face.

Annabelle was pale, and her eyes darted around fearfully. This terrified Bob even more than the wrath of Mother Nature that surrounded them. "Where have you been?" he asked.

"I was looking for someone, someone I thought I knew from my past." The guilt and disappointment in her voice was unmistakable.

"Who?" he asked. "Who were you looking for?"

She looked at him, seemingly confused. "I don't know."

"Are you sure you're okay?"

"I'm fine." Annabelle hung her head, seemingly sinking deeper into despair.

"Annabelle," Bob said, sounding desperate, "what is it?"

She lifted her head and looked at him, her eyes empty. "You don't want to know."

~~~

Paul Hart was still monitoring the chaos in the dance hall

through the mirror. It was like watching a live production of a traumatic movie scene. By virtue of his satanic power, he had single-handedly placed every person on board in harm's way.

The storm continued to wreak its havoc on the ship and its passengers. If the situation turned catastrophic, not a single person would survive. But the deaths of others in the tragedy was merely a bonus. Hart's only real target was Annabelle.

Unbeknownst to her, Hart had been following her since their fateful meeting in the fall of 1991, when he had requested her company while disguised as an angel of God. The young and devout Sister Annabelle had swallowed the hoax hook, line, and sinker. His motive for deceiving her looked to be moments away from paying off.

He kept a steady watch on his prime target, closely monitoring her in the mirror. He looked on as her husband tried desperately to reach his stricken wife. He touched Annabelle's mirror image with the tip of his finger, running it across her neck and down toward her chest. He watched in amusement as blood gushed from the glass and spilled down into the sink.

~~~

The storm and the powerful quake escalated, viciously battering the ship. The tension on board rose as panic-stricken guests desperately groped for a foothold on the deck. Passengers crawled and clung to whatever sturdy structure they came across. Some wandered in shock, unable to make sense of the tragedy around them.

A sudden calm came over the ship when the public address system came to life. "May I have your attention, ladies and gentlemen," the captain's voice boomed. "This is Captain Richard Patterson. We apologize for the disruption in your voyage. We are currently cruising through a severe storm, accompanied by an ocean quake. The sudden and severe weather has thrown the ship off course. I advise everyone to remain calm. For those of you able to return to your cabins, please do so at this time. If you are unable to return to your cabin, please remain where you are. We will keep you updated on our progress through the storm. Thank you."

~~~

Bob Goldman stormed onto the bridge just as the captain was replacing the intercom.

"Mr. Goldman," the captain exclaimed. "I was just about to page you. I—"

"What in the hell is going on?"

The captain tried in vain to calm him, but Bob could see fear in the captain's eyes. "What is it, Patterson?" he shouted. "Tell me—now."

"We have no way of . . . there is no possibility . . ."

"What do you mean, no possibility?"

"We're lost," the captain said, hanging his head. "The magnitude of this storm, the quake, it's like no other I've ever experienced. Worse—and this is really odd—our weather radar showed no signs of an impending storm. None. Last time I checked, it showed clear skies all the way through to our destination."

Bob Goldman sighed. Wearily, he stepped away from the crew, silent and shivering in terror. He turned to the window in time to see a powerful lightning bolt hit the front of the ship, knocking out the power on the bridge. Seconds later, a monstrous wave swamped the ship, pulling it sideways and throwing them off balance.

~~~

Annabelle's suspicion about the angel consumed her. Could it be that he was the mysterious mastermind behind the tragedy of her wedding night? Or perhaps this had something to do with her pregnancy, her child conceived out of wedlock.

When she thought about her pregnancy, the child conceived by way of deceiving her future husband, an unexpected truth rose to the surface. Her sacred encounter was not a calling from God, but from his enemy. Satan, in disguise, had lured her into a dark and evil plan.

"Honey," Bob screamed above the panic-stricken crowd, staggering his way through the chaos to meet her. When he reached Annabelle, he pulled her close and the two of them fell back against a pillar. He looked into her eyes, which were moist with tears. "Let's get out of here," he urged, grabbing her hand.

"Where are we going to go?" she asked.

"To our suite."

"Wait!"

"Why wait?" he asked. "Let's go."

"There's something I need to tell you."

Bob stopped and turned. He looked at Annabelle intently.

"I know this is going to sound awful and confusing, with everything happening around us, but this is all my fault."

~~~

Hart leaned over and kissed the center of the mirror. He stared at the print of his lips as it quickly vanished from the surface, giving way to a sudden burst of fire. The flame rocketed from the mirror's surface and fused with the wind and lightning. Seconds later, a deafening roll of thunder rumbled through, drowning out the screams of the passengers. Chandeliers crashed from the ceiling, cabin windows shattered. In the kitchen, cabinets came smashing down. The entire kitchen staff tried to flee in terror.

Hart was tapping into a higher dimension of satanic power. He felt strong enough to sink the entire ship. By the time it went under, he would be long gone. To the rest of the world, the tragedy would be an unsolvable mystery—an unstoppable and vicious act of God.

The water around the ship began parting. Hart looked on, smirking. In five minutes' time, two waves on either side of the ship had grown miraculously to match the high walls of the vessel. The ship rapidly sank down into the void between them.

~~~

Annabelle and Bob hobbled into their suite, exhausted and weary. Bob had grown numb to the terror raging on board. Moreover, he no longer feared his own death, likely only moments away. Annabelle's confession had left him feeling empty and unable to imagine anything but the most tragic of outcomes. But he was still curious; he wanted an explanation from his wife about how she was responsible for this nightmare. He felt the ship plunging as he sat at the foot of the bed, grief stricken.

Annabelle sat on the floor beside his right leg, trying to find the right words. "I never should have listened to my mother," she said regretfully. "I knew the priest's prophecy was meant for me."

"Prophecy?"

She nodded glumly. "The truth is, he deceived me, right from the beginning."

"Deceived you?" Bob asked. "Who deceived you? Who charmed you into this deception?"

"About a week after filming the last episode of *The Prodigal Doctor*, I was watching television. It was morning, and Channel 14 was airing its telecast of Father McClain's weekly sermon. In the middle of his sermon, he began talking about a prophecy." She paused before continuing. "Something inside of me responded when he spoke about a young woman watching him right at that moment. He started talking about how fame and fortune were unlikely for most and that there was a high price to be paid for such achievements. Right then, I developed this strong feeling. I knew in my heart that the priest was talking to me."

"We could drown at any moment," Bob snapped, "and you're telling me about some preacher's sermon? Some delusion you had that he was talking directly to you?"

"My mood swings, you remember those, right?"

"How could I not?" he said sarcastically. "They're burned on my brain, since they happened just a couple of hours ago." He was starting to lose his patience. Had his wife gone mad?

"I was afraid and desperate," she said. "I've been praying for months for the angel to return."

"Are you that delusional?" he asked. He decided to humor her. "And what was so crucial that you needed this angel to come to your rescue?"

"I fell prey to his sinister deception," Annabelle confessed. "I walked away from my life as a nun because he persuaded me to, by telling me he spoke on behalf of God. He told me to go out into the world, find a husband, have a child—a divine child, one that would be the living embodiment of God here on Earth. But then I got pregnant before we got married . . . He must have gotten wind of it."

Bob rose and walked to the other side of the room, glaring down at Annabelle in disgust. "Look, we're getting nowhere with this divine nonsense. I'm starting to lose my patience."

"I swear, Bob," she pleaded. "It's the truth. He came to me while I was at the convent and drew me to another world. He told me that God had a plan for me to fulfill, a special purpose—a prophecy. Even his appearance was angelic. How could I have known? How—"

Annabelle's pleas were interrupted by the roaring of waves engulfing the sides of the ship. Bob heard people screaming hysterically as they tried to scramble to safety. Though he felt the ship sinking rapidly, he had no clue that the wave had plunged four of the vessel's decks beneath the ocean in mere seconds.

~~~

In an attempt to flee the toppling kitchen, the chefs remained on alert. As they made their way through the kitchen doors, a powerful wave rushed in, drowning them.

A group of people managed to swim to the safety of the grand lobby, only to be met by huge waves that crashed in on them from every side. There were no survivors.

The rampaging flood swept dead bodies along by the dozens. Within minutes, the water began traveling toward the passengers' cabins.

~~~

Susan ushered her longtime friend Bill McCoy into the lobby of her quiet apartment building. Since her phobia of large bodies of water prevented her from taking the wedding cruise, Bill had offered to take her out for dinner that evening. Susan regretted not being able to participate in her daughter's wedding reception, and Bill McCoy was doing his best to cheer her up.

"So, why the ocean phobia?" McCoy asked as she pulled the keys from her purse.

Susan looked at him and sighed. "I lost my three best friends."

He frowned. "How?"

"Swimming accidents. And not all on the same day."

McCoy's eyes widened as he followed Susan inside the apartment.

"They were all in their early teens," she continued.

McCoy sighed, a quiet whistle escaping his lips. "I can't begin to imagine how devastating their deaths were for you."

"The grief was worse than I could have imagined," Susan said, setting her purse on the coffee table. "Imagine losing a dear friend three summers in a row."

McCoy shook his head and sat on the couch. "I can't

remember you ever sharing this with me before."

"It's not something I like to talk about," Susan answered, switching on the TV. "Besides, it was a long time ago, way before I knew you."

As Susan grabbed her purse from the table and headed to her bedroom, the phone rang. She was expecting a call from Annabelle, so she hurried back to the living room and lifted the receiver. "Hello, my beautiful, newly wedded daughter," she exclaimed excitedly.

"Mother . . . ?"

"Yes, I'm here, honey." She stood in front of the entertainment center, the receiver held tightly to her ear. Annabelle's voice had sounded oddly distant. The connection kept breaking up. "Annabelle," she called into the phone, "are you still there?"

Seconds ticked by, and no Annabelle. Susan detected what she thought was an unusual-sounding static, as if she were listening to a thunderstorm in the distance. "Annabelle?" she shouted. "Honey, you're scaring me." The distinct sound of thunder rumbled on the other end of the line. "What's going on there?" A new sound surfaced: people screaming hysterically. *What's going on?* A little over a minute went by, and still not a word from Annabelle. The line went dead. "Honey?" she shouted in vain. "Are you still there?"

Susan slowly pulled the receiver away from her ear and replaced it on the cradle. It rang again.

Susan picked it up. "Hello?"

"Mother?"

"Yes, Annabelle, I'm here. What is going on?"

"We're trapped in a storm," Annabelle shouted breathlessly. "I don't know how long I'll be able to talk."

Susan heard the panic in her daughter's voice. "A storm? How bad is it?" She shot a worried glance at Bill. "What do you mean, you won't be able to talk long?"

Bill was immediately at her side, trying to listen along with Susan.

The line went dead again.

Susan's heart raced, and her breath came faster. She looked at Bill one last time before everything went dark.

~~~

"Mother," Annabelle cried out, but it was no use. Her mother was no longer on the other end of the line. She pressed on in vain. "Mother," she screamed, tears streaming down her cheeks. "Can you hear me?"

Bob stepped closer, stood over his bride, and reached out his hand. "Let's get out of here," he told her.

Annabelle dropped the satellite phone to the floor in resignation. "Where are we going to go?" she asked, sobbing.

"Somewhere . . . safer."

Despite the fact that all hope seemed gone, Annabelle placed her hand in Bob's. Just as she got to her feet, a swirling burst of ocean water gushed in through what was left of their suite's windows. The violent flood swept them off their feet and slammed them against the back wall.

The water encircled them, rising at a rapid pace. Bob struggled to save Annabelle as she screamed for help. He managed to grab hold of her hand, the water having risen above their waists.

Bob held tight to Annabelle's hand as the water continued to rise. The newlyweds were able to tread water, but the ceiling was drawing nearer by the second. Annabelle gasped for air as the current threatened to drag her under. Bob dove beneath and tried to push his wife up to the surface, but the ceiling came too fast. Annabelle drew one full breath before her head hit the ceiling and the water engulfed her completely. Below the surface, Bob maintained his grip on his wife, but, as the life drained from her body, Annabelle became a dead weight in Bob's arms, and, together, they drowned.

The parted waves at last caved in and sucked the ship below the surface, burying the vessel at sea.

Chapter 18

BBC Breaking News

It was an unusual morning that drew millions of viewers to their television sets like never before. The anchor, Tim Brosna, appeared genuinely saddened as he read the report. His pale, grief-stricken features suggested he'd known Annabelle Smithson and Bob Goldman personally.

"Breaking news just reaching our news desk: Golden Globe Winner Annabelle Smithson and her new husband, billionaire Bob Goldman, along with their more than five hundred wedding guests, including staff and crew, died late last night while cruising the Atlantic aboard Mr. Goldman's personal cruise ship, the St. Gordon.

"Though the cause of the mysterious storm that damaged the ship and eventually drove it under the water's surface is still under investigation, sources say the vessel departed Felix Stowe Dock eight hours prior to the tragedy. Investigators have speculated that the catastrophe aboard the St. Gordon could very well be the worst shipwreck since the sinking of the Titanic in April of 1912.

"BBC News will keep you updated as this story continues to unfold. Thank you for watching. I'm Tim Brosna."

~~~

Three weeks later

The tragic death of her only child sent Susan Smithson into deep mourning. Annabelle's fearful last words haunted her, and the disturbing memory of the sounds of the storm and the panic-stricken passengers threatened to linger in her mind indefinitely.

Guilt and regret consumed her more than anything else. She thought back to the day Annabelle had tried to talk to her about Father McClain's sermon. But she'd just blown her off, even thought that Annabelle had become narcissistic as a result of all her fame to think that the priest was talking directly to her.

She pondered the events of that day with great remorse, wishing she'd been more attentive to her daughter's peculiar mood. She realized now that Annabelle may have known she was on a path leading to unavoidable tragedy. It dawned on her, too, that Annabelle had been right about the prophecy Father McClain spoke of from his pulpit.

Susan blamed herself for her daughter's death. By grossly misjudging the situation that morning when Annabelle had asked for help, she had ignored an opportunity to help Annabelle avert tragedy. But it was too late. It pained her to know that her daughter would be alive today if only she had taken her seriously and not judged. If only she'd listened and persuaded Annabelle to return to the convent. The guilt was strangling her.

Susan suffered another long, sleepless night as the memory of that day ran continually through her mind. After going over the "what ifs" for what seemed like the hundredth time, she reluctantly scooted off the bed and walked to the window. Wearily, she pulled the curtain aside and peered out her eighth-floor window, immediately spotting a white Land Rover Discovery as it drove into the neighborhood and parked at the curb across from her apartment building's entrance. Curious, Susan continued watching the SUV, straining to get a look at the driver. Inside the vehicle sat an unfamiliar middle-aged African-American woman.

~~~

Eleanor had to find the woman who was Annabelle's mother. Her sources had pointed her to this apartment building. She surveyed the building from the front seat of her SUV, and her eyes came to rest on the building's main entrance.

The neighborhood was quiet—too quiet. Without another person roaming around, she decided it was safer to remain in the car. A woman alone, dressed in a gold-and-white cloak, could raise suspicion in anyone who happened to be watching.

Eleanor had been unexpectedly pulled into this tragedy, and though she didn't know why, she felt compelled to trust her instincts and follow God's command. She was pursuing a woman she had never even met, a woman whose identity was revealed by way of a prophetic vision. She knew people would think she was crazy. Heck, even she felt a little crazy, but nonetheless, she couldn't walk away from the vision, a vision that had led her to Annabelle Smithson's mother's front door.

Her anxiety grew as she continued to sit, scanning the apartment building's grounds from the driver seat. She knew time was running out. She must track down Susan Smithson before it was too late. She had to warn her of the divine revelation God had summoned her to deliver.

It was eleven o'clock, and Eleanor was growing weary. She'd been in her car, searching for Susan Smithson, since the crack of dawn. Her eyes still fixed on the entry doors, she spotted what she thought might be Susan's familiar face exiting the building. She straightened, all of her senses on alert. As the building tenant hurried down the front walk and passed in front of her car, Eleanor knew for sure that she'd found the person she was looking for, but before she could roll down the window and call for Susan's attention, Susan hopped into her car and drove off, seemingly in a rush. Eleanor started her engine and followed the Volvo down the road.

When Susan pulled into a filling station, Eleanor pulled in directly behind her, the Land Rover nearly coming into contact with the Volvo's bumper. Close up, Eleanor could see that Susan Smithson was heavily laden with grief. She didn't even seem to notice that she'd been followed.

~~~

Susan filled her tank and drove off into the traffic. Fifteen minutes later, she pulled into the parking area of the train station. She hurried into the terminal and bought a ticket for a train bound for Sloax.

She stepped up onto the train and sat quietly in a window seat near the rear of the car. She didn't bother to look up when another passenger sat down beside her moments later. Susan lifted her head and gazed out the window, unable to stop her eyes from filling with tears.

As the train disembarked and picked up speed along the rails, tears began streaming down Susan's face. From the corner of her eye, she spied the woman sitting next to her digging into her purse. The woman pulled a tissue out of a small plastic package and politely handed it to Susan.

"Thank you," Susan whispered, mustering a small, pained smile.

The woman smiled sympathetically. "It's my pleasure."

As Susan dabbed at her tears, she drew back in surprise. The woman sitting next to her was the same woman who had driven up in front of her building. "I know you. I mean, not exactly . . ."

"You did see me, then. I wasn't sure." The woman extended her hand. "I'm Eleanor Griffins."

"I'm Susan," she replied hesitantly. "Susan Smithson."

"Nice to meet you, Susan."

"Nice to meet you, too." She scrutinized the woman carefully. "If you don't mind me asking, who—"

"Looks like it's been a horrible day," Eleanor

interrupted.

Susan hesitated, but finally answered, "More horrible than you think."

Eleanor tilted her head. "Oh? How's that?"

"I lost my one and only child—my daughter."

"I know."

How do you know? Susan thought. *You don't even know me.* Susan looked away and gazed out the window. Though she had withdrawn from the conversation, she realized that talking to this woman offered her a small bit of comfort—the first she'd had felt since Annabelle's death.

"I'm sorry," Eleanor said. "Where are my manners? This must be awfully disconcerting for you."

Susan turned back to face her.

Eleanor smiled. "You see, I'm a prophetess."

"A prophetess?" Susan repeated, confused by the woman's explanation.

"You don't believe me, do you?"

Susan hesitated. "Well, it's just that I . . ."

"Perhaps you're not a woman of faith," said the prophetess. "Of course, you sure look like one to me."

Susan scoffed, rolling her eyes. "Faith is my greatest enemy."

Eleanor looked genuinely concerned. "How can that be?"

"Faith should've saved my daughter, but it didn't," Susan cried. "She was pregnant, for God's sake."

"Of course faith saved her," the prophetess exclaimed. "She is saved."

"Saved by the arms of death. Down in the belly of—"

"No," Eleanor practically shouted, and then, seemingly catching herself, she quieted and leaned closer. "Your daughter is not dead," she whispered in Susan's ear. "She is merely lost."

Susan arched an eyebrow. Fiercely skeptical, she studied

the so-called prophetess for a long, anxious moment. "Who are you talking about, woman?"

"Your daughter," Eleanor replied confidently. "I know you don't know me, but you must believe me. I'm not playing mind games with you, Susan. I could never do that to someone."

Deeply suspicious, Susan continued to eye the woman. In the space of five minutes, she'd traveled from pain to comfort to utter bewilderment. "I'm riding on a train, but it doesn't seem real."

"What are you trying to say, Susan?"

"That maybe I'm still at home, in bed, having some kind of wild dream . . . or nightmare. I'm not sure which."

"I know it seems hard to believe, but this is not a dream, Susan. This is real. I've been trying to track you down since the crack of dawn to unveil this mystery."

"I'm sorry," said Susan, refusing to look at the woman. "I think you must be mistaking me for someone else."

"You are the mother of Annabelle Smithson, are you not?"

Susan froze, continuing to stare straight ahead.

"Now you know I'm not delusional," said Eleanor. "I'm only doing what I've been instructed to do, which is to pass on a secret meant only for you."

"I'm getting off at the next stop," Susan said curtly when the train began to slow.

"Are you sure you're going to be okay?"

Susan looked at the woman, incredulous. "I don't really see how that's any of your business."

Susan disembarked and took the station's escalator down to the street-level exit. As she hurried along, the hair on the back of her neck rose. Susan concluded that Eleanor Griffins was still following her. Like a ghost's shadow, the so-called prophetess stalked her every move.

Susan spun on her heel and confronted the insufferable

woman. "What do you want from me? I don't know you, and you certainly don't know me."

"Does it really matter?" Eleanor asked. "What matters is my mission."

"Mission?"

"My mission. I never would have been called to find you if you thought for a moment that Annabelle was really dead. If you truly believed your daughter was gone forever, we would not be standing here having this conversation."

"How ignorant do you think I am? Who in the world would dare to believe such nonsense? My daughter is dead, Ms. Griffins," Susan shouted. "Dead."

"It's entirely up to you to believe me or not," Eleanor said. "But *I* am not the issue here. This is about you making a choice—a choice of faith."

Susan stared at her impatiently, wondering how much more she could take.

"What I am saying is that it takes faith to wholly embrace this mystery."

"You're crazy, lady."

"But you believe in my work, Susan," she said. "I know it inspires you. Why, then, can you not believe in my message?"

Susan tilted her head. "Your work?"

"My paintings. As I stand here before you, I see many of my paintings hanging on the walls of your living room and bedroom. I'm convinced you once had deep confidence in me when I was an artist. But you've taken for granted the divine gift that only God can bestow on the one he divinely chooses to work his purpose."

Susan had been so caught off guard by this woman's message that she hadn't even recognized the name of her favorite artist. She humbled herself and spoke calmly. "So, where exactly is my daughter, then?"

"Only God can answer that."

Susan swallowed down her frustration. "Why did you give up your career as an artist?"

"I didn't," she answered, smiling. "I'm still an artist. I still paint. Only now, my paintings are inspired by a new light."

"A new light?" Susan asked. "What does that mean?"

"I'm an artist, divinely called as a prophet," Eleanor replied. "God uses my hands to reveal future events—through my art, on my canvas."

"Are you saying that you foresaw the tragedy that killed my daughter?"

"Yes. But I'm not empowered to avert disasters that are destined to occur."

Susan felt her anger rising again. "You know what I think?"

"Not unless you tell me."

"I think you're trying to deprive me of my feelings about the things happening around me—including you."

Eleanor looked at her, puzzled. "What are you getting at, Ms. Smithson?"

"No matter what you believe or say to me, I still feel like I exist in this . . . dream world. Nothing around me—even you—seems the least bit real."

"I'm not sure what to say about this 'dream world' you speak of, Susan," Eleanor replied. "But let me ask you this: Have you ever wondered why Annabelle's body was the only body never recovered from the wreck?"

~~~

Susan quietly entered the empty sanctuary, still baffled by Eleanor Griffins' parting question. The prophetess's words had swirled in her mind while she ran errands the next day, triggering an impromptu visit to the church to talk with the priest. She entered a pew, knelt, and prayed. When she opened her eyes and looked up, Susan found herself face-to-face with Father Chapman.

"Good afternoon, Susan," he greeted warmly.

"Hello, Father."

He smiled. "What a surprise, seeing you this time of the day."

Susan rose to her feet. "I know, Father," she said flatly. "This is unusual."

The alarmed look on the priest's face confirmed Susan's worst fears. She knew she was a mess, but his wide-eyed expression suggested that her perpetual state of agony had gone from bad to worse, and had taken a toll on her outward appearance.

"Is everything okay?" he asked, his voice conveying genuine concern.

Susan pondered for a moment. "Things are not going well, Father," she replied with despair.

He nodded sympathetically. "You don't seem yourself."

"No, I'm not myself at all, I'm afraid."

The priest offered her his arm. "Why don't we step up to the altar so we may petition the Lord in prayer together."

"Thank you, Father," Susan replied, taking his arm.

Once they reached the altar, Father Chapman hurriedly fetched a chair from the far end and offered it to Susan. "I might be wrong, Susan," he said hesitantly, "but the spirit tells me that your current state of mind isn't just about mourning your daughter's death. I sense it's a bit more than that. Has something happened?"

"Yes, Father Chapman."

"You loved your daughter very much."

"Yes. I gave birth to that beautiful girl, and no mother should have to experience the death of her child."

"Her death has left you with some very deep emotional scars," he said. "May I offer you a word of comfort?"

Susan nodded.

"Remember this: death is not a mystery. The perishing of our mortal bodies has been around from the very beginning, and it will remain until God decides otherwise. But death is not the end of life, but rather, the beginning of a new life."

She sighed and nodded.

"So, something has happened," he said. "Is this something spiritual? A family matter?"

"Both," Susan replied, bowing her head.

Father Chapman gently removed his glasses and set them atop the Bible in his lap. "So, what's troubling you?"

She lifted her head. "I have a question."

"Okay."

"This might sound weird, but it's something I'm trying to wrap my mind around." She locked her eyes onto Father Chapman's. "Have you ever looked beyond the natural?"

"I'm sorry, but I'm not gifted in foreseeing the future, if that's what you're getting at."

"What about the gift of prophecy?" she asked. "Do you have any personal experience with prophecy at all?"

The priest raised an eyebrow. He took a long, deep breath and exhaled. "I honestly don't operate in the prophetic gift at all. Preaching the message of the Lord is what I'm ordained to do."

Susan was surprised. "So, in your thirty-something years as a priest, you've never, at any point in time, experienced something unearthly?"

"Well, I don't know if I would go as far as to say I haven't had divine experiences, but they are not frequent—and are perhaps not as deep as one would expect. But, yes, God, in his divinity, has spoken to me on occasion."

"Okay, now we're getting somewhere."

"What's your point?"

"I ran into a woman late last night. Well, to say I ran into her isn't quite accurate. More like, she tracked me down and followed me." Susan paused, coming face-to-face with the priest. "She claimed to be a prophetess of God."

The priest seemed intrigued but also skeptical. "Did she

state her name? Her religious background?"

"She said her name was Eleanor Griffins. If she is who she says she is, then she used to be a very gifted artist—a painter."

"Eleanor Griffins," Father Chapman repeated, nodding. "Yes, I know the name."

"You know her?"

"Well, not personally," the priest replied. "But her story is well known in the church. Some time ago, she converted her life to serving God. She claims he made her a prophet. I've talked to other clergy who have met her in person and they seem to think that she's the real thing."

"Forgive me, Father. This may sound judgmental, but I am not convinced this woman is for real. I believe she's falsely claiming the title of prophet."

"And what has led you to this conclusion?" the priest asked, his brow furrowed. "I *can* say with confidence that Ms. Griffins is a woman of God."

"She told me on the train that she had a vision, and . . ." Susan hesitated. "And in that vision, the Lord revealed that my daughter is still alive—as in, not dead. Now tell me, isn't that despicable? Is this woman trying to torture me?"

Father Chapman's Bible slid to the floor, along with his glasses. He picked up the items and composed himself. "This woman, she actually used the word 'prophetess' in describing herself?"

"You just gave me the impression that you believed she's a prophet of God."

"Yes, but . . . but a prophetic vision from God, one of this magnitude, would have to be based on the testaments of two or more prophets in order to verify its authenticity. Well, that or . . ."

"What, Father?"

"Either you need to get a second opinion or"—he cleared his throat—"you need to ask yourself if this is merely a matter of faith."

"Faith?"

"Faith."

"Do you truly believe that Annabelle could have survived the shipwreck?" Susan asked.

"What I can tell you is that God, in his divinity, never lies. If Eleanor Griffins revealed this to you, it's my opinion that the revelation is truly from the Lord. I have no reason to doubt her. The question is, what do you believe, Susan? What does your heart tell you?"

Susan remembered the feeling of peace that had come over her when Eleanor Griffins spoke to her for the first time. "If Annabelle is still alive," she said, searching the priest's eyes, "then where is she?"

"Jonah lived in the belly of a whale for three days—you know the story. After those days of darkness and anguish, the whale vomited him onto the shores of Nineveh."

"But that was centuries ago."

"The wonders of God are ageless, Susan."

"Father, I'm afraid," she said, tears spilling over.

"Don't be," he said, smiling gently. "Miracles still happen, for those who believe."

She stared at the priest, her cynicism rising to the surface again. "Why are you trying to find truth in this fairytale, Father?"

~~~

An early-morning knock at the door the next day startled Susan as she sat on the couch, coffee in hand, ruminating over her conversation with Father Chapman. She shuffled to the door and opened it a crack. To her horror, she found Eleanor Griffins standing on the other side. *How in the world did she know which apartment was mine?* The woman's unexpected visit sent waves of fear rippling through Susan's body. She thought—hoped—she'd seen the last of the so-called prophetess, having walked away from her that day at the train station.

"What do you want?" Susan asked, not bothering to mask her annoyance.

"Good morning," Eleanor Griffins replied, overlooking Susan's irritable greeting.

"Don't 'good morning' me," Susan barked. "You've made my life more miserable than even I could have imagined. You and your damned *visions*."

"Miserable?"

Susan scoffed. "Don't you get it?"

"Well, then it's God you're angry with, because I'm just the messenger." She paused. "Susan, ask yourself: Why would God go out of his way to make your life miserable? Why would he inflict unnecessary pain on someone who has already had enough pain for a lifetime?"

Susan stared at her for a long moment, wishing she had an answer to the question. She pulled the door wide open. "Come in."

Eleanor smiled. "Thank you."

Susan regarded the prophetess skeptically and motioned to the sofa. "Have a seat." She grabbed her cup of coffee from the end table and took a sip. "So, how did you find my apartment? More of your 'divine insight'—isn't that what you call it?"

"I am a prophetess, yes."

Susan sighed impatiently and set her coffee cup back on the table. "Don't you have a home, somewhere to be?"

"I do."

"Look, I don't mean to be rude, but why are you here? And, more importantly, why are you here so early?"

"I understand your frustration," said Eleanor. "But like I told you on the train, I'm on a divine mission."

"Well, it must be a pretty desperate mission, Ms. Griffins," she said, glancing at the clock on the mantel. "Because I don't recall anyone ever showing up on my doorstep at this ungodly hour."

"It was important that I see you. It couldn't wait."

"So what is this mission that is so important that it couldn't wait? And please, don't tell me it's another senseless revelation about my deceased daughter."

"It's not."

"Well, then?"

"You're obviously still skeptical."

"And if I am?"

"Your doubt concerning this situation is making things awfully challenging for me. I'm afraid that if you continue to fail to embrace Annabelle's return from captivity, she won't have the motherly support and love she'll need more than ever."

Susan stared at Eleanor Griffins for a long, uncomfortable moment. "You are driving me insane, lady."

Eleanor Griffins straightened. "It's the truth," she said resolutely.

"I must have been out of my mind to let you in here," Susan said, shaking her head. "I believe it's time for you to leave." She walked to the door and yanked it open. "Now, before I call the police."

"Just remember, Susan," Eleanor said as she approached the door, "one day you will need my help, and you will seek every means to find me."

"Maybe I will, Ms. Griffins," Susan said. "But not today."

Chapter 19

A team of explorers launched an expedition along the Westminster Shoreline Woods aboard a chopper on a sunny Monday afternoon. Heading the four-man team was forty-eight-year-old Max Taylor. He was busy snapping photographs of the scenery from the helicopter's open door when an unidentifiable object on the beach came into view. He laid his camera aside and squinted, trying to make out the strange object. It was the body of a woman, dressed in an elaborate wedding gown.

As the chopper circled low around the area, Taylor could see that the body had not been lying there long, perhaps washed ashore within the last hour or two. "Hey, you guys," he shouted to the others, pointing. "Look there."

"What?" they shouted back in unison.

"There's a body—look."

The three other members scrambled to the door and looked down. By then, the pilot had gotten wind of it and hovered lower in an attempt to land.

"Don't land this chopper, Alec," Taylor yelled.

"Wonder who it is?" asked Maurice, one of the crew.

"Heck if I know," another member of the crew, Marvin, replied.

"Shouldn't we get closer, Max?" Alec asked. "See if we can help?"

"No, not right now," Max replied. "We've got no idea who she is or what kind of a situation we'd be getting into."

"It's a woman lying on the beach, Max," the pilot shouted back. "We can't just leave her there. She might be hurt, or worse. We should at least get close enough to identify the state she's in."

"How sure are you it's just a woman, Max?" Collins asked. "We could be messing with a ghost or some kind of evil mermaid."

Taylor glanced at the young crew member, not bothering to hide his amusement. "What in the hell are you talking about, kid?"

"Think of it. The closest town to this haunted beach is a hundred kilometers away."

"Haunted beach?" Taylor asked, screwing up his eyes. He looked at the body and back to the kid. "Mermaid?"

But the kid wouldn't let up. "Maybe you aren't seeing what I'm seeing. They do call this the ghost coast of Westminster."

Taylor glanced at the other crew members, both of whom were trying to suppress laughter. He looked back at the kid. "Looks like a woman to me, Collins, probably drowned."

"Not to me."

"Just what are you seeing that I'm not?"

"So we're just going to let her lay there and rot?" the pilot interrupted. "What's the point of arguing, gentlemen?" He looked at Max. "Do you want me to get closer to investigate or not?"

"No way," Collins blurted, scared to the teeth.

"We can't just leave her there," Alec said.

"I've never seen a drowned body in an outfit like that," Maurice said. "One thing's for sure, this was no swimming accident."

The crew regarded each other silently. The issue about the bridal gown plunged them all into grave trepidation.

"So why are we afraid, if it's just a dead woman?" Maurice asked, breaking the silence.

Max Taylor studied the body and looked back at the

others. "The body looks too natural, too polished for a dead person."

"Excuse me, gentlemen," Alec spoke up. "The decision's been made—I'm going to have to land this thing before we run out of fuel." He set the copter gently down on the sand and killed the engine.

"Well," Maurice said, "I guess we've arrived at the moment that will truly define our excursion."

"Who's man enough to step out?" Maurice asked.

"Wait," Marvin exclaimed. "It could be an ocean goddess, just waiting to snatch us all and pull us deep into the ocean." He threw an amused glance at Collins, who shot him a dirty look in return.

Taylor secured the camera strap around his neck. "What is this, some joke to you all?" he shouted. "That could be somebody's wife or daughter—maybe even someone's mother, for Christ sake."

"Oh my God," Maurice called out. "You guys see that?"

Taylor and Marvin flanked Maurice and looked out the window, just in time to see the woman roll over onto her side. They exchanged nervous glances and looked at Collins.

"What?" said Collins.

"Looks like you were right, kid," Taylor said. "The woman's not dead."

Taylor surveyed the scene in disbelief. Collins leaned in beside him, seemingly as stunned as the rest of them.

"Well, let's find out who she is," Marvin said.

"You guys go ahead," Alec said. "I'm staying here."

Max Taylor jumped out of the helicopter.

"Where are you going?" asked Collins.

"What Marvin suggested," Taylor replied. "Finding out who she is."

The crew and pilot watched him closely as he made his way across the sand. Halfway to the body, he turned back and beckoned his colleagues.

A visibly shaken Collins was the first to jump out and follow. He shot a glance at Marvin. "You coming, scaredy cat?"

Marvin narrowed his eyes at the kid. "Max," he screamed.

But Max Taylor kept his eyes on the woman as he drew nearer.

"Max!"

Taylor glanced over his shoulder. Collins was about fifty feet behind him, with Marvin in hot pursuit. Max turned his attention back to the woman, who had moved again and was now lying on her back.

His heart began to pound as he reached the unconscious woman. He watched as a wave gently swept up and washed away the sand beneath her heels. Max pointed his camera at the body, inexplicably drawn to the potential danger that loomed beneath the surface. He stooped lower to snap a photo but immediately drew back. The curve of her midsection was unmistakable; the woman appeared to be several months pregnant. *Good God.*

Taylor took a deep breath, his composure returning. He lifted his camera and snapped a dozen photos of the woman.

Marvin arrived on the scene. "Jesus, Max, what are you doing?"

~~~

Susan hadn't slept since Ms. Griffins' visit. Not that she'd slept much before that. The idea that Annabelle could have survived the ship disaster began to take hold, but, strangely, the revelation triggered more fear than anything else. There was no conceivable way someone could have survived such an ordeal, and yet, she wanted to believe it was so. Was Annabelle immortal, or some kind of a ghost? Whatever the truth was, Susan was haunted by the words of the prophetess, and, after six months of vicious torment, it seemed she could no longer endure the emotional agony.

Perhaps Susan's sanity would be restored if the prophecy came to pass. *Yeah, right.* But as she looked realistically at the futility of the situation, it was difficult to see how her mental state could improve at this point.

At midnight, Susan dimmed the bedside lamp and curled up in bed. As she lay there, praying for sleep, the phone rang. Susan sat up in bed and stared suspiciously at the phone on her nightstand.

Ring.

Her heart raced. *Only bad news prompts phone calls at this hour*, she thought.

Ring.

Susan hesitated, holding her breath. When the ringing finally ceased, she breathed a sigh of relief.

Seconds later, the ringing started again. The caller obviously wasn't giving up, but Susan was determined to ignore the call. Her breath quickened as she watched the phone, tempted to pull the cord from the wall.

Ring.

Susan reluctantly placed her hand on the receiver, but before she could pick it up, the phone quieted again. She turned on the lamp and glanced at the caller ID. Her mouth went dry. It was Annabelle's home number—the number Susan had never worked up the courage to disconnect. "Oh my God," she whispered.

Again the phone rang, making Susan jump. She snatched up the receiver before thinking. "Hello?"

"Mother?"

Susan's hand trembled violently, her heart thumping out of her chest. "An—" Her voice caught. "Annabelle?"

"Yes, Mother," the voice on the other end replied. "This is your daughter. This is Annabelle."

Susan's hand went limp, and the receiver slipped from

her grasp, dangling from its cord off the side of the nightstand. Susan stared straight ahead in shock. Unable to speak, she listened to the distant-sounding voice on the other end of the line.

"Mother? *Mother?*"

Chapter 20

Father McClain awoke early Tuesday morning with an eerie feeling in his gut. He longed to embark on his long awaited mission to pursue and conquer his arch-enemy, and he sensed that today he would learn something about the mission God had laid out for him years before.

His breakfast was served promptly as usual, the dining table spread lavishly with mouth-watering entrees fit for a king. McClain walked into his castle's Victorian dining room feeling an unusual hunger, but, strangely, he lacked an appetite.

His chef arrived with a pitcher of iced tea. "Have you watched the news this morning at all, Leonard?"

"No, Father," the chef replied, pouring the tea. "Are you concerned about something?"

"No, it's just . . ." He hesitated, not wanting to alarm his servant. "Just be alert, good man. We're living in perilous times."

The chef nodded. "I am very much aware," he replied. "Thank you, sir."

~~~

The sun at nine o'clock was sunny and bright. Yet, despite the torture of having been held captive in a dark and mysterious universe, Annabelle managed to immerse herself in the glow of the beautiful day. She was trying to relish every moment of her miraculous salvation, after being hell-bound by the evil forces of darkness for months. But the luscious feelings lasted mere moments before her encounter with the Prince of Darkness returned to haunt her. She looked out the family room window and immediately drew back, her heart pounding.

Her mother, obviously noticing her sudden agony asked, "What's the matter?"

"They lied to me," Annabelle cried out.

"Who lied to you?"

"Those scientists or explorers, or whatever they called themselves."

Susan regarded her daughter quizzically.

Annabelle sighed. "I told them to keep it secret," she replied. "And they promised me they would."

Susan peeked out the window. She turned to her daughter, clearly astonished.

Annabelle stepped beside her mother, her eyes filling with tears. It seemed the entire media had showed up, and were anxiously waiting outside the mansion's gate. From their place at the window, Annabelle and Susan could see that they were eager to rush in with their microphones and cameras.

After they had surveyed the situation for several minutes, Susan drew the curtains closed. "It's no use getting upset, Annabelle," she said. "There's nothing you can do about it."

"Oh yes there is."

"No, honey—"

"I want them off my property and out of my life. I've had enough trouble."

"It's their journalistic right," Susan said in return. "You're a public figure and a popular one at that. And, in case you hadn't remembered, you just came back from the dead."

Annabelle walked off, annoyed, and threw herself onto the sofa. "So what do you want me to do, Mother? Invite them in?"

"I didn't say that," Susan replied. "But you have to

remember, you're still a movie star, still famous. Even when they thought you were dead, your fans still celebrated your life every single day."

Her mother's words triggered something in Annabelle's subconscious. She swiftly grabbed the remote off the end table and switched on the television. Sure enough, as she flipped through the channels, she found a BBC Breaking News special report in progress about her recovery. A photograph of her lying unconscious in the sand was flashed on the screen as she listened to the newscaster read the report: "Rumors about the mysterious return of Annabelle Smithson continue to abound. Beneath the surface lies this mystical question: did Annabelle Sm—"

She switched off the TV. "I can't listen to this."

"Just try to stay calm, honey," Susan said. "It will all be over soon enough."

~~~

As rumors continued to spread, more and more viewers tuned into the BCC network. At 11:30 that morning, an updated special report interrupted the regular news schedule:

"Good morning. I'm Robert Rodstein. We interrupt regular programming to bring you this breaking news report. Rumors about the shocking discovery of actress Annabelle Smithson have increased over the last few hours. As we strive to solve this puzzling mystery, new revelations state that the body discovered yesterday afternoon was, in fact, the very-much-alive body of the Emmy-winning actress. Our correspondent Betty Rice is outside the home of Annabelle Smithson. We join her now as she unveils more details."

"Thanks, Robert. I'm standing at the multimillion-dollar mansion of Annabelle Smithson, whose presumed death in the tragic sinking of the cruise ship St. Gordon shocked the world just over six months ago. But today, we learn of an equally shocking story that has stunned the country and the entire world. Since late last night, we've been hearing rumors that the thirty-year-old actress was discovered alive yesterday afternoon on an abandoned beach forty-five kilometers south of Gosforth by a team of scientific explorers. Sources say that the screen actress was found in stable condition.

"Robert, just a few moments ago, someone peeked out from that front window," the reporter said, pointing. "And the woman we saw looked an awful lot like the 'late actress.' So the only question now is, did Annabelle Smithson miraculously survive the devastating shipwreck, or did we just see a ghost?"

Annabelle pressed *off* and tossed the remote onto the coffee table. "Ghost?" she repeated, disgusted. "Did you hear that? This is exactly what I was worried about."

"Settle down, honey," her mother soothed. "You're obviously not a ghost."

"I'm afraid about the spin they're putting on this," Annabelle said, fear creeping into her voice.

Susan sat beside her daughter on the couch. She could see how wound up she was getting and knew that it wasn't good for her or the baby. She was worried that if she didn't do everything in her power to console Annabelle, her daughter would sink further into despair. "Darling, ask yourself: Is it possible for a ghost to be pregnant?"

~~~

Since first hearing about Annabelle's recovery, Father McClain had been monitoring the news constantly. Unlike the other viewers, the priest wasn't overly shocked by the extraordinary events that had taken place. He was almost relieved by the news, having awoken on this day with an uneasy feeling and instinctively realizing the time was

Michael D. Benson

drawing near. Annabelle Smithson's miraculous return from the dead was the moment of truth and just the beginning of a battle to unravel the mystery meant for him alone to solve.

Father McClain listened closely to the details of the story, hoping for a sign indicating his need to act and launch his pursuit of the powerful demon God had commissioned him to destroy. The mission, he realized, would test his faith, and would likely endanger his life, as well.

~~~

The crowd of journalists huddled below the spacious front porch of Annabelle's home. McClain observed that the actress appeared well as she made her first live appearance on national television since having been declared dead in the ocean tragedy. From the top step of the porch, Annabelle smiled tightly. Her swollen belly stretched out before her under the designer maternity clothes she wore. She was over seven months along now.

The priest studied the television with deep interest as Annabelle, with her mother at her side, bashfully waited as photographers snapped her picture. The reporters peppered her with questions, and Annabelle finally spoke up. "Before attempting to answer your questions, I wish to first make a brief statement to my fans and the rest of the world."

Chapter 21

Exactly one week since the scientific explorers had found her washed up on the beach, Annabelle awoke severely agitated. Guilt consumed her as she thought of Bob and their wedding guests, all of whom had lost their lives in the tragic sinking of the *St. Gordon*. They were dead because of her; she had been the target. Her depression resulted from her acceptance of that grim reality.

Because of the dark clouds hovering over her, Annabelle reasoned that she would never again live a normal, fulfilled life. Could it be that the secret covenant she had unwittingly initiated with the Prince of Darkness had taken its toll? The unsettling mystery behind her pregnancy haunted her. She felt irrevocably trapped by the circumstances, unable to imagine life ever returning to what it was.

As Annabelle drew open the drapes to let in the sunlight, she was surprised to spot a cream-colored Rolls Royce Phantom slowly entering the circular drive. Instantly, she was reminded of the car Bob owned. As the car stopped in front of the house, Annabelle noted the license plate: *CLERGY*.

~~~

The door opened tentatively, revealing the face of Annabelle Smithson. When their eyes met, Father McClain detected that his presence warmed her, perhaps offering a comfort she hadn't experienced in months, even years.

"Good morning, Ms. Smithson," he greeted her kindly.

Annabelle Smithson leaned forward, almost as if she intended to embrace him, but stopped short of falling into the priest's arms. "Good morning, Father McClain."

"So you know who I am then?"

She nodded, smiling shyly.

"I hope it's okay that I've come to see you. I mean, is this an appropriate time?"

"I don't know that there'd ever be an 'appropriate' time, Father," she replied. "Nothing seems normal or right anymore."

"I understand," he said kindly. "But I beg to differ, and that's why I'm here."

She stepped aside. "Please, come in."

"Thank you," the priest said, stepping across the threshold.

"I must admit, you took me by surprise," she confessed, ushering him into the family room. "I've only just woken up."

"I'm terribly sorry for showing up unannounced, especially so early. I wouldn't have, except that the matter is of some urgency."

"It's okay," Annabelle replied. "A servant of God needs no invitation. Please, have a seat. Can I fix you some breakfast?"

"I believe, as the one who barged in on you, that the least I could do is make you breakfast. Jesus washed the feet of his disciples, saying, 'For the son of man came not to be served, but to serve.'" The priest smiled and looked into Annabelle's weary eyes. "My mission as a servant of God is to serve. And I am here to serve you, which is part of my mission."

She stared at Father McClain questioningly. "I'm really not sure who you are, Father, aside from catching your telecast once or twice. Forgive me if I'm skeptical of your kindness, but there are far too many devils masquerading as men of God these days."

McClain was genuinely hurt by her words, but he knew

full well that this innocent girl had fallen prey to crafty deception. Her suspicion of him was well founded and perfectly understandable. He decided to play dumb. "My guess is that you have good reason for making such a statement."

"Very perceptive, Father," she replied. "So what wind blew you my way?"

"Maybe we should have a word of prayer first." He bowed his head, and Annabelle, surprisingly, followed suit.

"Merciful and everlasting Father, the God who reigns in Heaven, and the universe, and throughout eternity: this day I seize the honor to sit in the presence of your beloved daughter—this precious soul of yours who holds within her the beauty of your creation.

"By your divine power, restore her life, Lord. Mend her mind and spirit, and, most of all, redirect her course of destiny and purpose to the woman you created her to be so that she may encounter your glory again. With these requests I welcome your blessings, in the name of your Son. Amen."

"Amen," Annabelle uttered quietly.

When they lifted their heads, Annabelle regarded him curiously. "You're awfully concerned for my well being, Father. Why?"

"It's part of being a true believer in Christ—caring and supporting the brethren, putting others ahead of myself."

"I'm not sure if I should admit this or not, but I felt a sudden transformation when you arrived on my doorstep, sort of an instant bolstering of my spirit. I couldn't help thinking God must have sent you here with a purpose in mind."

"Perhaps he has, Ms. Smithson," McClain replied, smiling.

Annabelle smiled back.

"Well, now that we've gotten that out of the way, may I

go ahead and make you some breakfast?" he insisted.

She laughed. "You can't be serious."

"Oh, but I am."

"Well then," she said, "perhaps next time. Truth be told, my appetite is a little off these days."

"I'm sorry to hear that. Next time, then."

"So, Father, tell me why you've come. It's a bit strange for a powerful man of God like you to visit a woman like me."

"While I understand that it may come as some surprise to you, your life plays a major role in my ministry, as does the unborn child you are carrying."

"You want to know something?" Annabelle asked.

"Tell me."

"You seem to possess a divine insight. I'm of the opinion that you are well aware of my short life expectancy. Now tell me if I'm right."

"I don't believe that it's the will of God to shorten your life."

"You foresaw my future," she insisted, "every detail of the tragedy I endured."

He hesitated. "I saw a prophecy, Ms. Smithson, not your future."

"How could you not have known it was me?"

"Sometimes visions—revelations, prophecies—aren't vivid enough to discern the actual identities of the people they involve."

"Do you suppose, perhaps, that's because secrets are sometimes the best way to spare someone anxiety?"

McClain locked his eyes onto Annabelle's. "You're hiding something. I'm sure of it."

Annabelle visibly flinched. She pondered for a moment before speaking again. "Perhaps I am, but how do you know?"

McClain straightened, his senses on alert. "I studied your

entire press interview from start to finish. I couldn't help but see how flustered you became when certain questions were asked."

"And?"

"Well, I discerned that the enemy still has a very strong hold on you, and has left you with a wealth of dark secrets."

"You're right, Father," she said. "And I would never trust the media with something of that nature. The question is, can I trust you?"

"You can trust me," McClain said resolutely. "With me, you will be saved."

"What do you want from me?" she asked, perhaps too harshly.

"You mentioned something during the interview, something I found deeply interesting."

"You'll have to be more specific. I can't claim to remember much about that interview."

"You mentioned seeing a strange fellow—someone who seemed dangerously suspicious—but then he vanished. What I want to know is: What happened when he vanished?"

Annabelle looked thoughtful for a moment. "If I recall correctly, the storm began about five minutes after I lost sight of him."

"I see." McClain did his best to mask his alarm.

"So, you're searching for clues, are you?"

"Just a matter of curiosity, that's all," he said, trying to remain casual. But McClain had strong suspicions about this mystery guest, the "wedding crasher," as he'd come to be known. Could he have been that powerful demon, the one McClain had been commissioned to conquer?

"You should know," said Annabelle, "I'm quite sure that mysterious and sinister man is the one responsible for sinking the ship."

"Why would I believe you?"

"Father, the prophecy was spoken from your lips."

"But the prophecy didn't reveal the tragedy in detail."

"Hmm, I wonder why?" Annabelle muttered.

Father McClain redirected the conversation. "Have you decided to which church you will share your testimony?"

"Come again?"

"Would you consider giving your testimony at Salisbury Cathedral, on my *Hour of Power* telecast?"

She rolled her eyes. "I'll think about it."

Chapter 22

McClain stepped to the podium after the choir finished their hymn. Not only was he feeling spiritually fulfilled, but a heavy dose of excitement stirred inside of him. This morning's worship service was destined to become the most historic event his church had ever celebrated. In minutes, a change in protocol would occur when he surprised his mega-congregation by inviting Annabelle Smithson to the altar. Despite her initial reaction to his offer, she had eventually accepted his request, and quite graciously.

On this fateful Sunday morning, the congregation would buzz with excitement when Annabelle unveiled the mystery that had set off the devastating chain of events that ended in tragedy. With her testimony, Annabelle would shock the world by finally revealing how she survived the *St. Gordon* disaster. At her own risk, she would unearth the secret that had held her captive in a world inhabited by dark angels.

"Greetings to you, children of God," said the priest after a moment of silent meditation. "This morning, there will be a shift in the usual protocol. I am proud and humbled to announce that we have a very special guest in our midst. By virtue of divine ordinance, she is a woman of God—saved and sanctified. Without further ado, I hereby suspend my sermon so that she may share her testimony, her miraculous life-changing story.

"My brothers and sisters, please help me welcome with open arms, with the love of God, Ms. Annabelle Smithson."

The congregation came to life, giving Annabelle a

rousing standing ovation.

Annabelle tentatively rose up from a reserved pew at the front and waddled to the podium.

"Thank you," she said. "Thank you very much." Annabelle smiled shyly, overwhelmed by the congregation's warm welcome. As she stood at the front of the church, flashbacks of those dark months spent in captivity surfaced in her memory. "I don't really know where to begin." she said as the applause subsided. "I must confess that it took a great deal of faith for me to revisit the house of God. Because of this, I want to express how grateful I am for the invitation to speak, and the spirit of love and support you've shown in welcoming me so warmly." She paused for a moment, pondering. "My testimony begins with a long story, and with the belief that, behind every calamity, there are explanations and reasons to consider. Coming through dangerous circumstances has taught me a life lesson which I will never forget. A writer once said, 'Experience is a great teacher.' I've come to realize that saying is quite true."

Annabelle paused again. She struggled to put into words this complicated story, trying to recall the exact incident from which all the other events had erupted—from the second the horrific storm had battered the ship, to her death, to her experiences in the dark world beneath. She drew a deep breath and began. "When I first spotted the unwelcome guest that night, I thought he was an angel. I was convinced that my prayer had been answered. However, after he seemingly vanished into thin air, my senses told me otherwise—that there was something treacherous about this stranger, perhaps even deadly." Her eyes started to fill, but she blinked back the tears. The congregation sat in silence, clearly mesmerized by her presence.

From his podium on the other side of the altar, Father

McClain spoke up. "How did you know?" he asked.

Annabelle remained silent. The question embarrassed her. How could she explain that she simply knew, that it was instinct and nothing more?

The priest continued, "You mentioned to me that at the instant of death, you felt as though you had been resurrected and placed into a horrible dream, that you found yourself wandering in an unknown domain ruled by the Devil."

"Yes," she exclaimed. "Exactly."

Right then, Annabelle's memory flashed back to that dreadful moment when she had arisen strangely from the bare ground and discovered she was still alive. By then, it was midafternoon. But the sun had disappeared, and partial darkness had set in.

"Tell the congregation what you told me last night, during our telephone conversation."

"I entered through an old, rusty gate, and though I seemingly walked alone, it was not of my own will. I felt an invisible force pulling me in." Annabelle remembered back to when the demon spirit had ushered her into a huge temple. "The demon was the most frightening creature I had ever laid eyes on. Its body, although human-like, was like that of a monster, and the head was of a bird. It spoke in the voice of a full-grown man. It led me to the middle of the center aisle and vanished." Annabelle's eyes darted nervously around the sanctuary. "I had arrived in the middle of a dark ritual, a satanic one, I believe. A congregated mass of demon spirits, dressed in black gowns, chanted quietly on their knees with their heads bowed. When I looked before me, I saw a throne in the center aisle upon a raised platform, about four feet from the floor. Over the throne, a gruesome-looking dragon hovered, with a cluster of serpents' heads furiously waving from its neck."

Annabelle paused and grimaced. It was as if she were

reliving this dark time. She swallowed hard. "Suddenly, lightning struck. Fire blasted from tombs, setting the dragon ablaze and burning it to ashes. Seconds later, the Devil resurrected out of the ashes, taking the form of an angel, and sat on a throne."

Father McClain interjected again. "What came into your mind at this moment, after you realized you'd wound up in a place of devil worship?"

"At this point," Annabelle replied, "it dawned on me that the dark ritual I was witnessing was related to the source of power used to sink the ship."

McClain drew a breath. "I know this must be difficult for you, but, for the benefit of the congregation and the millions around the world watching, can you tell us the reason this dark shadow was cast upon you?"

"Yes, I can," she answered, swallowing thickly. "I believe it is because . . . I'm carrying Satan's unborn child."

A collection of horrified gasps escaped from the congregation.

Annabelle pressed on as the murmurs of the crowd grew. "Satan has made it clear that he will do everything he can to possess my child's soul."

Chapter 23

On Wednesday, July 19, at 11:55 p.m., Annabelle gave birth to a beautiful baby girl—a child destined to reign as the dark princess. Father McClain, Susan, and Annabelle's doctor, along with two midwives, remained by her bedside. They all looked on in amazement as Annabelle cradled her newborn daughter.

The joy of the child's birth made Annabelle quickly forget about her painful dilemma. The dark secret surrounding the birth of the baby, which had haunted her continuously, vanished. She felt restored, her sanity regained. From this point on, Annabelle was determined to make a dramatic turnaround. How wonderful it was, this abundant joy of having a child that, just like that, could conquer the torment of this seemingly never-ending nightmare that had raged deep within her for years.

An hour after her daughter was born, a young nurse rolled the infant cart into the room. Father McClain and Susan had left the hospital. The nurse explained that she was transporting the baby to the nursery so that Annabelle could get some sleep. Annabelle was reluctant to let go of her baby, but the nurse was insistent. Tenderly, the nurse reached for the baby and laid the newborn in the cart. Annabelle gazed at her daughter for a long moment before the nurse quietly wheeled the infant away.

A feeling of dread washed over Annabelle as she watched her daughter disappear around the doorway. Lying back on the pillow, she thought about the events that had taken place just twenty-four hours earlier, when she had finally broken her oath of secrecy. There was simply no way of knowing if she had done the right thing—if breaking the oath would restore her life or if her actions had risked her eternal damnation. Whatever the aftermath of her public confession, she knew one thing for sure: it had triggered the consequences she had coming, good or bad.

~~~

Father McClain startled awake at two a.m. to the sound of the phone ringing. He reached for it without hesitation, remembering that Annabelle had named him as an emergency contact. "This is Father McClain," he answered groggily.

"Yes, Father, this is Dr. Charles Bass, from Scott Memorial Hospital."

"Yes, of course, Dr. Bass," McClain replied, sitting up in bed. "How may I help you?"

"Father, I'm terribly sorry to disturb you so early, but you were listed as an emergency contact for Ms. Annabelle Smithson, and . . ." The doctor hesitated.

The priest swung his legs over the side of the bed and stood. "Yes, of course. What can I do for you?"

"Well, I'm afraid I have some bad news."

"Oh?" His heart skipped a beat. "What is it, Doctor?"

"I'm very sorry to have to tell you this, Father, but Ms. Smithson has passed away."

"What?" he exclaimed, incredulous. "But how is that possible? I just left her a few hours ago. She was fine— stable. She had a perfect delivery. For heaven's sake, how did she die?"

"I'm sorry, but at this point we haven't any clue. We haven't been able to find an immediate cause. To be quite frank with you, I've never encountered more curious or mysterious circumstances."

The doctor's response gave McClain pause. He stood beside the bed, dumfounded, the receiver hitched to his ear.

"Father McClain?" Dr. Bass called out. "Father, are you still there?"

"I'm here," he said, barely registering Dr. Bass's words. "Thank you for calling." His arm went limp, and the phone fell to the bedroom floor. Father McClain's heart raced wildly. He tried to come to grips with what he instinctively knew was the reason for Annabelle's sudden death. He staggered back to the bed and sat, allowing grief to wash over him.

Before long, the grief was replaced by guilt. He understood all too well how he had contributed to Annabelle's death. He had, after all, persuaded her to break her oath of secrecy. Perhaps she would still be alive if he hadn't been so insistent that she share her story with the world. He had truly believed that God, through his divine protection, would shield her from death.

McClain hung his head in shame and wept for Annabelle, who had unwittingly—innocently—become a pawn in the Devil's game, only to be exploited by someone she should have been able to trust.

Chapter 24

"McClain," an enraged Cardinal McCartney shouted, storming through the doors of Salisbury Cathedral. "If I was God, I'd release my wrath on you and make you regret the day you chose to go beyond being a servant of God and tried to step into his shoes altogether."

McClain looked up from reading his Bible, his eyes widening in shock. "I've done nothing to deserve this harsh rebuke."

"I warned you, McClain," the cardinal continued, jabbing his finger into the priest's face. "Now look at the misfortune you've caused. That woman would be alive right now if you hadn't pressured her to unveil her devilish secret—a secret that had nothing to do with anything, for that matter."

"You sound worse than a pagan, Cardinal," McClain lashed out. "How could you be so naïve?"

Cardinal McCartney stared at him, his eyes narrowing. "Naïve?"

"Yes."

The cardinal backed up and eyed the priest skeptically. "What is this dark secret—this 'oath of secrecy' that bound this poor woman to the despicable demands of Satan?"

"Calm down and just listen for a minute." McClain paused. "Do you really want to know?"

"Don't you think I deserve to know," the cardinal replied, "seeing as it took the soul of an innocent victim?"

McClain sighed heavily and looked at his colleague. "Annabelle Smithson told me that Satan had transplanted an enormous amount of evil power into the infant while the baby was still an embryo. Look, maybe it was a mistake, but her death—"

"Mistake?" Cardinal McCartney said. "Is that what you're calling it? It's a damned travesty, Father. And you're to blame."

"I thought, and you know this as well, that when it comes to the battle between good and evil, angels and demons, the Devil's greatest stronghold is to keep his prey in bondage."

The cardinal looked at him, confused. "What are you saying?"

"It may interest you to know that this dark secret played out as Satan's ultimate weapon," McClain explained. "He managed to lure her into bondage through this ordeal, and then he threatened her—under oath—to conceal what she knew. And if she was to break this covenant, her death would be imminent. He fears that if his dark secret is exposed, his enemy could then win the fight."

"Well, his dark secret's been exposed, but at what cost?" the cardinal said. "An innocent woman is dead."

"Understand this, Cardinal. I did everything in my power to protect her. Moreover, you must understand that it is now my life that is at stake here, not yours. I am the one who has been summoned to foster that child. Don't you think that I need to have as much knowledge as possible about this child who will rise to become a great threat to the kingdom of God?"

"What became of the prophetic vision?" the cardinal asked sternly. "Didn't it already reveal everything you needed to know?"

"Obviously, you don't understand just how big of a threat the dark princess is," the priest replied. "And in answer to your question, no, the vision did not afford me every single detail, and I feel compelled to learn everything

I can so that I will be able to carry forth God's purpose for me."

"And you thought that by persuading Annabelle Smithson to break her oath of secrecy to the Devil himself, you would find a clue?"

The priest stared at the cardinal. "Yes, that's exactly it."

"I'm deeply disappointed in you, Father McClain," the cardinal said disdainfully. "Look, you need to read the writing on the wall. Are you now convinced that the dark princess is a powerful adversary?"

McClain stepped closer to his colleague until they were practically nose to nose. "In case you hadn't noticed, Cardinal, the adversary in question is an enemy God has commissioned me to pursue. How am I to pursue someone—or something—before I have all the facts?"

Cardinal McCartney stared at McClain in disgust before storming out of the church.

Chapter 25

A week after her daughter was laid to rest, Susan moved into Annabelle's home, having taken custody of baby Tabitha. She missed Annabelle terribly, but was grateful for the privilege of raising her granddaughter.

The following day, bright and early on a Tuesday morning, Father McClain paid her a surprise visit.

"I thought you were a late sleeper, Father," said Susan as she welcomed him at the door.

"I hope I didn't wake you," McClain replied.

"No, no," she replied, smiling. "Please, come in."

McClain stepped into the foyer. "Thank you."

"I've been up since five o'clock," Susan said as she shut the door. "There isn't much sleep to be had when there's a newborn in the house."

The priest nodded. "Of course. I should have thought of that."

Susan ushered the priest into the living room. "I have to admit, it's even harder when you haven't taken care of a little one in over thirty years."

"I can imagine."

"Make yourself at home. I need to finish up preparing the baby's bottle in the kitchen."

"How is the baby?" the priest asked.

Something in the priest's tone alerted Susan's concern. "Very well, thank you," she replied over her shoulder as she walked back to the kitchen.

McClain sat quietly on the loveseat, his usual place when he came to visit. He gazed at the portrait of Annabelle on the wall, and her photograph sent memories cascading through his mind. In the short time they'd had to get to know each other, he had developed a deep bond with her. He realized that he missed her company most of all.

Susan returned to the living room, interrupting his reverie. She sat down on the couch directly across from the loveseat. "Annabelle told me you made breakfast for her every morning."

"Yes, absolutely."

"You are a true servant of God, Father."

"Thank you. I do try to be."

Mrs. Smithson nodded, her expression thoughtful. "No wonder you're here so early. You must be accustomed to your breakfast routine. I appreciate the visit, Father, but now that Annabelle is no longer with us, you certainly don't have to—"

"No," he interrupted, and realized he'd spoken perhaps too harshly. He exhaled and mustered a tight-lipped smile. "I came to check on the baby."

Susan's earlier discomfort surfaced again. "You seem to have a special interest in this child."

"Does it bother you?" he asked.

Yes, it does, only I'm not sure why. "I didn't say that."

"I am simply fulfilling the duty that God has entrusted me with."

Susan regarded him quizzically. "And what if I had been asleep?"

"But you weren't asleep," he said, smiling in a way that made her skin crawl.

"You're ignoring the point."

"Not at all. You're telling me that it's not right that I should stop in to see the baby so early in the day, no?"

"Well, yes, but—"

The priest locked eyes with her, sending a chill up Susan's spine. "Ms. Smithson, do you have any idea of the dark mystery hovering over this child? I hate to be the bearer of bad news, but trust me, it's for your own good. You have not been anointed to parent Tabitha."

"With all due respect, Father, what are you talking about? I am Tabitha's grandmother—her only family, for God's sake."

"That baby is as important to me as my ministry."

"Wait a minute," Susan said, her eyes narrowing. "Are you suggesting that your aim is to father my granddaughter?"

The priest hesitated. "Let's just say there's more to it than simply fathering the child." He straightened. "I'm here to make clear that God has given me a task, and I am bound to carry it through."

Susan frowned. Her anger was reaching a boiling point. She rose silently and walked to the window. "And just what do you think gives you legal rights over my grandchild?"

"If you care about the well-being of this world and all the people in it, you would allow me to do what I'm trying to do, which is to save us all from plunging into the depths of Hell."

Susan spun on her heel, incredulous. "Are you some kind of crazy person, Father?"

"I am not," he replied, indignant. "I was divinely commissioned by God to foster this child"—he hesitated—"well before her mother even conceived."

"Father McClain, you are insane," Susan screamed, unable to contain her rage. "If there is a God, he wouldn't rip a child from the only family she has."

~~~

One week later
Susan laid baby Tabitha gently in her crib. For a long moment, she stared at the baby, who slept ever so sweetly as the afternoon sun streamed through the nursery window. As Susan stood over the crib, lovingly gazing at her

granddaughter, a dark shadow crossed Tabitha's face.

Susan glanced toward the window to find that the sun had disappeared behind a cluster of dark, ominous clouds. A grave darkness engulfed the mansion.

She gaped at the spectacle outside the window. There was something decidedly sinister about this sudden change in the weather. Susan sensed the distinct presence of evil looming in the house. As darkness set in, an acute sense of dread came over her.

Could she be dreaming? Was this some kind of nightmare? But it seemed so real. She stared out the window in disbelief as the lake, just a short distance from the back yard, disappeared from view. The rose garden vanished as well, making room for the creepy forest that materialized in its place.

Susan trembled as hissing noises emanated from the forest, as if from a brood of serpents. The hissing grew louder as a band of revolting monsters sprang out of the forest, followed closely by another group seconds later. Susan backed away from the window in terror as the creatures made their way toward the mansion, surging forward like blood-thirsty vampires. She rushed to the crib to gather up the baby, only to find that the crib was empty. Susan's eyes darted around the room, frantically searching for her granddaughter, as a group of monsters slammed into the bedroom window. Susan screamed and fled the room.

Once out of the nursery, Susan found that the house was no longer familiar. She raced down a flight of rickety old stairs and dashed across a living room that looked as though it belonged in a two-hundred-year-old haunted house in the woods, long since abandoned. She felt the floor give beneath her feet and looked down just as the rotten wood gave way, pulling her down into the basement. She landed on her back with a thud, barely conscious.

The furious howling of monsters reawakened Susan's

senses, but she lay helpless and broken on the floor. Her eyes darted around the room fearfully. Everything had happened so fast. Unable to move, Susan was convinced that death was near. She stared at the remains of the ceiling, with its rotting beams and thick, dangling spider webs. Suddenly, the creatures stormed in on her from the rusty windows and shattered walls, swooping in violently and hovering above her.

Susan screamed as loud as she could, but she barely heard herself above the ear-splitting cries of the repulsive creatures. She could only watch in horror as the creatures used their claws to rip off her clothes and tear into her flesh. As her blood spewed onto their faces, Susan heard herself scream again before everything went black.

When Susan drifted back into consciousness, she found herself in bed. She jumped up and rushed to the bathroom. She switched on the light and approached the mirror, her eyes filling with terror. Her pajamas were drenched with blood. She lifted her top to find deep grooves and bruises all over her torso.

Panic consumed her. She hurried from the bathroom and ran to the baby's room, her heart pounding. She approached the crib, looked down, and exhaled in relief. There lay Tabitha, sleeping soundly, unharmed.

At 3:30 a.m. Susan lay on the floor of the baby's room, staring at the ceiling and refusing to return to sleep. She willed herself to stay awake despite her exhaustion, for fear of resuming the horrible nightmare. She told herself it was only a bad dream brought on by lack of sleep. After all, taking care of a newborn was not the job of a woman in her fifties. But she wasn't entirely convinced the events had taken place only in her mind.

Susan stood, checked on the baby again, and reluctantly walked away from the crib. She squatted fearfully in a corner of the room and quietly began to weep.

Chapter 26

Eleanor Griffins dropped her brushes into a bucket, as usual, at exactly six o'clock in the morning. She gathered tubes of acrylic, and her sketch pad, and locked them up in the storage cabinet. Her night's work had been pleasant, but long—a tough and fulfilling seven hours. She had started and finished a new painting of a terrifying prophecy.

Eleanor had recently converted the basement of her five-bedroom house to an art studio, a place to work and display her work. The walls held many of her most sacred paintings, ones that foretold treacherous events.

She slipped off her paint-speckled apron, hung it on the inside of the closet door, and stepped to the sink to wash the paint residue from her hands. Eleanor affixed her latest canvas on the wall next to the others, and headed upstairs. In the kitchen, she prepared her usual cup of tea—a post-work ritual to which she had grown accustomed years ago.

As she stood at the sink, filling the kettle, Eleanor was startled to see a car pulling into her driveway. *A visitor, at this hour?* She turned off the tap, set the kettle on the counter, and headed for the door just as the visitor pressed the buzzer.

She pulled open the door, and her eyes widened in shock. A haggard and barefoot Susan Smithson stood on her doorstep beside a carriage that held a very young baby. For several moments, Eleanor simply stared, speechless, taking in Susan's alarmingly disheveled presence: sunken eyes, dirty dress, greasy hair. Susan's appearance gave the prophetess pause. This was not the woman she had met a few months ago.

"Mrs. Smithson, is there something I can do for you?"

"Yes," Susan replied flatly.

Eleanor stepped aside. "Please, come in."

Susan stepped inside, pushing the carriage in front of her.

"It's a long drive out here from your place," said Eleanor. "It must be something awfully important. Please, have a seat, make yourself comfortable."

"Thank you," Susan replied, her voice barely audible.

"I must say I'm surprised. I don't get visitors out here very often, much less before dawn."

Susan smiled, seemingly embarrassed. "I wanted to apologize for being so rude to you all those months ago."

Eleanor shrugged. "Oh, please, I completely understand," she offered sincerely. "A prophet is not welcome in his hometown." She paused, smiling. "It's a high price to pay for my calling, but I'm used to it."

"I feel so ashamed . . ."

"Why?"

"You were right," Susan confessed. "I was so immersed in my own pain and guilt, I wasn't listening to the voice of God."

"The spirit of God is always right. Remember that," said the prophetess. "So, tell me, why are you here now?"

"It's hard to explain."

"Something's happened?"

"Yes," Susan replied, bursting into tears. "With such divine instincts, you must know why I am here."

Eleanor smiled knowingly. "Perhaps. I might have an idea, a hint."

"Last night, I was viciously attacked . . . by a nightmare."

"Tell me everything that happened."

"Well, at first I just thought it was a dream, and I suppose it was, really, but when I woke up, the wounds were real—scratches, bruises, blood."

"Did anything unusual or odd happen prior to the dream?"

"No," Susan replied. "Not that I can think of."

Eleanor eyed Susan's pitiful state, noting the fear in her eyes. "So what is it, exactly, that you want from me? What are you hoping to find out?"

"I was hoping," Susan said, choking on a sob, "hoping you could help me figure out what really happened. Was it a dream, or real, or . . ." Susan bowed her head and dabbed her tears with her sleeve.

Eleanor reached for a tissue and lifted Susan's chin. "Susan, I don't wish to scare you," she said, dabbing at the wretched woman's tears. "But I believe the nightmare was a warning." She sighed. "You're lucky to be alive." She looked down at the baby, sleeping peacefully in her carriage. "And Susan?"

"Yes?"

"If it were me, I wouldn't keep that child another day."

Susan drew back, horrified by Ms. Griffins' advice. "What is that supposed to mean?"

"It means you shouldn't be mothering this child," the prophetess warned. "You were never intended for the role. Nor was your daughter, for that matter."

Susan's fury mounted. "You can't be serious."

"Do you even know who this baby is?"

"Of course," Susan cried. "She's my grandbaby, and she's all I have." Susan did her best to calm down. "So, that's your advice? Just abandon her?"

"I'm not saying you have to abandon her, Susan, but I do believe there is likely someone more suitable to look after the specific needs of this child."

Susan placed her head in her hands. "What am I missing here?"

"You aren't missing anything, but rather refusing to see

what's in front of your face—spiritually speaking."

Susan pondered Eleanor's words for a long moment. "Perhaps you're right," she admitted. "But there are certain things that are simply inconceivable."

Eleanor smiled sympathetically. "Why do you insist that this baby is meant for you to raise?"

Susan looked at her, incredulous. "Give me one good reason, in the name of God, why I should forfeit my rights as guardian over my own grandchild?"

"Oh Susan, I shouldn't have to tell you," Eleanor replied. "The reasons are all around you, even as we speak."

"Oh yeah? Tell me, where are these reasons? Because I'm clearly not seeing them."

The prophetess looked at the baby and back to Susan. "What does God have to do to open your eyes to the dark angels surrounding this child?"

"Both her biological parents are dead, for Christ's sake." A fresh stream of tears ran down Susan's face as she stared lovingly at Tabitha. "She needs me."

Eleanor shook her head. "No, and I suspect that I'm not the first one to tell you this."

Susan sobbed, her anguish threatening to swallow her whole. "It's not fair."

"Fair?" the prophetess repeated. She rose from the sofa and looked down at Susan. "You wanted my advice. If you are unwilling to take it, then ask yourself: Are you willing to drink from the cup of tribulation? Because, for as long as this child remains in your possession, that will be the sum total of your life."

Susan quieted and looked away. The prophetess, realizing her question had fallen on deaf ears, leaned over into Susan's face and asked one last question. "Are you willing to pay the ultimate price for custody of your grandchild?"

BOOK THREE
The Dark Moon Banquet

Chapter 27

First Vamps' meeting, 1:00 a.m.

It was warm for the hour, even for summertime, as the old, beat-up school bus cruised down the secluded M466 highway. On board was an elite group of loyal occultists from the secret society known as The Vamps of the Knights of Beelzebub—or known more simply as The Vamp Society.

In the pitch black of early morning, the bus rolled to a stop in front of an enormous, two-sided steel gate at the highway's abrupt end. On the side of the gate, a warning sign had been posted:

DANGER ZONE
DO NOT ENTER

The gates opened automatically, and the bus traveled through, slowly making its way down the single-lane gravel road, heading deep into a dense forest. The dusty road, about a mile and a half long, ended at a hidden lake.

The lake itself looked to be about a quarter of a mile wide, and in the middle of the water stood a brick mansion. Atop the mansion's vast roof was a monstrous sculpture of a seven-headed beast ridden by a woman adorned in a scarlet robe.

The Vamps, dressed in black cloaks, disembarked the bus and lined up along the edge of the lake, facing the front entrance of the mansion. Together they gazed upon the image of the beast, looking on in allegiance at the sculpture erected in honor of their Grand Master, Satanist Paul Hart.

They chanted to the statue, a ritual performed every time they arrived here at this secret domain, in order for each to retain the power to magically enter the mansion. A powerful wind swept up around them and, one by one, each man shape-shifted into a giant bird, soared over the lake, and dove into the mansion's foyer. Inside, their human bodies returned as they proceeded into the main chamber.

The windowless chamber was lit with hanging torches which illuminated the engraved images of monstrous dragons on the walls. Each man took his seat on a stool along the customized half-circle concrete bar built in the center of the room.

Paul Hart swooped in, seemingly out of nowhere, making a lightning-fast landing on the opposite side of the bar. For a moment, he quietly paced the floor, arms folded, as the Vamps looked on questioningly. No one dared speak up, for each could plainly see the rage in their leader's eyes. His expression oozed vengeance, and his jaw muscles twitched.

The Vamps looked up in alarm as the ceiling began to rattle. Seconds later, a muscular hawk swooped low into the room and landed, taking the empty seat at the end of the table.

"Vamps of the Knights of Beelzebub," Hart announced. "I'd like to introduce you to Dorcas, a stranger to this body, this covenant, but not a stranger to this kingdom. I will unveil her mission in due time."He cleared his throat. "We are gathered here tonight because the kingdom has, once again, come under the fire of an adversary."

The Vamps regarded each other questioningly. "Adversary?" one of them called out.

"Yes," Hart replied. "A man who wishes to alter the destiny of this kingdom by unlawfully taking custody of the baby dark princess. I do not intend for him to get away with it, of course. Not this time around."

"Did you say dark princess?" asked a bald, middle-aged Vamp seated to the left of Dorcas.

Hart leaned over and spoke into the Vamp's face. "The infant is twelve weeks old today, Zachaeus. Do you know what that means? Twelve weeks of her destiny and power have been flushed down the drain. Bear in mind, the fate of the dispensation lies in the power bestowed upon that baby." Hart paused thoughtfully. For several seconds he pondered in silence, and then continued. "The child belongs here, with us, under this roof. This is where she ought to be reared and groomed, in order to inherit the throne."

"Who is this enemy?" another Vamp, Zodiac, asked cautiously.

Hart grinned malevolently. "Father John McClain, a name familiar to everyone in this room. By some means, McClain managed to snatch the child and has deemed himself her foster father. The job was made easy for the man, being that her parents are dead." He took a long, deep breath. "She must be redeemed," he shouted, "as quickly as possible."

"How did the priest acquire custody of the child in the first place?" asked Berekiah.

"That's not important," snapped Hart.

"What if we just kidnap her?" Dagon suggested. "Shouldn't be that difficult."

Hart regarded Dagon sternly. "If kidnapping her was an alternative, don't you think she'd already be living under this roof?"

Iuvart spoke up. "Sounds to me like Father McClain needs to be eliminated before we can redeem the child, no?"

Hart nodded. "Correct. But the job is not as easy as it sounds. This religious fanatic didn't just conquer our powerful beast, he destroyed the creature completely. Now ask yourselves: Where does this mere mortal get his power?"

"Every conqueror has a secret which he uses to slay his conquests," Nevi replied. "Let us find out what McClain's secret is."

Hart smiled his sinister smile. "Ah, from the mouths of fallen angels," he said. But thoughts of Father McClain's custody of the baby cast a dark shadow upon Paul Hart, breeding a fear unlike any other he had known. Imagine if you were thrown into a cage with a rattlesnake. How would you tame the poisonous viper to escape being bitten?

~~~

A new revelation had surfaced. The Gnostic knowledge unveiled that the Devil's arrival in the earthly realm was swiftly approaching. His kingdom was on the brink of collapse, and he was well aware of it. For this precise reason, the Devil had shifted much of his power to his then unborn child, who, in turn, would grow up to succeed him.

As a result, the priest's life was now at stake.

Tabitha was now four months old, and disturbing thoughts nagged at Father McClain. Imagine raising a child, knowing the baby will grow up and turn into a powerful beast. Imagine that this child will one day emerge as the dark princess and rise to threaten the world and the church, in particular. Imagine the danger you would encounter if her evil power was unleashed at age seventeen. What would be the repercussions if she discovered that you are her prime adversary—indeed, a threat to her destiny?

McClain remained constantly on alert, always preparing for the worst. He couldn't think of anything more dangerous—or more terrifying—than evil emerging when one least expected it. He reminded himself that God was in control; He had a perfect plan. God had commissioned him to bond with this child. Soon, Father McClain will discover, deepening a relationship with her, will reveal the Adversary in question.

Chapter 28

1:00 a.m., Tuesday

In the Lost Room, Satanist Paul Hart and his host of Vamps chanted fervently for ten minutes and quieted. As a hush fell over the group, McClain's castle—sitting high on a hill overlooking the Arun River—appeared in the mirror located in the center of the room. They scanned the panoramic view of the castle's courtyard in silence before the image shifted to the Fitz Land Chapel.

"If the secret of McClain's power is buried in this little church," Hart explained, "it makes our job infinitely more difficult. Remember, we still don't know the exact origin of this man's power, nor do we know just how much power he has."

"What has this got to do with kidnapping the baby?" asked Berekiah.

Hart turned to the Vamp, is eyes narrowing. "It appears you haven't been paying attention, Berekiah," he scolded. "Who here ever talked about kidnapping the child? You can't kidnap a child that already belongs here."

~~~

Father McClain looked around and realized he was strapped to his bed. But his surroundings did not resemble his master bedroom. He jumped as a strong wind blew open the curtain on the window just beyond the foot of the bed to reveal the face of a man staring at him from outside. Moments later, another face, exactly the same as the first, materialized beside the stranger. Then a third face, identical to the other two, appeared in the window, followed by a fourth. Terrified, McClain awoke suddenly, his breath coming hard and fast. It was only a nightmare.

After taking a moment to regain his composure, McClain scrambled from the bed and dashed to the chapel, where he knelt before the altar in prayer. Although he struggled to interpret what the exact details meant, he detected a distinct malevolent presence in the nightmare, and sensed that the Devil's minions were on the brink of waging a war against him. For the sake of the child, he must call down for divine intervention. The power was his for the taking; all he need do was pray.

~~~

One by one, each of the vamps pressed their backs against the mirror and, by virtue of their power, vanished through the glass. Seconds later, they shape-shifted into a band of flying werewolves and took to the sky on wings like sharks swimming in water. Within minutes, they circled above their target—the premises of McClain's castle. The werewolves had made the trip, which was a two-hour journey by car, in less than five minutes.

~~~

McClain's eyes popped wide open, and he stared heavenward in fury, causing a thunderous gust of wind to blast from the walls of the chapel and into the sky. By the time the werewolves felt the violent intrusion, the clouds had scrolled open, letting through a powerful beam of light from a seemingly endless void, trapping them all as they hovered above.

Stunned, the creatures looked up to find a small troop of angelic soldiers circling in the air above them. The angels sat atop white, winged horses, their swords glinting as they pointed the weapons at the werewolves.

The monsters shrieked in fury as the twelve angels descended upon them, causing a violent clash between the two armies. The first angel to enter the mayhem managed to run his sword into the belly of a werewolf, sending the creature up in flames, his ashes blowing away on the wind.

Another angel cut off the head of an enemy who charged him. The werewolf burst into flame and plummeted toward the river below. Before the fire could destroy him completely, the creature shape-shifted into the body of a man and escaped on foot. But the angel pursued him on his flying horse, catching up with him as he ran along the banks of the rushing river. The angel plunged his sword into the creature's back, setting a fire inside his belly. Within seconds, only ashes remained.

A werewolf fell through the ceiling of a nearby house and landed on an antique table, splitting it in two. The creature writhed on the floor, shrieking in pain as his body transformed back into that of a man. Having managed to flee from the heat of the fight, Satanist Paul Hart scrambled to his feet, his hair still ablaze. He raced from the room and into the nearby bathroom, where he submerged his head in the toilet bowl, dousing the fire. To his horror and disbelief, his entire scalp was burned.

With his face contorted in pain, he yanked a towel from the towel bar and dabbed at the searing lesions on his skin. His entire head throbbed as he examined what looked to be third-degree burns, scars he would likely carry forever.

~~~

Bright and early the next morning, McClain peeked through the window of his study. Something strange immediately captured his attention. Down the street, in the distance, a crowd loitered along the river. His stomach lurched. While he didn't know exactly what had transpired, he was sure it had something to do with his disturbing nightmare. He rushed from the house and toward the riverbank.

The priest made his way through the throng of onlookers, only to back away once he'd reached the scene.

His heart raced, and he struggled for breath. Ashes and smoke belched from the river, the foul smell of burnt flesh polluting the air.

Tabitha's nanny greeted him when he returned to the castle grounds. "Good morning, Father."

"Good morning, Sarah," he replied soberly as he passed her on the way to his study. He paused. "Sarah, could I have a word with you?"

"Of course."

He ushered her into his study and closed the door quietly behind him. He motioned for the nanny to have a seat in the chair opposite his desk. "What's your agenda like today?"

"Tabitha has an eleven o'clock appointment with her pediatrician, Dr. Caldwell."

"And after that?"

"I was thinking of taking her for a stroll in the park."

McClain shook his head. "No, don't," he warned sternly. "Apart from doctor visits, I want you to keep the baby indoors at all times. Do I make myself clear?"

"Yes, perfectly," Sarah replied, taken aback. "Is that all, sir?"

"There's one more thing. How are you doing? With your duties, I mean."

"Perfectly well, sir," she said tentatively. "Are there concerns?"

He pondered for a moment. "Forgive my memory, but you've been Tabitha's nanny for how many months now?"

Sarah straightened. "Four months and two weeks," she replied confidently.

"Yes, of course. Have you, at any point during that time, encountered anything strange while living here and taking care of the child? Scary dreams? Night terrors? Anything of that nature?"

The nanny raised an eyebrow. After a long pause, she shook her head. "Not that I can recall. May I inquire as to why you're asking me this?"

"Oh, I don't know. I've just been bombarded with some very strange feelings lately, that's all."

"Strange feelings? About what, exactly?"

He realized his cryptic words were causing confusion. "Look, Sarah, I'm bringing this to your attention because I'm concerned for your safety."

She looked puzzled. "I'm sorry, Father, but I'm not sure I'm following you. Tabitha has been a perfect baby, and I love taking care of her very much."

He was obviously failing to get through to the woman. Somehow she had managed to steer clear of any unusual activity, and it was up to him to come clean and explain the situation. "You mean all this time here, you haven't come across anything upsetting, or . . ." He hesitated, clasping his hands under his chin. "Sinister?"

Sarah looked into the priest's eyes and tilted her head. "Is there something I should know?"

The priest exhaled. "Maybe, maybe not. You see, recently, I uncovered that the ghost that sank Tabitha's parents' ship has unleashed himself. He is out to abduct the child." He paused, locking eyes with the nanny. "I fear you could wind up in the middle of the ordeal."

Chapter 29

Cardinal McCartney marched into the castle's conference room and sat politely at the table. A couple minutes later, Father McClain walked in and took the seat next to him.

The cardinal spoke first. "I wish to apologize for my outburst some months back," he said. "It was not a very Christian thing to do."

The priest smiled at his longtime colleague. "Your apology is accepted."

McCartney nodded in appreciation. "So, what's this meeting about?" He looked around at the otherwise empty room. "And where are the other members of the clergy?"

"Actually, I scheduled the meeting for six o'clock," the priest replied. "I wanted you here an hour early because there's a revelation I need to share with you . . . in private."

"What is it?"

"I was attacked by a nightmare on the night before my neighbors discovered smoke erupting from the Arun River."

The cardinal's expression darkened. "Attacked? By a nightmare?"

"It was him," the priest replied solemnly. "He appeared in my sleep."

"Who?"

"The Devil's right-hand man," McClain replied. "Remember Annabelle's testimony? The stranger she claimed mysteriously boarded the ship?"

McCartney eyed him skeptically. "How could you

possibly have known it was him?"

McClain sighed and sat up in his chair. "Do not forget, Cardinal, that I am profoundly gifted by the spirit." His tone was indignant. "But, if you must know, it was his hair."

A small smile appeared on the cardinal's lips just as the butler swept into the room and whispered in McClain's ear.

~~~

Prophetess Eleanor Griffins sat idle on the rocking chair beside a large stone fireplace in the great hall, waiting to see Father McClain. She stared up in admiration at the eye-catching eighteenth-century accents in the room: human and animal masks carved into the ceiling's support beams.

The priest entered the room and smiled, seemingly relieved to see her. "Thank you for coming on such short notice, Ms. Griffins," he said.

"Servants of God do not delay when they are called," she returned, standing.

He extended his hand. "Father John McClain."

"Prophetess Eleanor Griffins," Eleanor replied, shaking his hand.

"I've heard some very inspiring testimonies about you, Ms. Griffins, about how God has blessed you with the gift of prophecy."

Eleanor nodded. "The visions I've encountered take a strong level of faith to believe and embrace."

"Well, my level of faith has worked wonders during the past several years. I reversed a tsunami bound to level this great country of ours. Indeed, we stand here today because of my unrelenting faith."

"I'm grateful to you," she said. "But not all situations are the same, Father."

"I agree. I sense that, every morning when the sun rises, you hear the voice of God, whispering on the air."

"Quite clearly I hear him, yes."

He smiled at her. "I was just in the middle of a private meeting with Cardinal McCartney," he said. "Do you care to join us?"

Eleanor shook her head. "I'm sorry, I can't. I only have a few minutes today. What about breakfast tomorrow morning?"

McClain looked down and thought for a moment. "What time?" he asked, lifting his head.

"Well, I usually go to bed at six thirty in the morning. But for your sake, I can lose a couple hours of sleep."

"Well then, tomorrow morning it is."

"How do you like your eggs?" she asked.

He chuckled. "Scrambled."

"Tea or coffee?"

"Iced tea, if it's not too much trouble."

She gave him a quick nod. "See you at six thirty."

~~~

Paul Hart bandaged his wounds and wearily shuffled out of the bathroom. He took a seat in the living room, tortured by the thought of defeat. Despite the crushing blow, he vowed to continue the fight for the baby dark princess. Perseverance was his only option now.

As he sat in seclusion, Hart strategized a new plan—one well worth considering. His power had failed him terribly. In addition to his own battle scars, he'd lost five Vamps in the clash. He had to figure out a way to carry out the operation without alerting the angelic troops, and recruit more vamps before time ran out.

He thought about McClain's megachurch. His beloved congregation was the apple of his eye. His followers tended to be the weaker vessels. Perhaps if he were to prey on them, he could strip McClain of his power—perhaps even crush his faith.

"Yes," Hart muttered, a smile spreading across his face. "This is a promising plan."

~~~

The following morning, at 6:30 sharp, McClain arrived at Eleanor Griffins' home. After Annabelle died, he had stopped actively pursuing information on his adversary, but he was now looking to resume his search for clues. He hoped that in the prophetess, he had found the means for a deep awakening. He was convinced of her prophetic instinct and insight. He was certain, by virtue of her prophetic visions, that the prophetess would uncover his enemy's identity—an enemy the whole of humanity had to fear.

"Any strange dreams?" Ms. Griffins began, setting a plate of eggs before him. "Nightmares? Since Annabelle . . ."

"Strange dreams?" he repeated. "Not that I can recall. But nightmares? Yes. And they're getting worse, and more frequent."

"It's a never-ending struggle, isn't it?"

"Absolutely."

Ms. Griffins stepped into the kitchen and returned a moment later with his iced tea. "Heaven must surely have found favor in you, Father, allowing you to bond with that baby," she said, setting down the glass next to his plate.

"I beg to differ, Ms. Griffins," he replied, taking a sip. "I do not believe it's any kind of favor."

"Oh? Why is that?" she asked. "Don't you think God has a plan? I mean, you and I both know, He never makes mistakes."

"I know it doesn't make sense for a servant of God—a priest, no less—to question him. But my question is this: Why would God risk my life for such a purpose?"

She shrugged. "Only you can answer that, Father."

"I guess there are a lot of things I still don't understand."

"Ah, yes. The Lord moves in mysterious ways, does he not?" Ms. Griffins smiled. "He rarely reveals things all at once, and this is so we can deepen our faith in him."

McClain nodded.

"Follow me," she said, standing.

When they reached the bottom of the stairs, she flicked on the lights. "Take a look at the real world. Tell me what you think."

McClain stared in awe at the vast array of prophecies gracing the walls around him. Ms. Griffins' gifts extended far beyond being a talented artist or painter. Viewing her inspiring works was unlike any sacred moment he had encountered before.

Ms. Griffins broke the long silence. "I don't normally share these, but I have a strong belief that you play a role in some of them, if you look closely."

He turned his attention to the prophetess. "I feel the very same way, Ms. Griffins."

"If I may be so bold, I'm quite sure the identity of the enemy is among the works on these walls."

"I believe you're right," he said confidently. As he stood among the paintings, one in particular drew his eye, capturing his attention more than any of the others. He stepped closer and studied the painting of a terrifying prophecy about Tabitha.

She looked to be about twenty, and the painting depicted that she'd successfully made her rise to the throne of the dark princess. In the first year of her reign, a fierce battle was being waged against her and her dark kingdom by the eternal forces of light. The painting foretold that Tabitha would launch out of the Atlantic Ocean, riding the back of a monstrous, seven-headed beast, and lead an army of dark angels to a clash with another princess, who had apparently descended from the heavens with her angelic troops to battle the Princess of Darkness.

McClain slowly removed his glasses, growing more and more perplexed. As he examined the painting more closely, he began to notice something even more shocking than the revelation itself. Tabitha, the dark princess, and her rival, the Princess of Heaven, were identical. Indeed, they were twins. Father McClain looked at Ms. Griffins questioningly.

"You look skeptical, Father," she noted. "Is there a problem?"

McClain inhaled deeply. "I'm trying to make sense of this painting."

"You never will. Not by examining it from a human viewpoint, anyway."

"Is there a reason . . ." His voice trailed off. "Is it my imagination?"

"As a prophetess of God, I've learned that it is often difficult for people to believe in prophecies. People have a tendency to go out of their way to prove me a liar."

"Don't get me wrong," he said, looking back at the curious painting. "I don't doubt you or your prophecies, Ms. Griffins. I'm just a bit confused here."

She furrowed her brow. "About what?"

"How is it possible that the Princess of Light perfectly resembles the dark princess—as though they are identical twins?"

"Ah, is that why you are so drawn to that one, Father McClain?"

"Well, not initially, but now I'm not so sure."

"It's all part of the mystery of God. And until that prophecy is fulfilled, the mystery will remain unsolved."

"But it looks as though Tabitha and the Princess of Light are blood-related."

"It doesn't just look like it," the prophetess replied. "They are."

McClain looked at her, deeply puzzled. "How is that possible? I was in the hospital room the night Annabelle gave birth to Tabitha. I, of all people, would know if there had been a twin sister."

"Or perhaps you wouldn't know," Ms. Griffins suggested. "Annabelle did indeed give birth to two children—twin sisters—and two extremely powerful, opposing forces, at that: a child of darkness and a child of light. And between them, a final war will be fought."

"Impossible," he argued. "If that was true, I would know. I would have seen it. And don't you think the signs would have revealed it?"

"Not necessarily."

The priest backed down reluctantly. "So, according to this prophetic vision, Annabelle carried a set of twins?"

"In earthly terms, yes. They are twins. From a spiritual standpoint, however, they are not twins, but enemies."

"Then the Princess of Light is mortal?"

"She is flesh and blood," the prophetess replied, nodding. "She's an earthly being, just like you and me."

"We're talking about a life that cannot possibly exist, Ms. Griffins."

"Oh, she exists. Her being simply hasn't manifested itself into our world yet."

"This doesn't make any sense."

"Well, no. Not until you decipher the revelation behind this strange mystery."

"You must shed some light on this, Prophetess," he demanded. "You must have some clue to understanding this unbelievable revelation."

"I'm sorry, Father McClain, but delving into the core of this prophecy is beyond me."

"You're just being unreasonable," he said, frustrated. "Don't you think, since I'm linked to this prophecy, that I deserve to have some deeper knowledge of it?"

The prophetess sighed in resignation. "Fine. The painting predicts the Red Battle of Armageddon. Armageddon is the dispensation of evil, when the world will be on the verge of being ruled by the young child you are fostering.

"On the contrary, the Princess of Heaven, as you see there, was conceived by way of immaculate conception. Her birth was divinely ordained and empowered by God to annihilate the dark princess and topple her reign."

Chapter 30

Seven years later
Salisbury Cathedral's thirtieth anniversary
Evening service

It was an unusual time for such an event, but nonetheless, Father McClain stood at the entrance of the cathedral's grand lobby, greeting faces and passing out the service bulletins. Congregation members reached for the bulletins as they passed the priest and filed into the sanctuary.

Among the congregation sat Satanist Paul Hart, disguised as a believer. Like an assassin on a secret mission, he sat in a middle pew in one of the center sections. A church service, due to commence at nightfall, seemed like the opportunity he'd been waiting for. Tonight, Hart vowed to terrorize the congregation. Moments from now, he would cast an evil spell and disrupt Father McClain's special service. As for the staff, he planned to turn them into stones. The members of the choir would transform into wild beasts.

For the time being, however, the Satanist kept a close watch on the faces of folks pouring into the church. His eyes roved around the vast sanctuary, monitoring the various service-related activities. His counterpart, the demon Nevi, was expected to join him shortly. With her resilience, Hart was certain that everything he'd plotted was bound to succeed.

Ten minutes before the service was set to commence, the organist took her place next to the choir and began keying the introductory hymn. Hart turned and eyed the young woman as closely as he could from his place below the balcony. She looked to be in her early twenties. Her obvious innocence prompted him to take his mission to a whole new level.

She was quite attractive, and appeared to be one of the many McClain followers who'd been fattened up for the Devil's pawn; in other words, a soul worth preying on. Hart was obliged to snatch her at once, even before the ceremony began. In a matter of seconds, the monster inside him would be unleashed, pounce, and carry her away.

Paul Hart closed his eyes and bowed his head under the false pretense of praying with the rest of the congregation. As he sat quietly, the monster grew inside his body and finally unleashed itself like a ghost escaping the body of a dead man. The monster, called Jabberwock, launched up and stormed into the realms of the unseen, swiftly transforming into a giant dragon with two heads, that of a werewolf and a man.

To Jabberwock's dismay, the entire domain was heavily guarded by an army of angelic troops. On wings they soared and circled the length and breadth of the cathedral, shielding the structure from his evil power. He tried to pull back, but it was too late; the monster was trapped in their midst.

The worship service began promptly, but Paul Hart's plans had shattered. His inner monster was trapped in a serious confrontation with McClain's army of angels. No use in hoping; he already knew the outcome. Jabberwock would never return. His efforts had once again been thwarted, his immense power rendered useless—at least, for the time being.

A woman minister stepped behind the podium. "I would now like to introduce our youth choir," she announced enthusiastically as the kids filed onto the steps of the altar.

"The children have prepared a special song for just this occasion."

Hart was drowning in an intense state of agitation, his nerves fraying at the edges. His mood changed considerably, however, when his eyes zeroed in on a particular girl singing in the front row of the choir.

Tabitha.

The teenaged choir director bowed to the crowd and turned to face the youngsters. Hart examined Tabitha carefully, his need to get close to her nearly overwhelming his senses. His eyes tracked her every move as she approached the microphone. After a moment, his tension began to ease. What were his chances of succeeding now, since Tabitha was but a small seven-year-old girl who happened to sing in the children's choir?

~~~

Enraged, Jabberwock soared across the sky on a rampage, swooping and dodging the squadron of angels. So swift and ferocious were his tactics that the angels could barely contain him.

Jabberwock pounced on the shoulders of one of the angels, his giant claws gouging its skin. The archangel, hovering far above, plucked a star with the tip of his rapier and pointed it at Jabberwock. The star launched from the angel's sword, billowing with fire, and swept the monster from the injured angel. Jabberwock burned, his ashes disintegrating into thin air.

~~~

"Due to time constraints," said Father McClain, "I cannot share the full details of this revelation, but there is a woman here, visiting the church for the first time, whom I wish to address. God, in his infinite wisdom, has shared with me the issues you confront on a daily basis.

"Quite recently," he continued, "the Lord unveiled to me that you need to be delivered from an evil spirit. I believe you know who you are. And if you are within the sound of my voice, I ask that you please come to the altar now." An uncomfortable silence washed over the sanctuary as Father McClain waited patiently for the woman to respond.

"Do not be ashamed, child of God," the priest spoke again. "Not only does the Lord want to redeem you from your bondage, He wants to save your marriage of eight years, a marriage that has been thrust into jeopardy due to excruciating circumstances—your inability to conceive a child. Surely you don't wish to walk down the lonely road to divorce court, do you?"

A woman rose from a pew in the rear of the church, turning the heads of hundreds of church members.

As the thirty-something shyly made her way to the altar, McClain removed his glasses, set them on the pulpit, and stepped down to meet her."What is your name?" he asked, once face-to-face with the blond-haired, blue-eyed woman.

"I'm Catherine Crawford," she replied nervously.

"Mrs. Crawford," the priest said, "is this your first visit to Salisbury Cathedral?"

She trembled as she spoke. "Yes," she said. Her tired, bloodshot eyes blinked back a host of tears. and her heart raced as she stared solemnly at the priest.

McClain reached for her hands and took them in his own. He was silent for several moments before he spoke again. "I feel the monster inside of you," he said. "It's female. Indeed, you are heavily laden with this demon, and the spirit looks to be taking up permanent residence within you." He looked into the woman's eyes kindly. "You've been wondering why you can't conceive, yes?"

The woman nodded, her eyes filling again.

"It is because the demon is consuming your husband's seed for her own breeding. But tonight, we shall banish her from your body forever."

Unable to hold back any longer, the woman broke down

in sobs.

Father McClain placed his palm on the woman's forehead. "Please kneel before me, Mrs. Crawford." He remained quiet, meditating for several seconds. He felt her body tremble under his power. "Demon of barrenness," he called out, "you, evil spirit, are holding captive this child of God. Tonight, by the power of the most high, I command you to leave this woman's body. In the name of Jesus and in the name of God Almighty, I cast you out of her womb. From the mighty hands of God, I will destroy every trace of your being. Leave her, devil."

The woman collapsed, dropping unconscious to the floor.

McClain knelt and looked down at the woman's face. Her eyes were open and unblinking, staring up at him as she lay stiffly in a trance. McClain wasn't a hundred percent certain the demon had abandoned her body. He waited impatiently for a sign, worried that the monster, if still around, could break out, reignite, and retaliate stronger than ever. He prepared himself to confront the creature head on.

~~~

Tabitha watched, mesmerized, as her father tried to exorcise the demon from the poor woman. Tabitha's need to observe every detail intensified. The tension in the church grew as darkness settled in. The woman clutched at the priest's robe before throwing back her head in a powerful convulsion.

Tabitha remained focused on the scene as the demon-possessed woman jerked violently on the altar. When she realized her father had disappeared from her sight, panic rose inside of her. She scanned the congregation to find that her father's followers were caught up in the rapture, as well. When the woman finally quieted, a grave silence fell over the sanctuary.

Seconds later, Tabitha drew back in terror as a huge bird with the heads of numerous babies slipped from the woman's body. The creature fluttered its wings and took to the air and was immediately met by an angel of battle who appeared in the sanctuary. The angel blasted a cloud of flame from its wings, kindling a fire that snatched the demon and sucked it into the outer darkness.

Tabitha, becoming hysterical, screamed in terror.

McClain spun around in alarm just as Tabitha came crashing into his chest, screaming uncontrollably. He held onto her tightly, trying to give her some measure of comfort, but her screams continued.

The possessed woman rose quietly from the altar, seemingly composed and in her right frame of mind. She looked on, speechless, at Father McClain as he tried to sooth his daughter.

"It's okay," the priest soothed. "I'm here. Look around, see? We're all here."

Cardinal McCartney stepped up to the altar and stood beside the priest and his hysterical daughter, whom the priest finally managed to calm. The cardinal knelt down in front of the girl. "What's wrong, Tabitha?"

Tabitha stared down into the cardinal's eyes and turned to look around the room at the choir and the congregation. "I . . . I . . . ," she stammered. "Everyone disappeared." She looked at her father. "Even you." She turned to the congregation. "But here you all are."

The crowd looked on in concerned silence.

"What happened?" her father asked cautiously, trying to quiet his looming fears. He knelt down in the cardinal's place, and McCartney stood and stepped back. "Tabitha, look at me."

Tabitha obeyed, but McClain saw in her eyes that she'd glimpsed the unseen realm of darkness, and it had cast a spell on her. McClain's fear grew as he accepted that his daughter had reached a turning point. She was under the spell of evil now, and for the moment, he felt powerless to stop it.

Her father rose and whispered into the cardinal's ear. Tabitha scanned the congregation, frantically searching for the middle-aged bald man with the hideous scars on his head. She remembered that the evil had erupted the moment her eyes had met the mysterious stranger's.

The priest reluctantly stepped behind the pulpit. "I sincerely apologize for the disruption," he said. "Unfortunately, I am unable to proceed with the service this evening, but I am leaving you in the capable hands of Cardinal Frank McCartney. Thank you for your understanding."

Father McClain grabbed hold of his daughter's hand and walked her through the exit behind the altar.

Chapter 31

Satanist Paul Hart returned to his evil mansion filled with renewed confidence. Although Nevi was still outraged, Hart assured her that they'd found the light at the end of the tunnel—a gleaming beacon of hope. His quest to capture and annihilate Father McClain had been crushed, but the sudden appearance of Cardinal McCartney shielded his fate.

His intuition about the devout cardinal surfaced when Cardinal McCartney took over the service's proceedings after the priest's hasty exit. Hart managed to acquire important knowledge about the man as he observed him presiding over the last fifteen minutes of the mass. The cardinal was indeed a faithful believer, but he possessed many flaws. Compared to the priest, the cardinal was barely grounded in his faith. God could never entrust such a man with the power to accomplish mighty things.

Hart sensed that McClain's faith ran much deeper, but his level of respect for his colleague was perhaps a foolish bet. Nonetheless, their relationship went beyond the sharing of common faith. It had more to do with the bond of brotherly love. Because of that deep love, Hart sensed that the priest had great confidence in the man, perhaps more so than in any other within his devout circle.

Hart walked in from the patio to find Nevi in the colonnade, pacing the floor. "We failed," she shouted.

Hart shook his head. "Not so."

"Look at this child's surroundings," she said. "She's lost track of her destiny and is heading down a slippery path."

He looked at Nevi and arched his eyebrow. "A soldier who gives up too early in a fight is not fit for battle."

"There was no battle," she replied. "We lost before it began—again."

"Says who? How could you be so weak?"

"If I am, I have every reason to be."

Hart pulled her close and kissed her passionately. "Do not worry, my dear. I have a Plan B."

"What are we talking about here?" she asked, pushing him away.

A sly smile spread across his face. "I'm talking about the cardinal."

"We missed the squirrel, so go for the rat?"

"Exactly. McCartney is the rat, and quite capable of leveling the forest."

"Hmm," Nevi replied. "Something I should know?"

"The cardinal has access to the priest's private life. And he has many weaknesses. By putting myself in the position of striking up a conversation with the good cardinal, I am confident that things will dramatically turn in our favor."

Nevi eyed him skeptically.

He drew her close again. "Trust me."

~~~

McClain ordered a decaf coffee while awaiting the arrival of the prophetess Eleanor Griffins. He looked up just as she strode through the door of the diner.

"Have I kept you waiting long?" she asked, rushing over to greet him.

He shook his head. "Just a few minutes or so."

She sat across from him. "Sorry, it's been a long day."

The waiter arrived with his coffee and set it on the table. "Can I get you something, ma'am?"

"The same, thank you," she replied.

The waiter gave a short nod and stepped away.

She laid her coat down on the seat beside her. "So, how

was the thirtieth anniversary celebration?"

McClain sighed and took a sip of his coffee. "Things did not go as I had hoped. In fact, that's why I asked you to meet me. I was hoping you could shed some light on a certain event that took place during the service."

She looked at him, concerned. "I must tell you, I didn't have a good feeling about it."

The waiter arrived with the prophetess's coffee, set it on the table, and slipped away quietly.

"Well, then you won't be surprised," McClain said. "Remember when we first met, you mentioned that the struggles we confront are an endless battle? Well, I hadn't thought about those words in some time, until they came back to haunt me last night."

"I think you'd better tell me the whole story."

"I will," he replied. "But before I forget, that painting you sketched, the one foretelling the possessed woman whose womb was bound by a demon? It was spot on. She came to the service, and it was exactly as you predicted. Her name is Catherine Crawford. I was able to expel the demon, and she's doing quite well now, right as rain, but . . ."

"That's when the trouble started, yes?"

"Yes. Just as I felt the evil spirit leave her body, the child went into hysterics."

"She saw something, then—something that frightened her?"

"I'm not sure how best to describe her reaction," McClain said. "The magnitude of it seemed out of proportion to the circumstances, at least from my view. She was in a full-blown panic. Since then, she's been acting very strangely, as though she's lost her senses."

"Have you asked her about it?"

"Over and over, but since muttering a few confused statements after the incident, she hasn't spoken a word—

not to me or anyone."

Ms. Griffins looked at the priest intently. "What do you believe happened?"

"I believe she saw something that the rest of the congregation, including myself, did not. I believe she may have glimpsed Mrs. Crawford's demon. What else could it be?"

The prophetess nodded. "You might very well be right, Father."

"I wish I weren't."

She smiled sympathetically. "I understand. But think about it. The child was born a supernaturally possessed princess, endowed with the power of Satan. By her very nature, she possesses every attribute of the Devil. It was only a matter of time before she came into contact with her maker."

"But don't forget," McClain said, "she's innocent. Until the day she has full knowledge of her power and the woman she's destined to become, she retains the innocence of a normal child."

Ms. Griffins nodded, sipping her coffee. "So what happens next? Have there been any other signs?"

"I don't think so."

"Maybe you should pray about it."

The priest nodded. "Speaking of prayer, I need to ask a favor of you, if you don't mind."

"Go ahead."

"Would you mind taking a careful look at the painting of Mrs. Crawford? I wonder if there could be something connected to her situation that may have caused the ups—"

The prophetess eyed him knowingly. "Father, this is not the time for denial."

"I just want to rule it out. I promise."

The prophetess looked him square in the eye. "What are you trying to find out? Do you believe she encountered the enemy?"

"Look," he replied, "I'm in the middle of an ongoing war with an enemy I don't know—"

"Because he is not identified by physical appearance," she interrupted. "Understand that this is spiritual warfare; the enemy in question has no physical identity or description. Neither is he mortal or immortal."

"Don't you see?" the priest said. "The incident might have afforded me a golden opportunity, one that could lead me to a clue."

"How exactly did you come to that conclusion?"

He sighed and reached for his cup. "My spirit tells me she encountered another force. That's why I need you to study that prophecy. Maybe the enemy is right under my nose."

"And just what do you plan to do if you discover who he is?"

~~~

It baffled Satanist Paul Hart when rumors abounded that Tabitha was enrolled at Beth-Haccerin School of Mysteries, a sacred institution run by the Ministry of John McClain. It was devoted to recruiting youngsters in their early teens and older to combat the principalities of darkness and evil.

By divine oracles, the sacred institution armed the sect of teens with in-depth knowledge for cracking the secret codes of the Bible and unraveling the mysteries of God. Ultimately, they were trained in how to tap into the secret knowledge of biblical codes that would unleash God's power. This enabled them to exist as supernatural beings. With Tabitha unwittingly lured into the organization, Hart's quest to groom her as the dark princess was in jeopardy.

Now that she was in her early teens, the urge to act was nearly overwhelming. The secret knowledge she'd attained so far made his quest ever more challenging and far from his reach. Even worse, if he was unable to secure her capture within a year, Tabitha could lose her destiny. By the time she gained knowledge of the woman she was destined to be, her devotion to God could very well strip bare the evil power embedded in her.

But Hart was a Grandmaster, and a master of the art of deception. He'd been thwarted by the angels' efforts to subdue him, but his confidence was bolstered by the memory of turning a once-devout nun into a movie star and, ultimately, the vessel for the Princess of Darkness. He was well aware that the power to entice his target lay in his ability to strike up a conversation with Cardinal Frank McCartney.

When Hart steered his car onto the campus grounds, he spied Cardinal McCartney walking to his car. Hart parked his car in the first available space and stepped out. "Cardinal Frank McCartney?"

McCartney turned to find a man with heinous scars covering his bald head. The man's black cloak gave the cardinal pause. "You must be a missionary," he said.

"Not exactly," Hart replied. "But my mission relates somewhat to the spreading of the gospel. Of course, we're not a large organization like the church. We're more of a secret entity."

"And you are . . . ?"

The Satanist extended his hand. "Paul Hart, end-times prophet, ordained by God. I was divinely called to unearth the mystery of Heaven being lost to a dark generation such as ours."

The cardinal eyed Hart up and down. "I thought you were a priest."

"You looked like you were in a hurry there, Cardinal," Hart said. "It doesn't seem like I've caught you at a good time."

"It's a perfect time, actually. I have nothing important on my plate at the moment."

Hart smiled. "Well then, good for me."

"What is it I can help you with, Mr. Hart?"

"Maybe we could sit down, get something to eat," Hart suggested. "I have something I need to discuss with you, but I've been running all day and I'm famished."

"I could use a bite myself," McCartney replied.

"Shall we head to the coffee shop?" Hart asked, gesturing to the greasy spoon across from the campus.

"I'm still curious to know," the cardinal said, picking up his hamburger, "how is it you know who I am?"

"The Lord works in mysterious ways, does he not, Cardinal?"

"I suppose."

"On that note, I have a question I was hoping you could help me with. Do you believe that people have come into contact with true prophets of God?"

"I can't speak for anyone else," the cardinal replied, "but I firmly believe in prophecies—as long as they are divinely inspired."

"Good answer, Cardinal. Now I'm convinced Jehovah has sent me to his faithful servant, a servant who won't waste my time."

"Sounds like you believe the Lord has sent you to me," the cardinal replied. "And this would be pertaining to . . . ?"

Hart leaned over the table and spoke with quiet intensity. "It's a revelation for the second half of your life, Cardinal." Hart paused and leaned back. "The Lord wants you to know he looks favorably upon you. And, because of this, he has bestowed upon you a new destiny, a destiny only you can fulfill for his heavenly kingdom."

The cardinal was immediately lifted by Hart's words, but he hesitated to respond. The message seemed too good to be true.

"What I am about to reveal," Hart said, "is not to be repeated. Trust no one with this information, not even the priest."

Cardinal McCartney eyed the man suspiciously, hoping not to reveal how much those words pleased him.

"The Lord trusts that you will keep this prophecy concealed. It's a secret to remain buried in your heart. Understand?"

McCartney's limbs began to tremble in anticipation. "I do."

"The Lord is about to shake up the ministry. It seems Father McClain's term of service is about to be terminated. Cardinal, you are predestined to succeed him."

Cardinal McCartney raised an eyebrow. "I don't get it," he said, suppressing a smile.

"Like I said before, God works in mysterious ways."

"No doubt he does, Mr. Hart." The cardinal was finding it more and more difficult to hide his delight.

"Here is the motivation behind it all," Hart continued. "You see, the name *church* has been around for ages. And it has not succeeded in the way that God had hoped. He feels that the symbolic attributes of the name *church* have faded away. And since God is extremely wise in his deity, he feels it is time for a major transition. Instead of the common church, the Lord has laid out a more suitable emblem, one that mankind can openly embrace and receive from a clearer view of his divine nature without any lingering doubts and skepticism. And guess what? You've been hand-picked to cut the ribbon at this phenomenal event, one that will radically change the world. Imagine, a whole city communing under one roof."

The cardinal couldn't believe what he was hearing. "You must forgive me, Mr. Hart. This revelation is beyond the outer reaches of my imagination."

Hart smiled. "It's nearly inconceivable, humanly speaking."

"I don't mean to question you or your divine insight,

but . . ."

"Feel free."

"You mention a whole city coming under the same roof. How is that possible?"

"Think about the millions of souls out there that have yet to be saved—millions that haven't heard about Christ. Surely you understand that it is not the will of God that they spend eternity in Hell. It is the hope of God that every soul escapes his wrath. That's why he looked down from his throne and chose you as one of the few that can help. The lives of those people will be at the mercy of your hands."

McCartney leaned back and exhaled. "My hands?"

"There is one final thing," Hart said. "God requires that you meet certain conditions."

"Conditions?"

"That's where my ministry comes in. Fulfilling this crucial call in your present state would be impossible." Hart paused, looking directly into the cardinal's eyes. "You must first be cleansed."

"Cleansed?" the cardinal asked skeptically. "How?"

Hart gulped some water from his glass and set it down on the table. "Don't be alarmed. It's just a season of preparation the Lord has prepared especially for you. It comes with the package."

The cardinal smiled. "Pardon me, Mr. Hart, but all of this seems rather unbelievable. What is this package you speak of?"

"Perseverance is not a viable option," Hart replied. "It's simply not enough. What this means is that a discipleship at this refined level will automatically give you access to a whole new dimension of God's supernatural power. As I speak to you here right now, the face of God is looking upon you, frowning because you've dangerously neglected the power of prayer. Now you understand why the cleansing process is so vital. It is a cleansing of your mind, body, and spirit, and it will work wonders."

The cardinal regarded him curiously. "And what's the name of your ministry?"

"The Gates of Heaven Tabernacle." Hart pulled a flyer from the Bible he'd brought and handed it to the cardinal. "Here is our address and information. On Fridays, we fast and pray. Please join us at your earliest possible convenience."

~~~

Tabitha walked out of the school's main entrance and sat alone under the shade of a large oak tree. It was recess, and about half a dozen of her peers were roaming about the property. The rest of the students were having lunch in the cafeteria.

As she sat in isolation, she sensed a presence. She could swear she felt someone lurking nearby, watching her. She glanced around the area and spotted a man parading back and forth along the edge of the woods across the street from the school.

When the stranger realized he'd caught her eye, he waved Tabitha over. She knew she shouldn't leave school grounds, but she was inexplicably drawn to the man. She cautiously made her way across the street. As she drew nearer, she stepped back in alarm. *The man with the scars.* For several seconds she remained frozen on the sidewalk.

"Your name is Tabitha, right?" he asked with a friendly smile.

She hesitated before answering. "Yes, I'm Tabitha."

"Well, Tabitha, I'll get right to the point," he said. "I'm here to deliver your answers from the gods."

Tabitha eyed the man curiously. "Who are you?"

"I'm a faithful messenger. The gods sent me to inform you that they've heard your cries—your concerns about those strange instincts you've been having."

She stared at him. *How does this man know my*

thoughts? She was desperate to understand what her dark thoughts meant, and perhaps this mysterious stranger could help. But he was so peculiar. Should she trust him? She had to admit, since spying him in the church all those years ago, there was something deliciously mysterious about him—a mystery worth unraveling. "If you are truly a messenger of the gods, why are you hiding? Messengers don't hide, do they?"

"Well, in this case, I'm afraid I'm forced to," the stranger explained. "My visiting you is forbidden. I have to avoid being seen by your peers. My meeting with you has to be kept secret, private—behind closed doors, if possible."

The bell rang. Recess was over.

"I've got to go," he said. "Will you meet me in private after school?"

"I can't," Tabitha replied. "I'm not allowed to meet with strangers."

"Stranger?" He smiled. "But I'm no stranger."

"My father makes sure the chauffeur picks me up right after school."

"Ah, yes, your father," he said. "Are you aware that Father McClain is not your biological father?"

Her heart started to race. "What are you talking about?"

"He's a werewolf in disguise, and cannot be trusted."

~~~

McClain arrived in his office exhausted from a two-hour board meeting. As he headed to the phone to retrieve his messages, his secretary hurried after him.

"Father McClain?"

"Yes?"

"The chauffeur has been trying to get hold of you for two hours now," she said nervously.

"What is it? Is there some kind of emergency?"

"The car broke down," the secretary explained. "Some

kind of engine failure, or so he said."

"How is that possible?" the priest fumed. "The car is practically brand new."

~~~

Satanist Paul Hart headed north on the A338 with Tabitha in the passenger seat of his 1978 Mercedes Benz, as Nevi relaxed in the backseat. "Hard to believe, isn't it?" Hart said, glancing at Tabitha. "You probably don't know what to think, do you?"

Tabitha sat in silence as she tried to take in what was happening, what Paul Hart had told her about her beloved father. "How is it possible?" she asked him, finally breaking her silence. "How could he be a hindrance to my destiny?"

"Do you know the real reason he enrolled you in that school?"

She shook her head.

"Well, I'll tell you," he said. "Their main agenda is to brainwash you and make you forget your true destiny. They hope to deny you the role which the gods have destined you for."

"I don't know," she replied. "This all seems really weird. How do I know that you're not the bad guy here, that what you're saying to me isn't some kind of clever trick?"

"I don't blame you for having doubts," Hart said. "The truth has been hidden from you for so long that it's perfectly understandable that you'd have trouble handling it."

"I don't mean to accuse you," she said, "but I can't fathom why you would lie to me about my father not being my father."

"What about your mother, Tabitha?" he asked. "How often does the priest talk about her?"

"She's dead."

"Indeed. And has the priest ever explained to you how

and why your mother died?"

~~~

McClain dialed the chauffeur's cell phone in a panic, his mind reeling back to a vision he'd had about Tabitha being abducted. "Where are you?" he shouted into the phone when the chauffeur answered.

"Still stranded in the middle of nowhere," the chauffeur replied.

"What's wrong with the car?"

"No idea. I was driving, and, all of a sudden, it just stopped, just like that."

Father McClain's heart skipped a beat. "Have you contacted Tabitha?"

The chauffeur hesitated. "I don't have the number to the school on me."

"Good grief," the priest yelled. He slammed down the phone and dialed the dean's office.

~~~

Late in the evening, the Mercedes steered into the court of Arundel Castle. The place was dark; the priest clearly was not at home. His absence seemed unusual for a late summer's evening. Tabitha guessed that he was out looking for her.

She led the strangers inside and took them on a brief tour of the castle. "How do you explain all of this?" she asked as they entered her father's study.

"It is not in my power to interpret the how or the why, or unearth the mystery of your destiny," Paul Hart answered. "Only you can do that."

"How?"

"By following your true path," he replied. "The truth is, you don't belong here. And until you are willing to leave and take residence where you belong, this mystery of your life will remain unsolved."

"Where's the chapel?" asked Nevi.

"In the west wing of the castle," she replied as they departed the study. "Why?"

"In that sacred room lies the spiritual power that has blinded you all these years," Hart explained. "But the good news is that your alienation is the secret weapon that will ultimately conquer your enemy."

She stopped in her tracks, staring at Hart disdainfully. "The chapel is where my father communes with God."

"Wrong," Hart objected. "You see, this is what he has made you believe, and you believe because you are merely a child. Sooner or later, you will learn the truth."

They strolled down the corridor, passing by the indoor swimming pool. The glassy, still water of the pool captured Hart's attention. This was the part of the castle he had longed to see. The crystal water, mirroring the ceiling, was an eye-catching sight. It was the breeding ground on which his satanic power promised to work great wonders. If he could convince Tabitha to rebel against Father McClain, the power to control her would come from this pool.

He broke away from the other two and walked to one end of the pool, where he closely examined the water. Tabitha and Nevi walked to the opposite end of the pool.

Hart looked across at Tabitha. "I sense that for most of your life, you have felt unhappy, dissatisfied. That's what happens when the call of destiny is squelched and left to cry out inside of you."

"Are you saying that by answering the call, I'll get the peace I deserve?"

Slowly, with his right hand, Hart pulled out *The Book of Evil* he'd had tucked under his left arm. He flipped through the pages, ripped one from the middle, and threw it into the water. He watched as it gradually floated to the bottom of the pool and dissolved.

"The truth has been revealed," Nevi said, turning to Tabitha. "The kingdom is depending on you; you are destined for the throne."

Tabitha turned to face the demon as Paul Hart reopened the book and again ripped a single page from the middle and threw it in the pool. He watched, smiling, as it sank and landed on the pool's floor.

~~~

When McClain approached the gate of the castle, an unfamiliar car—a black Mercedes—was pulling away from the spot where he usually parked. The man behind the wheel eyed him mockingly through the driver's side window as he slowly made his way past before speeding out of the driveway and down the road.

~~~

Tabitha shut herself up in her room, her insides churning with the events and revelations of the day. She felt an intense burning deep within.

She stared at her mother's portrait. Her mother's death, which had never had a profound effect on her, had suddenly become a source of deep pain and anguish. *Why now?* But Paul Hart had explained everything, and she was kicking herself for having fallen prey to the priest's deceit.

A knock on her door jolted her from her reverie.

When McClain stepped in, he immediately sensed his daughter's tension and resentment. Still, it didn't occur to him that all the things he'd feared since her birth had taken place in the space of the past four hours when Tabitha was missing.

"I've been everywhere, the school, the police," he began. "I even went to the news channels and reported you missing. You had me worried to death."

She lifted her head to face him. "I'm disappointed in you," she said sadly.

McClain sensed the hurt in her voice. "Why? What are you talking about?"

"Who is my real father? Where is he?"

The priest stared at her, dumbfounded. The question took his breath away.

"You raised me to believe that you're a man of God," she continued, "but I've come to find out that, all these years, you've kept the truth from me."

He sat beside her on the bed, struggling for words. "What evil has instructed you to say these words to me?"

"Evil?"

"The truth is not always easy to understand, and in this case, not necessarily something that would bring you comfort. In fact, quite the opposite."

"Why didn't you tell me you weren't my real father?"

"Would it have made any difference if I was?" he asked gently. "The truth is, I love you as my own. Can't you see how protective I am of you? My God, who would ever think that you come from the seed of another man?"

"What are you saying? That we somehow belong together? That there is some godly reason you raised me instead of my real father?"

He nodded. "Only problem is, you're the one who knows the reason."

"Did you kidnap me from my real father?" she asked. "I deserve to know who my real father is."

"He *was* Bob Goldman, a very wealthy and kind man." McClain sighed. "Now you've pushed me, against my will, to reveal the truth. But the question is, do you really want to know the truth?"

After a moment's hesitation, Tabitha nodded.

"Your father died, and his death is a mystery yet to be solved. But I'm certain, in time, the Lord will unveil the dark mystery of the tragedy that took his life and the lives of many others."

Chapter 32

Satanist Paul Hart was anxiously awaiting Cardinal McCartney's visit. He sat and stared out at the twilight, savoring the joy of having won Tabitha's affection, a move he perceived as a step closer to triumph over Father McClain. It dawned on him that, had he known then the hidden secret he'd only recently discovered, Tabitha would have been in his custody years ago. Nonetheless, she was securely in his clutches now, his latest strategy having succeeded.

He walked out onto the patio and stretched his arms upward, and a powerful gust of wind blew from the forest. A moment later, he lowered his arms, and the wind calmed. In the aftermath of the brief storm, rust- and green-colored dust clouds filled the air. The dust from the clouds covered the water, transforming the lake into a field of grass.

~~~

Cardinal McCartney drove his Jaguar into the woods, nervously making his way toward Hart's secret temple. He pulled into the front drive at 8:45 p.m. and gingerly stepped out of his car. The eerie silence surrounded him. The temple was huge and ornate, likely eighteenth century. "Good grief," he muttered as he stared up at the enormous structure, thinking it looked more like a haunted mansion than a secret temple.

To his surprise, the heavy wood front doors automatically swung open as he stepped onto the front porch. For several seconds, he hesitated, gawking through the entryway at the grand staircase. The alternate black and white squares that made up the floor of the foyer reminded him of an oversized chessboard. A huge wooden crucifix hung on the wall to his left.

When the cardinal stepped in, the doors closed. He jumped when he heard the voice of his host echoing from behind him.

"Welcome."

The cardinal spun on his heel to find Paul Hart approaching him from seemingly out of nowhere, like a ghost. "I'm thrilled to have you here at the Gates of Heaven Tabernacle, Cardinal."

"When you said it was in a highly remote area," the cardinal replied, "you certainly weren't exaggerating."

"Well, you get used to it. Come into the parlor." Hart gestured toward the attractive room to the left of the foyer.

McCartney sat on a brown leather sofa next to an antique chest. "The drive was certainly a long one."

"I hope it wasn't too taxing. It's just that we're more comfortable away from the noise and chaos of the city."

"I understand. I imagine it's easier to find one's spiritual center way out here in a place like this."

"You're the cardinal, so I imagine you would be the one most inclined to understand the supernatural gifts of an obscure environment."

McCartney chuckled. "I respectfully disagree, Mr. Hart. Being out here, I'm realizing just how accustomed I've become to city life. You are the one called to this particular ministry."

"I believe being confined to a remote area like this is more of a revelation of sorts."

McCartney raised an eyebrow questioningly.

"If you don't agree," Hart said, "think about it this way. Has it ever occurred to you that intense solitude is part of God's will? It brings glory to him in ways our minds can never conceive of."

"You have a point."

"And if I could tap into the mind of God, I believe we'd find that some of the bad things that happen could be directly attributed to the strains of living in society. Evil, heresy, debauchery . . . are these not the things that are easily found in the cities? On the other hand, it is the Lord's will that his saints live blemish-free lives away from all the corruptions which have enslaved countless sons and daughters. Since the Gates of Heaven Tabernacle is called to win souls to his kingdom, our isolation from the immoral effects of society was divinely ordained."

McCartney took a deep breath and smiled. "You make a convincing argument, Mr. Hart."

"Would you like a tour of this sacred mansion?"

"It would be a pleasure."

~~~

Paul Hart ushered Cardinal McCartney up to a midsized room on the fourth floor. The lights were so dim, the room was nearly pitch black. Behind a closed door, a group of devil worshippers masquerading as devout men were in the middle of a phony prayer, pretending to speak in tongues.

"This is the upper room," Hart whispered to the cardinal, "and these are mighty men of valor. In religious terms, they're prayer warriors—soldiers of God. In time, you shall know them each personally."

They headed out of the room. "Was that a prayer vigil?" McCartney asked.

"Not really. It's a custom we're wholeheartedly dedicated to. Every evening around this time, we seek the power of the Most High through prayer and intercession. It's the foundation on which the Gates of Heaven Tabernacle was built. We also believe, from the depths of our hearts, that when a child of God prays fervently, miracles will manifest on the heels of faith."

The cardinal nodded. "That's a very powerful

foundation, indeed."

They walked through a corridor to a flight of stairs that led to the basement. Hart noted that Cardinal McCartney appeared to have no clue that the operation was anything other than a legitimate house of God. Nor did he seem suspicious of Hart himself, who intended to crush the cardinal's faith.

"You all must have a special gift from God to endure such sacrifice."

"I believe we do," Hart replied. "But the reality is, only a select few are fit for this journey."

He led the cardinal into a secret underground room—the Dark Room, as they had come to call it. Before the cardinal's arrival, Hard had the room redone to resemble a chapel, one designed to capture McCartney's attention the moment he entered. "This is our chapel," Hart explained, "a room where mysteries are solved and dreams come true. And the destiny of a man, once lost, can be rediscovered. In this chapel, the quest for wisdom and direction is freely granted."

Like a tourist captivated by a breathtaking view, so went Cardinal McCartney. The bronze statue of the archangel Michael was affixed to the back wall. The round, gold altar was edged in shining gemstones. "Unbelievable," the cardinal exclaimed. "All these years, it never occurred to me that the deity of God could be revealed in such a remote environment."

"That's the attribute of God which you have yet to discover."

"I presume that this chapel is polished with many testimonials."

"Absolutely," Hart replied. "But for the sake of privacy, I will reveal no names. In this little chapel, leaders, officials of the government, all come here in disguise to seek the wisdom and guidance of God. They come in search of a higher power." Hart paused and looked at the cardinal. "I tell you what—they never leave disappointed."

The cardinal regarded him curiously. "Queen Elizabeth?"

"Twice a year, without fail," Hart replied, smiling. "Have you ever wondered why she's the greatest woman in the world, the longest reigning queen in history?"

The cardinal shook his head. "I can't begin to imagine."

"Oh, but you will, Cardinal. This chapel you are in holds the keys to the secret, and you are next in line. But it will take one thing to inherit the promise placed before you by God, so that you too may reap the bountiful blessings rightfully bestowed upon this ministry."

~~~

McClain awoke suddenly at the sound of his alarm. It was two o'clock in the morning, the time of night he routinely spent in prayer. But this time around, an unusual dread plagued him. Just a few minutes into his prayers, he lost the desire to continue. It was as though the light that prompted his need to pray had been abruptly switched off.

Tabitha had distanced herself from him. Her increasingly cold attitude toward him gave him every reason to believe that the monster inside her was on the verge of being released. If his instincts were right, she had uncovered the shocking mystery behind her existence. If that was true, he was certain the strangers who had taken her from school were responsible.

When the door of the master suite clicked closed, Tabitha pushed away the comforter and swung her legs over the side of the bed. Seconds later, she heard the sound of the priest's footsteps. Aware of the priest's usual routine, she listened as he made his way down the corridor. Several minutes later, when she noticed the headlights of a car shining through her window, she shuffled over and looked down. To her surprise, she saw the taillights of the priest's

Rolls Royce heading out of the gate. *Where is he going?*

His departure left her feeling strangely disappointed. As she stood and began pacing the room, Tabitha heard the quiet echoes of her name being whispered. She froze and listened to the voices resounding throughout the house, unable to ignore their calls. She crept from her room, scared but drawn to the relentless beckoning. She followed the voices through the house, eventually ending up at the swimming pool.

She soon realized that she recognized one of the voices. It was the voice of the man she had met two days ago, Paul Hart. She bravely crept into the room that housed the indoor pool, but not of her own will. She felt as if, under the power of a spell, a gust of wind was sweeping her toward the water.

Tabitha stood in the entrance, gazing around the room. She did a double take when she realized that the swimming pool had mysteriously transformed into a pool of boiling water. With the force still driving her, she stepped into the room and stood at the water's edge, studying the boiling mass. When the shock of what she'd seen began to wear off, she dipped her right foot into the pool.

The water calmed instantly.

~~~

Eleanor Griffins looked up from her drawing board at the sound of the doorbell. She glanced at the clock on top of her storage cabinet: 3:00 a.m. She hurried up the stairs to the front door and found a distressed Father McClain on the other side.

"Father, come in," she said.

"I apologize for disturbing you when you're working," he said as he stepped into the entryway. "I couldn't sleep if I didn't make this trip."

Eleanor sensed the tension in his voice, could physically feel the darkness that engulfed him. "Adversity is a virtue we cannot escape, especially as children of God."

"So true," he replied, his voice barely a whisper. "Things are exactly as you predicted. I believe I've seen the Devil."

She nodded.

"Look, I don't mean to put you through this, but would you mind if I took a look at the painting again?"

"Of course not," she replied, smiling sympathetically. "Follow me." She led him down into the gallery. "The Lord has just revealed to me an in-depth translation of the writings of John. I wondered if, when I complete the painting, it might benefit the church."

McClain ignored the prophetess's offer and instead stared at the painting he'd come to see. It was a painting similar to the Last Supper, but with McClain sitting at the middle of a long table. His entire ministerial staff was seated around him, each attired in a white ephod, except for the man on his immediate right, who was dressed in a black cloak and a veil concealing his identity. But the most distressing thing about the painting was that the priest's ephod was drenched with blood.

The painting rendered him silent for several minutes as he considered the unthinkable: that perhaps it was a sign of his gruesome end. Or perhaps the painting was the foretelling of an even darker story. The only thing he knew for sure was that he would soon learn the identity of his arch-enemy.

"You're awfully quiet, Father," said the prophetess, breaking the silence.

"I don't wish to say out loud what I'm thinking."

"Maybe you shouldn't take the painting too personally."

"Should a man ignore the revelation of himself? What does this predict? Death? Betrayal?" He turned to face the prophetess. "How do you interpret it?"

"It's a crisis of some type."

The priest looked back to the painting. "That blood is a

sign of a tragic death, not just a mere crisis."

"For years I have concealed this," she confessed. "Now you know your true destiny."

"*Death* is my destiny?"

She nodded. "You can only conquer your enemy through your own death. That is how it was divinely orchestrated."

He gazed at the prophetic painting for a long moment, numbness washing over him. How to comprehend such a thing, much less accept it?

"So tell me," Ms. Griffins said, "which one of your ministers do you trust the most?"

He looked at her, puzzled by the question. "I don't know. My mind isn't very clear right now. At the moment, I can't think of any of them that I would trust completely."

"None of them? You're sure?"

"No, why?"

"Well," she said, stepping up to the painting, "according to the prophecy, the man in disguise is a traitor. He's your Judas. For the price of your blood, he sold his soul to the Devil. But little does the Devil know that your death is the mystical means by which God will slay the dark princess."

"I find this all very hard to absorb," McClain said wearily.

"Remember the prophecy of the Princess of Heaven?"

"Very well."

"It's all about her," the prophetess said. "God knows he can trust you. He knows you are the only man willing to lay down your life so this immortal can launch into battle with the dark princess. She is the only force powerful enough to annihilate the dark princess and ultimately conquer the reign of evil once and for all." She paused, placing her hand on the priest's shoulder. "Father, your imminent death has been divinely ordained as the supernatural power which will pull her out of Heaven."

Chapter 33

The Dark Moon Banquet
One September night

The Vamps and a host of occult Grand Masters crowded the mansion's banquet hall, dressed in their black society robes. People chatted amongst themselves, goblets of fresh blood in hand, as satanic music softly echoed through the sound system.

A monstrous spider suddenly descended from the ceiling. Lightning escaped from inside of the creature, setting it alight briefly before smoke destroyed it altogether. Out of the smoke, Nevi emerged, wearing a red cloak with a wide, black collar.

Nevi greeted each of the Vamps with a handshake as she walked through the crowd toward the banquet table. She grabbed a goblet, raised her glass to toast the Vamps around her, and lashed her viper tongue into the blood for a sip.

Cardinal McCartney entered and scanned the room, the presence of evil overwhelming his senses. He surveyed the gathering disbelievingly—eerie music, drinking of blood, serpent's tongues sprouting out of the mouths of humans. The cardinal wondered if he was hallucinating. *This is the banquet Hart planned in my honor?*

His skin tingled as he observed a wizard stepping down the wall on the far side of the room as one would descend a staircase. The cardinal sensed something strange happening behind him. He turned in time to see a witch crawl out of the wall and fold into the crowd. Seconds later, a giant bat circled overhead and shape-shifted into a man, landing next to the banquet table.

A wave of dread washed over the cardinal as he realized he'd been a fool to trust Paul Hart. He swallowed hard and broke out in a cold sweat. Maybe it wasn't too late to turn back. The worst kind of fear gripped him as he ventured to think about what Hart had in store for him.

~~~

Father McClain struggled with his choices: die a gruesome death to save humankind from the wrath of the dark princess, or live and watch evil prevail. A devoted man of God, the priest was aware that evil had the potential to ruin God's plan, the world, and the human race. Chances were, once Tabitha reigned as the dark princess, God's quest to restore the world to its former glory could fail miserably. Meanwhile, the ordeal would cost him his life. But, for the sake of saving all of humanity, how could he possibly turn away from his sacred calling?

At his core, McClain was a vigilant soldier in God's army. Because of his devotion to God, he understood that this level of sacrifice was simply part of the cost of saving the world. It was also a gut-wrenching test of his faith. But what choice did he have? If the only way to conquer his enemy was through his own death, Father McClain would have to face his duty with courage.

Despite his distress about the prophecy, McClain responded with a humble spirit to an invitation extended to him from Mr. and Mrs. Crawford. At last, a child had been born into their union, and in celebration of their newborn son, they were throwing a cocktail party.

When McClain arrived at the welcoming home of Dan and Catherine Crawford, he was relieved to have been given a respite from his troubles. Dan Crawford greeted him at the door with an enthusiastic handshake and hug and escorted him into the living room, where a small gathering of friends and family sat together chatting and laughing.

Catherine walked in carrying a tray of champagne glasses, and she smiled widely at the priest, which warmed his heart. After serving her guests, she stood beside her husband in the middle of the room and motioned for the priest to stand on her other side.

"May I have your attention?" Dan announced. "Since our marriage eight years ago, Catherine and I have looked forward to this day—the day we got to officially celebrate the birth of our first child. It has been a long time in coming, as you all know, but after years of struggle and nearly losing all hope, we have finally been given our miracle: our new son."

The small crowd clapped and whooped enthusiastically.

"So tonight," he continued, smiling at his wife, "Catherine and I would also like to testify, with deep sincerity, that this moment wouldn't have been possible if not for the miraculous healing hands of Father John McClain."

Dan, Catherine, and all of their guests stood and toasted the priest.

When the toast was over and the crowd quieted, Dan tapped McClain on the shoulder. "Catherine and I would like to introduce you to someone," he said, motioning for the priest to follow him down the hall. When they reached the nursery, Dan brought his finger to his lips and winked. "Shh."

McClain quietly crept toward the crib and gazed upon the infant. His worries, for the moment, were whisked far away. This baby's existence, his innocence, breathed new life into Father McClain's faith. "What's his name?"

"Jeremiah," Catherine replied, appearing in the nursery doorway.

"Congratulations," McClain whispered, still gazing down into the crib. "He's a beautiful boy."

"Thank you, Father McClain," Dan said, his eyes glassy.

"For everything."

McClain shook his head. "Miracles come from God, and him only. I was just the vessel he used to channel his power. He is the one deserving of your thanks."

Dan nodded. "Father, could I trouble you for one more favor?"

"Of course."

"Catherine and I would like you to dedicate Jeremiah at your church. Would you please perform the ceremony?"

McClain pondered a moment, wondering if he would live to see that day.

Dan must have noticed the change in his mood. "Are you all right?" he asked, glancing questioningly at Catherine.

McClain sighed and mustered a smile. "I'm fine."

~~~

Cardinal McCartney bumped into Paul Hart at the entrance to the room as he tried to sneak away from the banquet. His heart pounded as he came face to face with the man who was clearly not what he said he was.

"Cardinal," Hart greeted him, smiling as if nothing was wrong. "I'm so sorry I wasn't here to formally welcome you."

McCartney stared at his host, incredulous. "I can't believe the things I'm seeing here, Hart," he said, fear creeping into his voice.

"Oh, this? Only the best for such a special occasion, Cardinal."

"Under solemn oath, you made me believe that you were a man of God—a prophet, no less."

Hart wrapped his arm around the cardinal's shoulder and walked him into the corridor. "I didn't make you believe, Cardinal. You chose to believe me." Hart paused and faced him, placing his hands on McCartney's shoulders. "Only you can control your own instincts, and apparently yours aren't too sharp. You should have known the kind of man you entered into a covenant with."

The cardinal pushed Hart away and tried to run, but Hart magically traveled from his position by the banquet room doors to block McCartney's way. "Where are you going in such a hurry?" Hart asked, his slick smile causing the cardinal's stomach to lurch.

"I'm leaving this despicable place."

Hart tilted his head in mock sympathy. "Oh, I'm sorry, but it's against the creed of the oracle to boycott this ritual. You can't escape—you belong here now."

"Let me out of here," the cardinal cried.

"Truth be told, I'd rather have the priest here instead of you," Hart teased. "But I'm afraid you'll just have to do."

Gripped by desperation, Cardinal McCartney forced his way past Hart, who laughed as McCartney ran toward the front entrance. As he burst through the doors and onto the porch, the cardinal froze in his tracks. A lake he'd never seen before surrounded the entire structure. He locked back at Hart, confused.

"It has no bottom, Cardinal McCartney," Hart said, stepping up beside him. "If you think what you witnessed at the banquet was horrifying, wait till you see the predators lurking under the surface in there."

McCartney stood staring, his mouth agape, as Hart vanished before his eyes.

~~~

Dan whisked Father McClain from the cocktail party yet again and ushered him upstairs to the family room. "I never believed that miracles could really happen," Dan confessed. "At least, not in our generation. Now I can proudly say that my son is living testimony that miracles still happen."

McClain nodded humbly. "Jesus strictly decreed, 'Signs and wonders shall follow them that believe. In my name, they shall cast out demons. They shall lay hands on the sick, and they shall recover.'"

"That was exactly my wife's situation," Dan replied, shaking his head. "I still can't comprehend how powerful and miraculous it all was."

"I have come across worse cases than yours," said McClain. "In my thirty-something years of ministry, I've seen families weakened, drawn into the captivity of Satan's dark kingdom."

"Can I tell you something, Father?"

McClain nodded.

"No disrespect to your faith, but I used to be one of those who wholly disregarded the idea of religion. Of course, I'm not suggesting that I'm a pagan. I just didn't believe in God. And not because I'm a civil engineer making a six-figure salary. I just didn't believe he truly existed."

"So what changed your mind?"

"The night Catherine came home after attending your service, I saw a confidence in her eyes I hadn't seen in years. The first thing she said when she arrived home was, 'Honey, we will finally have our baby.' The glow on her face, it was almost . . . heavenly.

"We lay in bed for hours that night, talking. She told me all about the service, and the healing—everything you did for her. So I thought to myself, no flesh and blood on the face of this earth has that kind of spiritual insight. Right there and then, I arrived at a conclusion: that God was speaking through you."

"So you now believe there is a God?"

"Absolutely. Who am I to deny this amazing truth?" He pondered for a moment. "But the issue that concerns me the most, when it comes to living this pure life, like you do, is the price tag that comes with it. Just the thought of it scares me to death."

"I'm not sure I'm following you," McClain said, his curiosity piqued.

"You know what I am talking about, Father," Dan

replied. "You're a great man of God."

"Sounds like something personal."

"No, no. I just mean that, even though I'm now a God-fearing man, I don't intend to strive to reach your devout standards."

"No one is exempted from the vicissitudes of life," the priest replied. "It's a reality that we, as humans, cannot escape."

"Not even a strong believer like yourself?"

"Not even me," he replied, smiling. "But the good news is, God always prevails in the end."

"The author Richard Winchester once said, 'Man's greatest and most powerful enemy is not the one he confronts in a raging battle. It's death.' It shocked me when he said that the way to defeat death is to face it. My thing is, we'll all die someday, but the manner in which death might come is what seems scary."

The priest nodded. "What's your point exactly, Dan?"

"My point is the very reason I wanted to speak with you." He paused for a moment and locked eyes with McClain. "As a devoted man of God, would you lose your life to save another?"

McClain hesitated, his mind reeling. All of the tension he'd been feeling over his duty to God came rushing back. He tried to calm himself by taking a long, deep breath. "If it is the will of God for me to die so that another may live, I will humbly accept my fate."

~~~

Despite Hart's threat, Cardinal McCartney treaded into the lake and swam to the other side, thankfully without incident. When he reached the opposite shore where his car was parked, he looked back at the mansion with an immeasurable sense of regret. He reminded himself that he would never again set foot in that wicked place. Then he climbed into his car and sped away.

About a mile into the drive, as he cruised along the lonely freeway, he flinched when a horde of large birds flew out of the thick forest. Peering through the windshield, he realized they weren't birds at all, but flying monsters with human heads. He increased his speed, hoping to outrun the vile creatures, but the monsters continued in hot pursuit.

He pressed the gas pedal to the floor, the car speeding dangerously out of control, but the creatures caught up to him quickly. They surrounded his car, slamming into the Jaguar like a swarm of vultures feasting on a carcass. The impact caused the car to swerve, and the roof, hood, and doors were all badly damaged. The creatures hissed like a brood of hungry serpents, the ungodly sound piercing his ears.

When he approached a curve in the road, he spotted another bird-like monster storming out of the woods. This one carried the face of a female, perhaps in her late twenties, and was the most ruthless of all. She swooped toward his car, head on, and broke the headlight upon impact. McCartney ran her over.

He glanced in the rearview mirror as another one hit the back window and smashed it, sending shards of glass into the back seat. At his first opportunity, the cardinal exited the freeway, only to find himself on a local, two-lane highway. He spotted the taillights of a tanker truck a quarter mile away, about 2500 feet away from the bridge that crossed the Hamilton River.

McCartney's heart pounded with fear. Though the swarming creatures hadn't followed him, he struggled to calm himself in the aftermath of the high-speed chase.

He looked ahead to find that he was only a second away from plowing into the rear of a tanker. McCartney veered into the oncoming lane, where a semi sped toward him. The operator slowed the vehicle and moved it toward the shoulder, but as the cardinal passed, his car swiped the tires of the eighteen-wheeler. The Jaguar slammed into the guard rail of the bridge, flipped into the air, and plummeted into the Hamilton River.

The operators of the tanker and the tractor-trailer rushed to the bridge and watched as the Jaguar disappeared under the water.

Chapter 34

An overwhelming crowd of students and professors packed into the auditorium of Winston University. Prophetess Eleanor Griffins was moments away from premiering her *Millennium of Prophecies* conference. At seven o'clock p.m. on the dot, the audience welcomed her with friendly applause as she approached the podium from backstage.

"Thank you," she said, grinning widely. "Thank you very much."

The audience hushed.

"The *Millennium of Prophecies* is more than a myth," she said. "It's more than an insightful glimpse into the perilous events that promise to shake the world, which the Bible has forewarned. The *Millennium of Prophecies* divinely guides the human race and arms us with awareness of the fulfillment of these dark and terrible days to come—events we should not disregard as we journey toward the end of our lives here on Earth.

"For instance, from the scriptures, we've been forewarned about the birth and rise of the dark princess. In the same scripture, the mark of the beast, 666, is revealed, and the end-times chaos and destruction before the coming of Christ. Yet, throughout the centuries, man has taken for granted this end-times wrath, which has been described as an extremely perilous time.

"As host of this event, I wish to encourage you all to

examine these prophecies, these revelations that could save us from becoming victims of eternal doom."

Over a dozen people in the crowd raised their hands. Ms. Griffins pointed at what appeared to be a freshman girl. "Yes, the blonde wearing the black T-shirt."

The girl stood up. "You mentioned the rise of the dark princess—"

"The Bible prophesied," she interrupted, "not me."

The girl nodded.

"Please, proceed with your question. It was just a point of clarification."

"My question to you is: How will we know when the dark princess roams the Earth? Will there be signs?"

"The Bible does not reveal the signs in detail," Griffins replied candidly. "But one thing I am certain of is this: Hell has already unleashed the dark princess into our world. She lives among us, and to date, there have been no signs of her presence. My advice to you is to be on alert." She paused and scanned the faces before her. "Because your best friend, your fiancé, even your spouse could be the dark princess."

"What's the meaning of the mark 666?" asked a middle-aged professor.

"Bear in mind, the number 666 is the mark of the beast, or the number of his name. During the dispensation of evil, this number will emerge as a seal of identity, stamped on the foreheads of millions whom Satan will cleverly deceive, making them his loyal followers.

"Now here is the scary part," she continued. "At this time, food will be severely scarce, and unless you bear the mark of the beast, you will not be permitted to buy or sell anything of that nature."

~~~

Father McClain pushed his way into the crowd filing out of the auditorium, keeping a look out for Ms. Griffins. The

Millennium of Prophecies had ended roughly five minutes before, meaning that he'd missed the prophetess's newest revelations—something he'd vowed he wouldn't do. The priest worried he might lose this one last chance to meet with her. He finally spied her in the lobby as she stepped out of the elevator. "Prophetess Griffins," he called, relief washing over him.

"Father McClain?" she asked, surprised to see him. "Looks like you've just arrived."

"Yes, I apologize for being so late," he replied. "I've been stuck in rush hour traffic for hours."

"I understand. I would have been late myself had I left home even ten minutes later than I did."

"Do you have a minute?" he asked.

"I have more than that. Join me at the canteen. I have to get something to eat before I drop."

~~~

The priest's solemn expression and pale skin alarmed Eleanor. His unrelenting worry about his duty and his fate consumed him. If not for her foretelling of his gruesome death, McClain could be any man sitting at the table with her. But the priest was a strong man, a man of deep faith. She had every confidence that it was only a matter of time before he found the courage to defeat his fears.

"Cardinal McCartney is missing," he said after they'd ordered their food. "It's been two and a half weeks since I've seen him. He seems to have abandoned his cottage, as well."

"Cardinal McCartney, you said?"

"Yes. Do you know him?"

She shook her head. "No, I don't. But you need to settle down. You can't let his disappearance upset you further."

"Somehow, this entire situation has gotten beyond me." He looked at her, his face anguished. "The situation has become untenable." He sighed despairingly. "I thought perhaps your wise insight, your latest prophecies, might help me find out what's happened to him."

"Too much knowledge, at this point, is not necessary," she said. "You already know what you are destined to do, and that's all that matters."

"I understand what you're saying, Ms. Griffins, but in that painting, the minister you claimed was the betrayer— well, I believe the cardinal may be the one."

"Oh, I see," she said knowingly. "So now you confess to know who among your brethren would most likely deceive you. You thought you could conceal the cardinal's misdeeds indefinitely, no?"

"You must understand, Ms. Griffins, my mind was in total disarray when you asked me that question. I couldn't comprehend anything, much less pinpoint a traitor. I've wrestled with the question tremendously. This is a man I love dearly, my closest colleague. Imagine what it's like to realize that he is the one who will end up betraying me."

Eleanor felt badly for the priest. "Has he vanished before?"

"Never. He's never missed a single church service or event, not since he was ordained."

"What do you think has happened to him?"

"I don't know. That's why I came here. I'm ... I'm afraid he might be dead."

She looked thoughtful for a moment. "No, he's not," she said confidently.

McClain grew silent. "Well, if that's the case, I'm convinced he has disappeared, at the very least. Yes?"

"Your church is on the verge of being engulfed by a dark, sinister cloud. Conspiracy is looming below the surface. And that conspiracy is going to attract the news media."

"What are you saying?"

"If you unearth the mystery of the cardinal's

disappearance, you might very well discover that, not only has he betrayed you, but he is also planning to launch an evil mission against the church."

"Look, the cardinal isn't perfect, but he's not a monster. He would never do anything like that."

"Not of his own accord. But perhaps someone else would exploit the cardinal's weakness, use him to get to you, to get to the church, by offering the cardinal something valuable in return for his betrayal."

The priest stared across the table at Eleanor and narrowed his eyes. "What are you not telling me? Do you know who's behind all of this?"

She sighed, knowing the priest wouldn't give up until she answered his question. "I suspect the cardinal has made an unwitting bargain with the Devil, and the only way out is for him to compromise. If war is raged against the church, it will likely be Cardinal McCartney's mortal body that Satan will use as a vessel to launch that war."

"And?" he asked eagerly.

She looked down. "I've said too much already."

~~~

ANBC Live Breaking News
7:00 a.m.

ANBC News was capturing live what looked to be a tragedy about half a mile across Bromley Harbor. The incident caused a horrific traffic jam along the street running parallel to the harbor. A fleet of Coast Guard boats patrolled the water, while police rescue units and ambulances flooded the area. Emergency vehicle lights flickered everywhere.

A crew of fishermen had made an emergency call when their fishing vessel collided with a floating car earlier that morning.An ANBC News chopper circled the scene, capturing the action as a crane lifted the vehicle out of the water.

Millions tuned in, and McClain happened to be one of them, closely watching the story as it unfolded. A male reporter on shore reported the details:

"It was about five thirty this morning when police responded to an emergency call from the crew on board a fishing vessel. The fishing boat nearly tipped as it came into contact with the drifting car a little over half a mile from Bromley Harbor.

"As you can see behind me, the car, a 1999 Jaguar JXT, is currently being lifted from the harbor. After a thorough search, police have identified the car as belonging to Cardinal Frank McCartney. Though the cause of the accident is currently under investigation, it's been rumored that the clergyman went missing a little over two weeks ago and remains missing today.

"We will continue to keep you updated as we receive more information about the accident. For ANBC News, I'm Glenn Carter."

Chapter 35

Silence fell over the secret temple where loyal Vamps and occult Grand Masters congregated under a full moon. Up on the platform stood a marble stone podium, the front panel graced with an engraving of a flying red dragon with seven heads, fire billowing violently from their mouths.

By midnight, Paul Hart was consumed with joy. For the past decade, he had yearned with every fiber of his being to witness the unfolding of this secret ritual. Now that he had finally won Tabitha over to the Kingdom of Darkness, Hart was convinced he'd taken a tremendous step forward in his quest to slay Father McClain. When Tabitha had at last discovered her rightful place with her rebirth into the occult society, Hart decided to host a ceremony in her honor. From this night on, Tabitha would gain absolute mastery over her evil power.

Hart stepped up to the podium to address the congregation of Devil worshippers. "Tonight," he said, "we celebrate a moment of great joy, one that the Knights of Beelzebub will commemorate for a lifetime. This glorious night is in honor of a major victory. And, just as a kingdom cannot exist without a leader, so it is with this kingdom. If evil is to prevail over good once and for all, a princess must rise to the throne to reign alongside the Prince of Darkness.

"For years we've relentlessly fought a battle with our greatest enemy to redeem the princess and restore her to her rightful place. After many years of captivity, fate has finally stepped in on our behalf. So, my fellow Vamps, it is with great honor and joy that I present to you the Princess of

Darkness, Tabitha."

Lightning struck as a human shadow flashed across the back wall. From the shadow, Tabitha materialized to take her place beside Hart, who adorned her with her robe and crown.

~~~

McClain woke up plagued by a feeling of dread. The pressure to conquer his fear had reached its peak, to the point that he was incessantly haunted by nightmares of his own death. It seemed as though everything which could have possibly gone wrong had done so. Cardinal McCartney had been missing for over two months now, and the mystery behind his car accident remained unsolved. Tabitha's mysterious disappearance had also taken its toll on his faith.

The priest was constantly aware of his looming death— the fatal end that would release the world from the reign of darkness. The fear of sacrificing his life for God's glory gripped McClain fiercely. Exactly what manner of death would he face? The prophecy predicted that the cardinal was the traitor, but who was the actual mastermind behind the ordeal? The Devil himself?

McClain departed the castle earlier than usual, en route to a meeting with Sister Anne Gish. The nun had called the priest at ten o'clock the night before, asking for a private, one-on-one meeting with him.

Anne Gish was a dean at Beth-Haccerin School of Mysteries. Unlike a regular classroom teacher, she was endowed with the gift of discernment. She'd recently discovered something odd about Tabitha that no one else had been able to detect. She sensed a deep-seated evil within the girl, and she worried that Tabitha's latent tendencies might endanger the lives of the other students.

Anne was not privy to the revelation about Tabitha; she had no clue that the girl would become the dark princess.

Nonetheless, Anne had tapped into the girl's potential for malevolence. With the sacred knowledge of God's power that Tabitha had acquired so far, Anne worried that the girl could demonize the institution. When she had called the previous night, she indicated that she'd come across further evidence of her suspicions.

When the priest arrived, Anne ushered him hurriedly into the faculty lounge and politely offered him a seat at one of the tables. "I teach the attributes and functions of angels and seraphim, and the divine power under which they function," she said, taking the seat directly across from him. "The reason I've called you is to bring some things to your attention concerning Tabitha."

The priest nodded, trying desperately to hide his anxiety about his estranged foster child. "Oh, like what?"

"She's been acting strange lately, and I am extremely concerned." She paused, searching his face for a reaction. "Father, are you aware that the school has been unable to locate your daughter for the past three days?"

McClain bowed his head, trying to think of a response. Of course he knew, but how could he possibly explain the circumstances to Sister Anne?

"You do see why I'm concerned, do you not?" She paused and sighed deeply. "And with what I've observed lately, well, if God could just open your eyes to see that there is something beyond natural going on with your daughter . . ."

Father McClain lifted his head to meet Sister Anne's gaze, but remained silent.

Sister Anne regarded him curiously. "Father, do you have knowledge of what is really going on here?"

He hesitated, fumbling for words. "She . . . she wandered away." *It isn't exactly a lie*, he thought.

"And how long ago was this?"

"Two mornings ago was the last time I saw her."

Anne looked upon him with a mixture of sympathy and suspicion.

"Tell me more about what you've observed, Sister."

"Over the last several weeks and months, her entire nature has done an about-face. My spirit tells me that she's in covenant with some very dark angels, if not the Devil himself. My sense is that she has tapped into his power, the very force of power this institution is devoted to destroying." Sister Anne Gish pondered for several seconds and said, "Point of confession, Father: she frightens me."

~~~

Satanist Paul Hart strolled out of the mansion and stood beside Tabitha at the lakeshore. "You must be accustomed to being out of bed well before sunrise," he said quietly. When she said nothing in return, he asked, "What's on your mind?"

"Nothing."

"Just think, Tabitha," he said. "The power bestowed upon you will allow you to turn this entire domain into a paradise with the snap of your fingers. Think about your reign as princess, the most powerful youth in the world. No wonder the thirst burning inside of you to pursue your destiny was unquenchable. Tabitha, you were destined for this moment, even years before your birth."

"Indeed, I was," she replied.

"Before the beginning of this universe, there was another beginning. Before humans became humans, we all existed as spirits, living in the age of innocence. And it was our destiny to depart that blind stage and be reborn into mortality, in order to inhabit a physical universe." He paused, looking into her eyes. "But it doesn't have to be that way."

"The priest never revealed this to me," she said.

"Of course he didn't. That is exactly why I'm sad to say, unless the priest is annihilated, your chances for fulfilling your destiny are very slim."

"How is that?" she asked, seemingly annoyed. "He can't be that bad, can he? I've known him for years."

"What will it take to convince you that that man is a monster? All these years, he's used his so-called religious influence over you as a stepping stone to hamper your destiny. Can't you see he is your adversary?"

"I see that," she replied. "But I am no longer under his roof. The bond has been shattered."

"So you think that alone is going to set you free? Do I need to remind you that you will soon have complete authority over mankind? There is a battle you must fight, Tabitha. Inheriting the throne comes at a high price."

"And?"

Hart hung his head and pondered. Seconds later, he looked her sternly in the eye and said, "I challenge you to choose between your destiny and your enemy. Which one will you give up?"

"I'm afraid to cause the bloodshed of an innocent."

"That's too bad. You cannot escape it." He turned her to face him, placing his hands on her shoulders. "I am not suggesting that bloodshed is the only way out. Maybe there's a way the monster can be brought to judgment. But it will take your influence."

Chapter 36

McClain was ever more aware that he must conquer his fear in order to face death with courage. Otherwise, the unleashing of the Princess of Heaven onto the Earth hung in jeopardy. If this failed to happen, the world would suffer bitterly the gruesome reign of the dark princess—evil prevailing over good.

The priest, of course, opposed the reign of evil. He didn't want to see that happen. In spite of his fear, his unwavering faith kept him composed, preventing him from acting rashly.

On a windy and rainy night, at exactly 2:00 a.m., his alarm sounded, waking him instantly. He stood and quietly prepared for his early-morning prayer ritual. As the priest slipped into his prayer robe, he felt an eerie presence drawing him toward the swimming pool. Despite the silent alarm of dread going off in his head, the priest bravely allowed the force to pull him along.

When he arrived at the pool, McClain found a threatening message seemingly written in blood on the surface of the rippling water:

You should know by now that angels will not always come to your rescue. If that were so, you wouldn't be reading this letter from the Devil himself. You are just another vulnerable soul who has lost hope in a god you've never seen and never will. You are stuck with the reality that your service to him is in vain.

Maybe by the time you finish reading the fine print, you will have already thought about the consequences that wait to devour you. I feel deep sorrow for your followers and those you have affected through this deceptive medium, only to look the other way from my inevitable reign as the dark princess.

Every breath you take, my desire to have your head on a platter strengthens. Soon, you will be brought to my cabinet as I celebrate my reign. Any good deed you perform will not go unpunished.

~~~

"Has she returned?" Eleanor Griffins asked, deeply concerned.

"No," he replied. "And I don't think she ever will."

Eleanor simply looked at him, uncharacteristically speechless.

"The situation has become more and more unpredictable," McClain said, wringing his hands. "Now that she's threatened me directly, I can only guess as to what her next move will be."

"I understand your worry," she replied. "The situation has gotten very shaky, especially with the Princess of Heaven involved."

"What is your sense of the events of last night, the message I received?"

Prophetess Griffins set aside her brush and removed her glasses. "Tell me exactly what transpired."

"She relayed a message to me in the water of the pool—in blood."

Eleanor winced. "It seems as though the dark signs are becoming more evident by the day."

"Exactly. Since you are a gifted prophetess with divine insights, maybe you can help me interpret the message, tell me what it means."

Ms. Griffins paused for a few seconds. "I see no interpretations. Only that the signs are evident. She is planning to bring her powerful evil into the world."

"So what would you do, if you were in my shoes?" he asked.

"Well, though I'm sure you've thought about it, I wouldn't abandon the castle. That will only make you a fugitive, and servants of God are not fugitives, especially those who know the crown of glory lies ahead."

"What if I did run?"

She locked her eyes onto his. "Do not attempt it," she warned.

"I'm human, just like everybody else."

"Yes, but you're special, Father, a man of great faith. If you resort to fleeing, you will disappoint God. You will defeat his purpose—a purpose only you can fulfill." She paused, softening her tone. "Why do you think the Lord has placed so much trust in you?"

The priest shook his head. "I wish I knew."

She pondered momentarily. "I've given you clues of comfort and of hope. Death is not the end. And if your death does not manifest, it will be impossible for the Princess of Heaven to fulfill her destiny: to slay the dark princess. It will be impossible for the heavenly princess to redeem mortal souls from the chaos of darkness the dark princess wishes to inflict upon the world. The Lord will hold you accountable if Satan is allowed to pronounce his harsh judgment on the souls of humanity."

~~~

The priest arrived home at midnight, exhausted from his meeting with the prophetess. A severe storm had been predicted and looked to be picking up speed. McClain was determined to sleep soundly through it. When he entered the master bedroom, the phone rang. He hurried to the bedside, assuming it was Ms. Griffins calling to make sure he'd made it home safely.

"Hello?"

"Dad?"

The priest's heart skipped a beat. He held the phone to his ear, speechless for several seconds, before he finally broke his silence. "Tabitha?" he said tentatively. "Honey, I've been so worried. Where are you?"

"I don't know exactly."

"What do you mean, you don't know?"

"I . . . I was kidnapped. I don't have long to talk. But you need to rescue me before—"

"What do you mean, you were kidnapped? How did it happen? Who kidnapped you?"

"I was picked up by a man who claimed you'd sent him to take me to the school picnic."

The priest tried to imagine who would do such a thing. "Where can I find you?"

"I'm being held hostage," she whispered.

"Where exactly are you, Tabitha? Can you give me any idea?"

"I'm stranded."

"Yes, I understand. Stranded where?"

"Some deserted mansion. The only way to get here is through Vamp Street."

McClain's breath caught. The street name triggered alarm from somewhere deep in his memory. "Did you say Vamp Street?"

"Yes."

The priest was starting to grow suspicious. "What city is that?"

"Springville."

"Springville?" He had never even heard of such a place.

"Dad?"

"Hold on," he said, reluctantly removing the receiver from his ear. He drew a deep breath and contemplated his next move.

He heard the distant sound of Tabitha's voice in the phone. "Are you still there?" she cried.

He held the phone back up to his ear. "I'm here. Listen, do you have any idea what you're asking me to do?"

"You vowed to protect me, remember?"

He hesitated. "You're right, I did promise you that."

McClain headed out into the severe storm, the darkness and the wet roadways making for a treacherous drive. The rain poured down heavily as powerful winds made it nearly impossible for him to keep his car on the road. He glanced at his road atlas, but knew it wouldn't do him any good. He channeled his instincts and drove in the direction of his daughter, who needed him. But getting to Springville proved tough, the dense woods making visibility nearly impossible.

The storm suddenly ceased as he pulled into the little ghost town. The houses and buildings along the narrow streets appeared to be abandoned. Most of the homes looked to be well over a century old and had fallen into varying degrees of disrepair.

He pulled over to a curb and stopped the car. As he leaned back against the seat, a red flame suddenly lit up the sky in the distance. He stepped out of the vehicle and watched the fiery image with intense curiosity. His heart pounded as he peered at the spectacle, unsure how to interpret what he was seeing. He reasoned that a fire burned in the forest below, but instinctively he knew it was a sign, a guide leading him to the mansion.

Father McClain ducked back into his car and drove toward the fiery beacon.

~~~

Paul Hart looked down from the grand staircase, vengeance flaring in his eyes. He eyed the priest closely as McClain strode into the foyer.

"Finally, evil has prevailed," Hart called out. "The predator has become prey."

Hart vanished from the staircase and materialized inches in front of the clergyman. "Looking for something?" he scoffed.

"Where is Tabitha?" McClain asked.

A grin slowly spread across Hart's face at the delicious thought that McClain would never return to society. "Do you know who I am, Father McClain?"

"I presume," McClain replied icily, "that you are the son of the Devil. I foresaw this moment many years ago."

Hart laughed. "You presume right," he said, extending his hand. "Paul Hart."

The priest kept his arms at his sides, regarding Hart's hand with disgust.

"You are wiser than the wisest king that ever lived, Father," Hart said mockingly. "You know, a poet once wrote, 'A long and slippery walk always has an end, just as it had a beginning.'" He locked eyes with McClain. "For years, I've hungered for this moment and have fought desperately to uncover the identity of my adversary, so that he might fall prey to my power. And now here you are, at the end of your long walk." He circled the priest, scrutinizing his every feature. "Perhaps it has occurred to you, considering the man you are, that there's a time and a season for everything under the sun."

"Where is she?" McClain asked again.

"Don't lose your credibility by acting like a fool," Hart snapped. "I assume you know the dark history of this domain. Anyone and anything that risks trespassing on this treasured landmark of Springville never returns alive."

"I couldn't care less about the history of this abominable place."

"Oh, but soon you will care—when the scourging fires of Hell torment you without mercy. It will be a moment of great anguish and pain. At least, for you."

"What are you saying?" the priest asked. "That all this was just a setup?"

"I was under the impression that you were a powerful man of God, a man endowed with great spiritual insight. But now I know that the simplest of tricks can charm the devout from his high horse. Where is your gift of discernment?"

"Your taunting is a waste of time. Nothing is destined without a purpose."

Hart chuckled and stepped back. "Absolutely. I can now relish the fact that we're getting somewhere, are we not?"

"What are you up to, Hart?"

"Ooh, McClain, don't pretend as though you're blind to the reality. Don't play innocent with me. You know good and well that, as we speak, a host of dark angels are celebrating this moment in a world our human eyes can't see. If I may ask, how could your trade—your so-called God-given purpose—obstruct the destiny of the dark princess?"

"I was fulfilling the will of God," McClain barked. "If you think raising Tabitha was an obstruction to your devilish plans, think again."

Hart raised an eyebrow, genuinely puzzled. "Did I hear you say 'devilish plans'?"

"You heard me."

"I think I know what your problem is, Father. You don't even know the real Devil."

"I wouldn't doubt it, if you are the Devil himself."

"Make no mistake," said Hart. "From the very beginning, Lucifer had a better plan for the universe, and all of humanity as well. The only reason these two supernatural forces are constantly engaged in warfare is because Lucifer has one goal in mind: to save the world from the fierce wrath of Heaven. To save the inhabitants of this universe from judgment by the one who claims to be the Creator.

"I'm proud to be part of this vision, to be working with every fiber of my being to block this unbearable burden. That's what the battle between evil and good, Satan and God, demons and angels, is all about. And I can assure you that, when all this is over, the kingdom of darkness will surely prevail."

Chapter 37

John McClain's mysterious disappearance sparked controversy within the walls of Salisbury Cathedral, leaving millions of his viewers to wonder what had become of England's most prominent priest. His disappearance, however, fulfilled the terrifying prophecy Eleanor Griffins had foretold. Growing concern lingered throughout the church and the country, with many speculating that the priest's disappearance was part of a grand conspiracy.

The possible conspiracy, and the dark cloud cast upon the church, drew the constant attention of the news media. Coverage of McClain's sudden departure aired continuously on every channel.

~~~

The night Father McClain arrived at the mansion, Paul Hart ordered a squad of guards to apprehend him. They disrobed him, attempting to strip him of his prominence and spiritual power, and threw him into the dungeon.

He who had once dined with kings and the queen of England was now being held in secret captivity. A man who had ministered to millions of lost souls by way of his evangelistic telecast was now bound to a small bed in a dark, dank mansion basement, pending Hell's judgment.

During those days, while confined in the dark, McClain managed to conquer his fear almost completely. It seemed as though there would be little chance for the light of God to shine, but, amazingly, God made his presence known. The priest would never have learned the extent of God's mysterious ways had he never been thrown into Hart's dungeon.

Though it was perhaps daytime, the dungeon was pitch black. McClain could never determine the difference between day and night as the eerie darkness lingered for days on end. McClain was ruminating on the many prophecies that had been fulfilled when a light suddenly appeared under the door, capturing his attention. He listened closely to the footsteps as someone approached his chamber.

McClain flinched when the individual pounded on the door twice and then barged in, holding a lit torch in his right hand. The priest's heart clenched as he sat up in mute shock. He rubbed at his eyes. "Cardinal?" he inquired, disbelieving.

"You looked surprised to see me, Father," Cardinal McCartney said. "Don't be alarmed. I'm not a ghost."

"The whole world thinks you're dead."

"Well, history has a way of repeating itself, often in ways that seem dire. I guess the drama of the mystery of Annabelle continues after all. Perhaps I am her, reincarnated."

The priest drew back, his eyes wide.

"Oh, don't look so shocked," the cardinal said. "You knew it all from the start."

"And to think, I went against God by doubting the prophecy pointing to you as the traitor," McClain shouted. "I couldn't conceive that you, of all people, would become my Judas and lead a revolt against me. I took the truth for granted, and now here you are—another prophecy fulfilled."

"Your Judas? This is not the time to point fingers, McClain. What does any of this have to do with being a traitor? I have nothing to do with you being here."

"Your very presence here suggests otherwise."

"I did not come here to engage in endless dialogue," the

cardinal said. "I'm here for one thing: to bring to your attention that this is a war that God has already lost. If I were you, I would seriously consider what I'm telling you. And dare not think that your faith will save you, because if that were the case, you wouldn't be here in the first place. God would've sent legions of angels in your defense."

"You think I'm that naïve, Cardinal? This moment was destined to be."

"Come on, McClain. Do you really believe you can defeat evil merely by your death? If that were the case, I'm sad to say you've fallen under the sway of deception. The dark princess has been unleashed, and right under your nose." He stepped closer to the bed. "What will it take to convince you that God will never win this war?"

"You've just mocked God, Cardinal. I'll pray he doesn't bring his fierce wrath upon you."

McCartney scoffed. "Seems like you have yet to accept the facts."

"You think I didn't foresee this?" McClain returned. "Of course I did. I just wasn't prepared to face it this early. But God has given me the grace to endure this persecution."

"I've known you for forty years," the cardinal said. "I'm warning you as a friend, as a brother, that it's time you place your faith in what I'm about to reveal. You must trust me on this."

"I trust no man."

"Do you know that, quite recently, I uncovered the truth?"

"Which truth?"

"That there is no such thing as God's righteous judgment," he replied. "The God we both think we are devoted to failed man from the very beginning. Why do you think he gave man free will? It is universally known but rarely acknowledged that the human race always chooses those things that are forbidden. It is this truth that Lucifer is trying to convey to mankind—the very same knowledge you and I fight blindly to conceal, cleverly framed in this so-called radical organization we call Christianity."

McClain looked at him, disgusted. "Your tongue speaks lies from the Devil himself. By no means will I fall for such deceit."

"You have three days before you are to face execution," the cardinal told him. "Three days to choose your fate: life, or merciless death for a vain cause."

Chapter 38

The mansion guards shoved Father McClain into the torture chamber. He trudged heavily, his shackles clanking as they bound him between two pillars and chained his outstretched arms to each of the structures. Paul Hart and Cardinal McCartney looked on as the torturer came up behind the priest, whip in hand, ready to execute his orders upon Hart's signal.

Hart approached the priest. "You are now at my mercy," he said. "Don't forget that." He glanced at the torturer and back to McClain. "I offered to give you back your freedom, if only you would agree to surrender your humanity and your faith in this wayward god of yours. But you turned down my generous offer, Father."

"I'd rather die," spat the priest, "than allow your will to succeed."

"Oh, really?" Hart replied. "If that's the case, I suppose I have no choice but to bring forth my wrath to its full extent." He snapped his fingers and retook his place beside the cardinal. In turn, the torturer lashed out hard with his whip across the priest's bare back.

McClain held back his tears. When the man drew back the weapon, McClain felt the welt rise on his back as blood trickled from the wound. On the fourth lashing, a scream escaped the priest's lips. McClain screamed louder with each lashing, no longer able to endure the searing pain. The secret chamber echoed with the priest's cries as his skin split repeatedly and began to peel. After the twelfth lashing, the priest let loose a blood-curdling scream that ignited a furious clap of thunder.

~~~

12:00 midnight

The Knights of Beelzebub assembled in a secret room in the mansion's judgment chamber. Tabitha, adorned in a gold robe and silver and gold crown, presided over the meeting from her high throne set in the middle of a platform at the front of the room.

Tonight, McClain would finally face judgment for treason against the Vamp Society and the kingdom of darkness at large. The crime leveled against him was the false bond he'd established with Tabitha at the age of her innocence, a move conceived to thwart her destiny in the hope that it would impede the dispensation of evil. Hart accused Father McClain for unlawfully claiming custody of Tabitha—a role he felt he rightfully deserved.

The clan of devil worshipers had taken their seats to witness the priest's secret trial in Sethi's Court. Paul Hart walked out of a private room to the side of the platform and stood beside Tabitha's throne.

Shortly thereafter, the double doors at the rear of the room swung open as two guards escorted McClain up the center aisle. He was pale, half-naked, with chains binding his limbs. The fragile prisoner's hair had grown wild during his captivity, and his long beard was gray.

Hart stepped down the marble stairs and studied the priest with disdain. "Take a good look at her, Father McClain," he said, gesturing toward Tabitha. "Tonight might be the last time you'll ever see her." Hart turned to the crowd and announced: "Some of you know this man, and to others, he is a stranger. As innocent as he appears, I assure you, he is guilty. For years he relentlessly devoted himself to altering the destiny of our beloved princess. He was, and has always been, our prime adversary. Since we have the power to judge the god he so adores, I believe it is fair that judgment begin here."

The Knights erupted with laughter, mocking the priest.

Hart took another stepped toward McClain after they'd hushed. "Father McClain, I'll ask you again: Are you aware that, one way or another, you served as a hindrance to my vision for this world?"

"I am aware of no such thing," McClain replied honestly. "As far as I knew, your vision was doomed to fail."

"But you admit that you knew from the start that this girl was not your daughter, correct?"

"Of course," the priest replied. "I've never claimed otherwise."

"Why then did you deny her the privilege of bonding with her biological father?"

McClain looked at Hart, puzzled. "Her biological father, as far as I know, is dead."

"And just who do you think her real father is?" Hart asked. "Are you aware that Tabitha occasionally comes into contact with him?"

McClain's eyebrows rose in surprise. "What, you raised him from the dead, just as you took his life?"

The crowd murmured.

"Who gave you the authority to raise her, Father McClain?"

"Raising her was part of my purpose. I faithfully fulfilled the task for which I was divinely chosen."

"Since you claim that your mission to adopt the girl was divine, why didn't you focus on nurturing her like a father should?" Hart stared at the priest. "Instead, you chose to involve yourself with all sorts of other matters rather than properly raise the child you claimed was your own daughter."

"What are you talking about?"

"Her destiny, of course," Hart replied, his anger flaring. "You kept things from her, important information about her birthright. You blinded her from the truth of who she really is and of what she's capable of becoming."

The priest's face reddened. "That is absolutely not true."

"It is true," Hart argued.

"What difference does it make now?" asked the priest. "She has obviously made a choice, earned her rightful place. She is saved, as you say. Her future and her destiny are secure. So on what grounds are you prosecuting me?"

Hart shook his head in sharp disapproval. "Sometimes one thing leads to another. This is not just about an infant you abducted eighteen years ago. It's about the new dispensation and your loyalty to this deity who is the master of deception. It is extremely unfortunate that he made you an enemy of this great revolution. That is the primary reason for all of this."

Cardinal McCartney walked quietly into the trial chamber and sat.

Hart pondered for a moment and spoke. "Now that your fate has come to claim you, I don't want to make things worse than they already are. So, one last time, I am offering you a choice. Your decision in this matter determines whether you will return to society as a free man or reap the consequences. Father, will you denounce your faith in God and unite with me for the rise of the new dispensation?"

The priest glared icily at Hart. "Over my dead body."

"Why do you insist on being such a fool?" Hart asked. "I am trying to avoid having your blood on my hands. Why are you pushing me?"

"My faith in God is a treasure. It's more precious than all the wealth of this world combined. It is at the heart of my loyalty to him. No amount of threats will lead me astray."

"Is this some sort of joke?" Hart asked, repulsed. "Let me remind you that there is no such thing as eternal life. It's nothing but an old myth. Now that the truth has been revealed, you may want to reconsider the foolish belief you've been holding onto for so many years. If you were to join me, you could spread the good news, instead of deluding yourself with lies of hope and resurrection. It's all meaningless, and yet the whole world has fallen for the lie."

"The truth about God can never be revoked," the priest shouted. "The power of his spoken word lives forever."

"Tell me, Father McClain, do you honestly live by the scriptures?"

"Of course I do. Why ask a question you already know the answer to?"

Hart exhaled in frustration. "I believe you have knowledge of the words written in the pages of scripture: 'He who does not bear the cross is not worthy of him. Right?"

McClain pondered in silence.

"Answer me."

"I know these words, yes."

"Are you surprised that I'm familiar with the scriptures, Father?"

The priest shook his head. "I'm not surprised."

"Now bear in mind, you will fulfill those written words from that holy book. I hope you know, the weight of the cross is very heavy, unbearable. But, as you well know, scriptures and prophecies cannot be broken."

Tabitha stood. "Give him another chance," she shouted.

"You heard his testimonies, Your Highness," Hart replied.

"Then torture him some more," she pleaded. "Maybe he'll come to compromise."

Chapter 39

McClain had been missing from the pulpit for five Sundays. As the tension mounted, the congregation was left to wonder who would be the next victim. Both Cardinal McCartney and Father McClain had vanished without a trace. Tabitha was also missing. Over the weeks, worry and uncertainty plagued the entire membership. With no revelations about the conspiracy, the staff at Salisbury Cathedral believed wholeheartedly that something evil had infiltrated its ministry.

On this fifth Sunday, the nuns arrived at the church to carry out their usual Sunday morning duties. Sister Betty arrived at the church at exactly 6:00 a.m. As she unlocked the front doors and stepped into the sanctuary, her eyes widened in shock. Moments later, the other three nuns hurried in behind her and gasped. Speechless, the four took in the terrifying spectacle before them.

Overnight, the sanctuary had been transformed into a place of demon worship. An eerie red light filled the sanctuary, and smoke from burning incense and a vast array of lit candles filled the air. On the altar, a monstrous sculpture of a horrifying beast with seven heads and ten horns had been erected. A mass of engraved images of flying dragons dangled from the ceiling on separate cords like a fleet of chandeliers.

"What is this?" asked Betty, unable to tear her eyes away from the terrifying sight.

Together, they crept further into the church, their hearts pounding as though they expected a lurking demon to show its face at any moment. Panic rose among them as they tried to make sense of what was happening.

Sister Martha muttered, "This is unbelievable."

"What happened here?" Sister Helen asked. "What do we do?"

"Look here," Theresa shouted from one of the aisles, and lifted a satanic book for them to see.

Betty and Martha didn't have to guess; they had already realized the church's Bibles had been cleared from the pews. Curious, Martha carefully picked up one of the satanic books and read to Betty the gold inscription on the cover. "'The Book of Satanic Knowledge,' it says."

"The enemy has turned this church into a sanctuary of evil worship," Betty said.

They exchanged nervous glances.

"That means we cannot tamper with anything he—"

"Of course not, Helen," Betty snapped.

The longer they stood, the more panicked Martha became. "Maybe it's time we ran for our lives."

"Wait a minute," Betty said. "I have an idea. Maybe if we put out these candles, we can stop the presence of evil."

"Don't try it, Sister," came a man's voice from the rear of the sanctuary.

The sisters turned and were shocked to see Cardinal McCartney walking down the stairs from the balcony.

"Cardinal McCartney?" Betty murmured, astounded.

"Don't look at me like I'm some sort of ghost, because I'm not." He stepped up to confront the trembling nuns. "What, you holy rollers can't believe the sudden change in protocol?"

"I'm sorry, Cardinal," Theresa spoke up, "but we're terribly confused about what's going on here."

"Confused?" he echoed. "About what?"

"Did you have something to do with this?" asked

Martha.

"Again, about what?"

"The priest's disappearance," Betty shouted. "You plotted his kidnapping."

"Don't be ridiculous," the cardinal replied. "Why would I do that? You seem to think you know everything, but you do not. If I were you, I would be careful of whom you accuse." He addressed them all. "What will you do now that your faith has been shattered? Now that the hope of eternity has failed the test of time? What will you grab hold of next?"

"Where is Father McClain?" Martha asked. "Was he the sacrifice used to accomplish this devilish mission?"

"I warned you: be careful," the cardinal replied icily. "And do not worry about Father McClain. He is saved, although there are some things he must answer to, certain realities he must face, before he returns to society."

"Whatever you have planned, it will surely not succeed," Betty cried. "Not in this sanctuary. I promise you, before the sun rises, we will call every member and spread the news. The doors to this church will remain closed. You might as well render your service to these empty pews."

"Make no mistake," the cardinal said. "Lucifer now possesses the key to life. He has finally redeemed his rightful place of authority, and Hell is destined to reign on Earth. This edifice has been singled out as the throne on which he will sit."

Chapter 40

The verdict was unanimous: McClain was condemned to death by way of crucifixion. But the priest remained brave. Little did Hart know, McClain's death would change things for the worse by instigating a total collapse of his dark kingdom.

By the same token, the unleashing of the Princess of Heaven, in disguise as a warrior, loomed. It hadn't crossed Hart's mind that the situation could change hands at any moment; God could make his counter move in a heartbeat. Hart was certain that the priest's death would finally end the war and Tabitha would take her reign as the dark princess, but Father McClain knew better.

~~~

To celebrate their impending victory, the Satanists hosted a wild feast. It was 11:30 p.m., and the priest was to be executed promptly at twelve midnight. Loyal members of the Knights of Beelzebub arrived at the mansion's ballroom in full attendance. They wore their official black cloaks and were seated at their respective tables. Tabitha was fully robed and wore a gold and emerald crown. She had taken her seat on the throne upon the marble platform. On her right was Paul Hart, and to her left, the demon Nevi.

Cardinal McCartney was sitting at a table up front when a strong feeling of guilt washed over him. His teeth clenched, and his face flushed. Like a murderer tormented by his crime, he was plagued by overwhelming feelings of regret. He sat, trembling, trying hard to compose himself. He knew it was too late to come to his senses; the plot was in motion, and Hart had given him a part to play. But he understood that the agony of being part of the plot to destroy the priest would haunt him forever.

When he could no longer bear his torment, McCartney nervously rose from his chair and quietly slipped out of the ballroom. Outside in the corridor, he collided with the guards leading McClain to his execution. The guards stopped in the middle of the otherwise vacant hallway.

"Excuse us, sir," one of the guards said.

McClain was still bound in shackles, a heavy wooden cross chained to his back. In that fleeting moment, the priest and the cardinal gazed at each other balefully. This would be the last time they would ever stand eye-to-eye. McCartney's guilt consumed him. Unable to look at the priest any longer, the cardinal hung his head in shame and quickly tramped away.

~~~

Paul Hart marched down the middle of the wide, U-shaped staircase and clapped, sending an echo through the ballroom. Immediately, his subjects hushed their murmurs. With torches raised, one group of men ceremoniously lined up shoulder-to-shoulder and faced another group across the room. Guarding the door were two centurions, fully armored for the execution.

"Our gathering tonight signifies a great victory," the Satanist spoke. "Tonight, the gods will celebrate this triumphant moment in ways they never dreamed. At last, the predator has been conquered." Hart paused and looked toward the doors. "And here he comes now."

The centurions pulled open the massive doors, and the executioners shoved McClain into the room.

~~~

McCartney hurried to his living quarters, closed the door behind him, and collapsed on the bed. He tucked his face into the pillow and sobbed bitter tears. The thought of watching McClain die a cruel death had become nearly unbearable—the stuff of nightmares. He could barely endure the crushing remorse which plagued him ceaselessly. He rolled over in despair and lay on his back, tears streaming from the corners of his eyes.

Too anguished to remain still, he rose from the bed, trudged to the bathroom, and slammed his head into the mirror, sending shards of glass crashing into the sink.

~~~

"Any final words for the dark princess, your one-time daughter?" Hart asked Father McClain. "This is your last chance to speak to her."

"You can kill my body," the priest replied disdainfully, "but my soul you can never destroy. I have learned that mortal death isn't the ultimate end. No battle ceases before its appointed time. And there will be no lasting ruler other than the King of Kings. I may face mortal death now, but after this, another enemy will rise—and she's a powerful one, at that."

"Only fools speak such nonsense, Father." Hart had no intention of taking the priest's words into consideration. "The only thing your words tell me is that you have no self-worth. And if that's true, I wonder how you can possibly care whole-heartedly for the people you claim to shepherd?"

"You could never understand why."

"Oh, but I do understand. And I assure you, when I see to it that you have finally left this world, a spiritual change will take over the Earth—a dispensation the human race is waiting to embrace—a new form of deity."

"Don't be deceived," the priest replied. "The battle has just begun, and it will be you and yours that end up in the pit of deception. But woe unto you, for you shall not live to see these things unfold."

~~~

McCartney rushed from his room and fled the mansion. But where could he go? Weighted with the guilt of having betrayed his longtime friend and colleague, to whom could he run for forgiveness and repentance? He stood on the front porch, frantic for the answer. He acknowledged his role in the shedding of an innocent man's blood, and admitted that he'd allowed himself to be lured by false promises. But confessing to himself wasn't enough; he had to somehow make amends.

The cardinal managed to hot-wire Hart's car, climbed behind the wheel, and sped away. He drove down the lonely highway at top speed, with no particular destination in mind. He only knew he needed to flee from the crucifixion—to get as far away as he possibly could. Several kilometers into his journey, McCartney came to a sobering realization: no matter how fast or how far he drove from the mansion, he could not escape his all-consuming guilt.

He slammed on the brakes and made a swift, unsafe turn onto a hidden road leading up the side of a mountain. His troubled conscience took over as he unconsciously raced up the dirt and rock incline. He nearly drove off the edge of a cliff before slamming on the breaks, realizing that he'd driven hundreds of feet up the mountainside. His heart raced in horror and regret as he uselessly groped for inner peace.

He sat in Hart's car, breathless, inches away from the cliff. In one swift movement, Cardinal McCartney pressed hard on the gas pedal and launched the car over the side of the mountain, plummeting to the valley below.

~~~

The lights dimmed as the executioners thrust McClain to the floor. The Knights of Beelzebub circled the priest, cheering in triumph:

"Bear your cross."

"Bear your cross."

"Bear your cross."

"Bear your cross."

"Bear your cross."

The executioners began the process of nailing the priest to the cross. The man at the base yanked the priest's legs into position and pulled a twelve-inch nail from the bag around his waist. He positioned the nail at the center of the priest's foot, raised his hammer, and drove the nail through McClain's flesh. McClain shrieked in pain as his blood splattered the face of the executioner.

After securing his second foot, the executioners knelt beside his hands and poised the nails over McClain's palms. Together they raised their hammers and drove the nails through to the wood. McClain cried out continuously, his eyes bulging in blinding, unbearable pain. His blood freely flowed from the wounds as the executioners stood and stepped back. Father McClain heard the cries of the Knights as if they were being shouted in the distance.

"Bear your cross."

"Bear your cross."

The chorus from the Knights soon hushed, and grave silence fell over the ballroom. The Knights looked on as McClain's body twitched in pain, his eyes rolling back in their sockets. In mere minutes, the priest's body would stiffen, and their leader would be free to reign. The mansion's guards stood at the ready to dispose of the body, which they planned to throw into the lake.

The Knights broke the circle when Paul Hart approached. He trembled in anticipation as he watched the priest draw his last breaths. Tabitha stepped down from her throne and strode to the scene, followed closely by the demon Nevi. Together, they gazed at the body, staring in triumph as blood trickled from the priest's wounds, his nose, and his ears.

Hart declared, smiling, "He didn't believe me when I vowed that I would feed his body to the predators lurking beneath the lake."

Chapter 41

Two hours later

While the mansion guards patrolled the shores of the lake, something mysterious captured their attention. As they focused on the lake's shadowy, reddish surface, they spied a beaming light glowing upward out of the water. Their eyes followed the light heavenward to find that the moon had turned blood red. They exchanged puzzled glances and noticed the trees and bushes withering before their eyes. Seconds later, the entire forest surrounding the property dried up, the leaves on the trees disintegrating into a rust-colored dust. They looked toward the sky again as a meteor the size of a soccer ball plummeted into the lake. Moments later, the lake water started to boil.

The guards stood, trembling, unable to comprehend what was happening around them. One of the guards fled to the mansion to inform Hart. The others watched in horror as the moon cracked open, revealing a red, winged horse whose rider looked to be a fierce woman warrior.

~~~

The feast, now at its climax, was expected to last until the first gleams of daylight. Rhythms of satanic music played through hidden speakers as the clan of Devil worshippers danced in great happiness. They were certain that by morning, England and the rest of the world would be shaken by the fulfillment of a major prophecy: the rise of the dark princess.

The crowd was startled as an earthquake shook the mansion violently. The powerful quake gained momentum, and the mansion trembled under its power. The Knights watched in disbelief as the walls started to crack, sending rippling veins threading through the bricks. The ceremony ceased and the crowd was beginning to panic when the center chandelier crashed into the crowd, crushing those standing beneath it.

Confused, Hart left Tabitha on the platform and hurried into his crowd of subjects. Quickly realizing he was powerless to calm the panicked Knights and the rest of his brethren, he dashed to the front porch to investigate.

He stood, stunned, in the glow of a red light mysteriously shining from the horizon, covering his entire domain. The lake water was boiling and belching a foul-smelling steam into the air. He stared, mouth agape, as the ground split along the shrunken forest and began caving in. When he looked back at the lake, he saw the boiling water quickly rising. He knew it would be only a matter of minutes before the foul liquid flooded the mansion. Dozens of trees had begun sinking into the earth as the first boiling waves lapped over the shores of the lake.

The stone railing, which Hart gripped in fear, suddenly shattered under his hand. Sensing a disturbance above him, he looked up in time to see the giant statue of the Beast crumble from the roof in pieces. An immense wave of anger spiraled up from deep inside him. Hart stretched his arms wide to halt the disaster, but to his shock, he no longer possessed any power.

He ran back into the mansion and back to the ballroom. Stripped of his power, he fled in fear, hoping to find shelter with the princess. On his way through the house, Hart collided with the two guards who had performed the execution. "Did you bury the body?" he asked, panic-stricken.

The two guards nodded.

"Where, exactly?"

"In the lake, sir," one of the guards answered, "just as you instructed."

"You're sure?"

"Yes, sir."

He exhaled, regret filling his mind. "Maybe that wasn't such a good idea, after all."

The guards looked at each other quizzically and back to Hart. "His execution?"

"No, you idiots," he barked, storming off. "I am talking about throwing his body in the lake."

"What's going on?" Tabitha asked anxiously when Hart returned to the ballroom.

He shook his head. "It's unexplainable," he replied miserably. "It seems like nature is trying to avenge McClain's death." He looked into her eyes. "I am unable to protect you. We all must fight for ourselves now."

"Protect me?" she said, clearly insulted. "I can protect myself."

He leaned in close to her. "We are on the verge of an invasion, Princess," he whispered. "Our chances of escape are very slim. And even if we could escape, where could we possibly go?"

Panic ensued as nature's wrath assumed its great power over the mansion and its grounds. Another earthquake erupted and again shook the mansion violently. The magnitude of the quake sent the remaining chandeliers to the ballroom floor as people ran for cover. The floor rippled, cracks appearing beneath their feet. The ballroom floor caved in on itself, leaving a gaping hole filled with tables and chairs.

The platform saved Hart and Tabitha. It was a miracle that the raised floor didn't sink under the strain of the quake. But just a few seconds after they breathed a sigh of relief, the hole in the floor grew, sending a crack toward the corridor outside the ballroom. The crack opened, and the hallway was swallowed up, quickly followed by the living area. The entire mansion was caving in on itself as Hart and Tabitha clung to the platform. They watched as everything, inside and out, fell victim to Mother Nature: walls, pillars, and the entire upper floor came crashing down around them.

In less than a minute, the earthquake had demolished the entire mansion. As Hart and Tabitha clung to each other on the small stage, they hoped the disaster would soon subside, but it was not to be. The lake waters, now out of control, flooded the grounds up to the very edge of the platform. Mysteriously, at that moment, the earthquake subsided. But Hart and Tabitha were trapped in the center of the platform amid a pool of boiling water.

As they gaped at the aftermath in awe and despair, Hart's regret grew. He had foolishly scoffed at the priest's prediction that his death would bring about the wrath of God on his kingdom. He had been arrogant and overly confident in his eagerness to unleash the reign of the Princess of Darkness.

They flinched at the sound of the roaring wind that swept up in the aftermath of the quake. Movement above turned their attention to the sky, where they gazed in awe at a female warrior dressed in red battle garments. She flew down toward them and landed on the platform.

Tabitha stared in shock at the face of the young woman, with her dark hair and golden eyes. She looked to be Tabitha's twin in nearly every way.

The warrior looked at Hart. "He told you, Hart, that there was an enemy more powerful than himself, did he not?"

Paul Hart gave her a tight-lipped smile. "I see. I guess that solves the mystery once and for all. The divine mystery the priest spoke so fondly of." He exhaled, narrowing his eyes at the woman. "Were you commissioned to avenge his death?"

Before the warrior could answer, Tabitha broke in. "Who are you?"

The warrior turned to Tabitha and smiled. "I'm the Princess of Heaven."

"Princess?" Hart repeated, deeply annoyed. "Look what you've done. Tell me, why does the Princess of Heaven wear the clothing of a warrior?"

She regarded Hart curiously for a moment before drawing her sword and swiftly cutting off his head.

Tabitha watched in horror as Paul Hart's body dropped to the platform and his head rolled into the boiling waters. Without wasting another moment, she shape-shifted into a dragon and took to the sky. The Princess of Heaven quickly spread her wings in hot pursuit.

Several kilometers away, Tabitha landed on the ground of a deserted park and returned to human form. Before the heavenly warrior could set foot on the ground, Tabitha drew a magic sword from her robe. The two princesses fought relentlessly for several minutes, but in the heat of the fight, Tabitha stumbled over a tree stump and fell back onto the ground. The Princess of Heaven quickly plunged her sword deep into her rival's chest until she felt the tip penetrating the ground. Tabitha, the Princess of Darkness, lay weak and helpless, the long sword lodged through her abdomen as blood gushed from the wound.

The Princess of Heaven, the fearless warrior, exhaled in triumph, having slain the dark princess. She gazed heavenward for several moments, relishing her victory. When she looked back down to retrieve her sword, she was astonished to discovered that only the sword remained, still lodged firmly in the ground.

Tabitha had vanished.

Epilogue

The hot midday sun beat down onto the seaside city. Without warning, the activity along the shore came to a standstill. Across the raging sea, the Princess of Darkness ascended from the ocean's depths in pursuit of her destiny. People stared in horror as the ravenous beast, followed closely by her dark angels, took to the sky on a rampage.

All of humanity was panic-stricken as they witnessed the dark princess's triumphant ascension.

From that day forward, terror and chaos reigned like never before.

Michael D. Benson believes that faith in God is all it takes to conquer the perils of life's disappointments and struggles. His unwavering faith in the Creator gives him a unique narrative voice, and his humble beginnings give him the inspiration for the stories he writes. Michael can relate to the spectacle of events he brings to life in his novels. Ultimately, his journey of faith, trials, and triumphs led him to pen the first installment of the *Judgment* series, an epic tale of the sinister, mysterious battle that rages between angels in the kingdom of Heaven and demons in the dark kingdom of Hell.

Michael loves nature and its unrefined beauty. He lives on the East Coast with his family and spends his leisure with his three sons. He's currently working on the second book in the series, scheduled for release soon.

Visit Michael D. Benson's website at
www.mikebensonbooks.com

MICHAEL D. BENSON

HELL'S JUDGEMENT

REVENGE OF
THE DARK PRINCESS

Coming Soon

www.ingramcontent.com/pod-product-compliance
Lightning Source LLC
Chambersburg PA
CBHW020912200626
46814CB00001BA/291